Imitation Island

Hope Harrington Kolb

PORTICO

Portico Publishing
14781 Memorial Drive, Suite 2491
Houston, Texas 77079
www.porticopublishing.com

Copyright © Hope Harrington Kolb, 2009
All rights reserved.

PUBLISHER'S NOTE
This novel is a work of fiction.
Names, characters, places and incidents
are either products of the author's imagination
or are used fictitiously. All characters are
fictional, and any similarity to persons living or
dead is purely coincidental.

Manufactured in the United States of America

Library of Congress Cataloging-in-Publication Data
1. Mystery - Fiction 2. Suspense - Fiction 3. Southern - Fiction
4. Sixties (1960's) in America - Fiction 5. Louisiana -Fiction
6. Chicago - Fiction

ISBN 978-0-615-32005-2 (Trade Paperback)

Dedicated to
Rev. Jerry Eugene Kolb
...my wonderful husband,
without whose
patient persistence
this project would
not have been
completed.

*"God works in a mysterious way,
His wonders to perform."*

*William Cowper,
English Poet*

PROLOGUE

"If you rescue that child again, I swear I'll get rid of you instead of her," the woman said, her voice as cold and hard as her face. She was only thirty, but he thought she looked fifty and sounded ninety.

The man who passed as her husband was beginning to think she might have been a witch in another life; he could hardly recognize her as the same woman who had drawn him away from the best wife in the world four years ago.

"I couldn't leave her in that place," he said grimly, trying to sound as harsh as she did, and failing miserably because of the softness of his heart.

Not that he was a particularly good man – he'd never had much of a role model, with a lazy, hard-drinking father and a mother who left him in the car while she went into bars looking for attention.

But he wasn't a murderer. There was something inside him that wouldn't let him leave that pretty little blonde angel trapped in a place where she would inevitably have died. She had looked at him so pitifully and tightened her arms around his neck in a way that made him wish he had never left his family behind.

Now he could never go back. But he didn't have to

become a murderer. This woman could scream and abuse him from now 'til doomsday, but he just couldn't do it, and he'd made up his mind he wouldn't let her do it, either.

"Do you have any idea what's at stake here?" She twisted her mouth around in a way that made him feel he would never want to kiss those lips again. It almost made him sick to think he ever had.

"I know what you're talking about," he said, "but it's only money. I know there's a lot of it, but nothing is worth doing that to a sweet innocent baby like that one!"

She shook her head and snorted scornfully.

"You know there's 'a lot' of it. What's 'a lot' of money to you? You've never had two dimes to rub together! You can't even *begin* to comprehend how much money we could make out of this deal. Millions, I tell you. Millions! More money than we could spend in three lifetimes. And you won't do a little bit of dirty work to get it."

She turned away from him and went on bitterly:

"Well, I will, if you won't. Or I'll find somebody else to do it for me. This is the chance of a lifetime, and for once I'm not going to lose it. If I had to pay somebody a tenth of the fortune that's at stake, it would be worth it!"

"You wouldn't be doing this if her mother was alive," he said accusingly.

He hadn't been here when the child's mother had died. He'd been told about her death and burial when he got back from an extended trip he'd taken, and he'd wondered then if it had been a natural death.

He'd opened the vault himself and checked the body as well as he could, but at that point, it had been impossible to tell. Isolated as they were, there had been no death certificate and no burial preparation. But he wouldn't put *anything* past the woman standing in front of him.

She said with a sneer:

"Oh? What makes you think I wouldn't do this if she was alive? I assure you *she* couldn't have stopped me! I know too much. I've been here a long time, you know. I was here when she tried to disguise herself, and I know why she did it...

"I could have exposed her any time I liked, but they'd have just come and taken her away, and we would never have seen a penny of her money, if she still had any coming to her, which I doubt.

"And besides, I'm betting that the other fortune is a bigger one, anyway. That's the one I want to get my hands on! And nothing in this world is going to stop me...certainly not you."

Several months later, he was still trying to protect the little girl he thought of as a blonde angel. And, except for depriving the child of all affection and many of her material needs, his former mistress hadn't tried anything...as far as he knew.

He would have left already, if it hadn't been for the child. He hadn't been near the woman he'd started calling a witch in his own mind ever since this last time he'd had to rescue her tiny victim. If he could think of a way to support the little girl and himself, he would take her away from here and keep her safe. But he knew he could get into as much trouble for doing that as for anything. No, the best he could do was to keep an eagle-eye on the evil-minded woman and the innocent child under her control.

The house they all lived in was huge, and there was no way he could watch over her every minute of every day. But if he could just protect her for a couple of weeks longer, she would be safe.

Her father – the owner of the house – was finally coming home after nearly three years abroad. And once the child's father was back, he could relax his vigilance and even leave the place altogether. He could hardly wait for that day.

But for now, he was responsible for the vast lawn and grounds around the house, and since he had let the place grow into a virtual jungle while the owner was overseas, it would have to be dealt with drastically and quickly. He had to spend long, arduous hours outside, trying to tame the wilderness he had allowed to take over.

And while he was doing this, the child disappeared. Without any warning or fanfare, she was just gone. At first he didn't notice it, but when he didn't see her one whole evening and the next morning, he realized that the tragedy he'd been trying so hard to avert had finally happened.

There was a smug smirk on the woman's face, and he was hot with anger toward her and cold with fear for the child when he demanded:

"Where is she? What have you done with her? You'd better tell me, or I swear I'll strangle you here and now."

His face was red with emotion, and his big fists were clenched; but she just laughed at him.

"*You* strangle *me*? You don't have the nerve to hurt a fly, and you know it. Besides," she added with a careless shrug, "what's done is done. It's too late now, even if I wanted to change my mind."

"What are you talking about?"

"That man I told you about – he's already taken care of things. It's out of our hands now. I guess I really ought to thank you for rescuing her. Now we can't be blamed for anything.

"It's all ours now. Even with him coming back here, it's all ours. He won't stay...I know him. He won't be able to stand it without *her*. And he'll have a child to love without that one.

"But he won't stay even for the child. I'll have access to everything again before you know it, and someday he'll leave it all to us, whether he realizes it or not. We'll be richer than we ever dreamed! Well, what do you say now?"

What he said was "Goodbye". He packed his bags and left that night, determined to find the child. It couldn't be too late. She'd only been gone one day and part of another. He would find her and rescue her.

The woman must never know, or they'd both be in danger – he and the little girl. What he was going to do with her after he found her, he had no idea. If he took her back home to her father, the woman would have his hide, one way or another – he knew that.

She had been determined to have *him* four years ago

and had gotten him. Now she was determined to have a fortune at her disposal, and she was willing to kill for it. She might already have done it once, he thought, remembering the child's mother.

He couldn't take care of a small child over the long haul; someone else would have to do it – but who? Surely somewhere out there, he could find people who would love such an adorable little girl – but where? There had to be a way to give her a good, safe life – but how? He didn't have the answers to those questions, and for the first time in his life, he prayed.

First he had to find her. He racked his brain trying to recall what he'd heard about the man who had taken the child away. He knew the man was a bad one who'd do almost anything for money, but he doubted he'd kill an innocent child in cold blood.

What would he be likely to do with her? Where could he have taken her that would end in her death without his having to do the deed himself? In almost a miraculous flash of insight, he guessed the place and headed for it immediately.

She was there – filthy, shivering, famished and thirsty, but mostly numb with terror, and the relief on her traumatized little face when he picked her up was reward enough for turning away from the chance to be rich at her expense.

He wrapped his cheap coat around the tiny shoulders that were trembling with fear and carried her to his old car, gently placing her in the back seat and telling her to please try to go to sleep if she could.

She seemed to be in a subdued state of shock, but he

could tell she trusted him, and it warmed his heart in a way he hadn't felt for years. He stopped for food as soon as he could, and when daylight came, he drove through the streets of the town they had come to during the night, praying again that God would show him what to do.

Passing a church, he heard singing spilling out through the open doors into the street, and he stopped to listen, pulling up to the curb down the street and shutting off the motor instantly. The child was awake now, and she listened, too, a tiny smile on her dirty little face.

Suddenly, he knew what he was going to do. Maybe God had led him to this place for some strange reason that he would probably never understand. He'd never had much to do with church, himself. His folks hadn't paid any attention to God, so he'd grown up a spiritual orphan.

But he knew these were the folks who built hospitals and had soup kitchens for the down-and-out and sponsored orphanages. It was the only place that he knew for certain wouldn't put her back out onto the street.

He waited until the singing stopped, and then he took the little girl in his arms and walked into the sanctuary, slipping into an empty back pew as unobtrusively as possible.

The congregation was standing with their heads bowed in prayer, and without waiting long enough for anyone to notice him, he deposited the little girl on the pew. He put his finger over his lips, warning her to keep quiet.

Then he slipped away, leaving her there, alone. But not before he'd pinned a note to her little dress, written on a piece of scuffed and dirty paper. He'd worded the brief message earlier this morning.

It read simply: "Her name is Avalon."

CHAPTER ONE

She'd had the nightmare again. Avalon woke up breathless, her heart pounding. The satin bedspread under which she'd slept so serenely the first part of the night was off on the floor beside her bed, evidence of the struggle she'd sustained in the wee hours of the morning.

She lay staring at the ceiling of her hotel room. Why did she keep having this dream, anyway? She'd been adopted almost as soon as she was abandoned and had been deliriously happy for the past twenty years with Lora and Eric Evans, her adoptive parents. Why couldn't she put it all behind her?

It was strange: she never had the nightmare anymore at home in Chicago, but only on the rare occasions when she was visiting this part of the world. Pulling on her robe, she got out of bed and went to the window to look out on a scene that was nothing less than idyllic.

Across the highway, which at this point was just a quiet, small-town street, a peaceful river wound its way through town, and she could see several of the hotel guests strolling under huge oak trees alongside water that shimmered like sapphires in the morning sunlight.

The small, old - fashioned hotel itself was a Southern

classic, with white columns across the front, and a broad verandah. An elderly black man and a young white boy sat at a small table playing checkers intently.

Others lounged in wooden rockers, sipping tea or coffee, inhaling the fragrance that floated from gardenia bushes and magnolia trees all around the hotel. It might have been 1866 instead of a century later, except for the long cars cruising the highway.

Before Avalon could retreat from her position, a dark-haired, clean-cut young man in his mid-twenties stepped off the verandah and walked across the grass to stand below her window, a mischievous look in his brown eyes. His solid strength contrasted sharply with her frail delicacy this morning.

Avalon and MacNeeley Evans were only two years apart in age and since childhood had been more like a close pair of twins than the cousins they actually were. They understood each other; and now Mac's playful grin faded as he looked searchingly into the pallid face before him.

Avalon smiled feebly to hide her distress. She'd never told Mac about her recurrent nightmare, and she wasn't about to start now. Mac had always been far too curious about her past as it was.

"Do you still want to take your little side-trip today?" he asked soberly, apparently alert to some subtle change in her, but too polite to probe. "It'll be a couple of hours out of our way, you know."

"You said yesterday you didn't mind," Avalon answered. "I haven't seen the place since I was ten, and I'm not likely to be this close again anytime soon. What made you think I might not want to go?"

Mac shrugged. "Well, I guess Columbia is still a hundred miles from St. Francisville, but are you sure that's far enough?"

St. Francisville, Louisiana. The town where she'd been abandoned at the age of two-and-a-half, filthy and so traumatized she didn't speak for another six months. After her nightmare last night, the mere thought of the place – as charming and historic as it was – gave her a sinking sensation, a little like falling off a cliff backwards. But, as Mac had said, St. Francisville would be a hundred miles away.

"Yes, I still want to take my little side-trip," she said quietly.

Mac nodded, and she closed the window as he walked away. Her hands were clammy and her mouth so dry she could hardly swallow as she made her way into the tiny hotel bathroom. She flipped on the light and turned on the water in the sink to brush her teeth, but her slender, delicate fingers shook so, she couldn't hold the toothbrush.

For a few moments, she just stood and stared at herself silently in the mirror, seeing the horror of her dream still reflected in her dark green eyes. Her ivory complexion was now deathly white, her honey-blonde hair as tousled as a toddler's. No wonder Mac had been suspicious!

Finally, she splashed water on her face and drank a swallow or two from a plastic cup, then tried to brush the tangles out of her hair. She managed to maneuver her long, thick mane into a French braid and hung her favorite pair of silver loops in her small, shapely ears. Then she pulled on a pair of aqua capris and a matching silk shirt in preparation for meeting Mac for a late brunch in the hotel's coffee shop.

As they faced each other over hot coffee and a basket of buttered, home-made biscuits kept warm by a linen napkin, slices of fresh cantaloupe, and scrambled eggs with crisp bacon and a side of grits, Avalon talked animatedly. She hoped Mac wouldn't question her further about how pale she was after last night's harrowing experience.

He didn't. But once they left the restaurant and started driving, he was more silent than usual and glanced at her sharply now and then. Avalon looked her most cosmopolitan as they neared the small Louisiana town; and yet – with her perfect profile, long blonde hair and dark sunglasses, seated low in the little silver sports car, she seemed to melt into the milieu like sugar in Southern tea.

"This is almost like driving into the past for me, Mac," she said abruptly, discomfited by Mac's scrutinizing gaze. "I can still remember going down this road with Mother and Daddy – I always leaned up from the backseat of the car to talk to them. They were my best friends even when I was just a kid, you know.

"We came here when I was six and moved away when I was ten. But even after these past twelve years in Chicago, it feels like we left just yesterday!"

She could almost feel the scorching sidewalk under her childish feet as she played hop-scotch with her little friends in front of the house she'd loved so dearly, and she could almost see the tiny hummingbirds that had hovered like brilliant jewels outside her bedroom window on soft summer mornings.

Waves of nostalgia were washing over Avalon, but Mac, who seldom set foot out of Chicago, said with a grimace: "So why did you want to come back to this place again, anyway?"

She looked at him with fond amusement.

"Oh, Mac, it won't take long to see everything I want to see! I guess I wanted to do this because I doubt I'll ever come back here once Mother and Daddy are gone. I don't think I could bear the memories without them."

"Don't you ever wonder about your real parents, Avalon? I mean, your natural parents? I know I would, in your place, even as close as you are to Uncle Eric and Aunt Lora."

He turned and looked at her earnestly.

Avalon had heard the question many times, but it took her by surprise this morning. Had he been able to read her mind, after her nightmare last night? She shifted uncomfortably in her seat.

"I know it's hard for you to understand, Mac, but I've never had any desire to know my 'real' parents, as you call them. I'm *glad* Mother and Daddy never found out who they were!"

What an understatement *that* was! Avalon was the adventurous type, doing things in Chicago that scared her parents speechless and made Mac scold like an old sergeant-major. But she did have one deep fear that turned her cold: that of finding out who she "really was", as one of her less diplomatic friends had put it.

"You know, Mac, Mother and Daddy are just Eric and Lora Evans to you – your favorite aunt and uncle. But to me, they're like angels in disguise – they changed my life from what must have been a hell on earth, into a fairytale of support and love!

"They're patient and kind, cheerful, fun-loving, unselfish, dedicated, wise...everything parents ought to be. How can I explain to you how painful it is to admit to myself that two people I've never laid eyes on brought me into this world and might still be in it somewhere?"

That knowledge was an internal wound that pulsated with pain whenever touched by a thoughtless word or even her own thoughts. But as close as they were, Mac had never seemed to understand this.

"After all, why *should* I want to know them?" she went on, fighting down the bitterness she was always tempted to feel when this subject came up.

"Apparently, they didn't need me back then, and I certainly don't need them now. Besides, I don't think it's a good idea to dig into the past. You might find something you'd rather not know. Personally, I think it's just asking for trouble."

They were still a few miles out of town when the next bend in the road brought Avalon's more pleasant past back so poignantly it almost took her breath away. There it was, set well back from the road: the two-story white house where she and her adoptive parents had lived those four precious years of her childhood, with the wide porch across the front, surrounded by deep-pink crepe myrtles in full bloom, tall magnolia trees and gardenia bushes, their ivory blossoms smooth and fragrant.

Only the azaleas were missing, and she knew they had bloomed briefly in the Spring. But the gardenias made up for them. She could smell them from the road. Childhood memories rose up like warm, motherly arms, wrapping her in feelings so sweet they brought tears to her eyes.

"I can understand why you liked this place when you were little, Avalon," Mac said, glancing at her and frowning as he always did when she became emotional, "but I hope this isn't going to take long. It doesn't strike me as being a very exciting spot."

Avalon laughed and wiped her eyes.

"Oh, come on, Mac! We'll only be here for a few minutes. Surely you can stand a little peace and quiet *that* long!"

She pulled off the road in front of the house and shut off the engine. "Just listen," she said softly.

For the next few moments, silence enveloped them like a warm mist, the only sounds a gentle rustling of the leaves in the tall trees above them and the liquid melodies of a mockingbird who, grateful for an audience at last, burst into a virtuoso concert. Avalon could feel the sultry solitude of the place soaking into her soul.

Then the silence was broken as a door opened and closed, and a man in his late forties came out onto the porch. His brown hair was obviously thinning on top, but his lean frame, encased neatly in a knit shirt and jeans, was young for his years. When he started down the steps toward them, Avalon and Mac got out of her convertible to meet him.

"Hello!" Avalon called out as if to an old friend, putting out her slender, well-manicured hand to shake the man's hand when he reached them.

"I hope you don't mind our stopping like this, but I lived in your house when I was a little girl, and we were passing by so close, I just couldn't resist swinging by to see the place again."

She beamed on him with the warmth that had melted many a colder heart on the sidewalks of Chicago.

"By the way, my name is Avalon Evans, and this is my cousin, Mac Evans. I do hope you don't mind!" she apologized again as she introduced him to Mac.

"Not at all!" the man laughed as he shook Mac's hand.

He introduced himself as Bob Marshall and had the outgoing, open manner of a born Southerner, so his next words were something of a surprise.

"I understand perfectly," he said with an engaging grin, "because my wife was born here and didn't leave until she was twenty, and we moved back from Boston several years ago to buy this house. We wouldn't move back East on a bet, so I can sympathize fully with your attachment to the old place! Please – come on in."

He motioned toward the house in a welcoming gesture, and the three of them started toward it together.

"You'll meet my wife, Megan – "

They all traipsed up the steps of the wide verandah and into the house, and as he closed the front door behind them, Bob Marshall called out:

"Meg! Company!"

The interior was cool and dim, and Avalon noticed an old rug with beautiful, muted colors on the floor of the entry hall. A small crystal chandelier lit the area and cast a gentle glow over the antique furnishings.

This had been a warm, comfortable house when she and Eric and Lora Evans had lived in it twelve years ago, but there was a refinement about it now that appealed to her innate love of understated elegance.

It was a quiet house and a peaceful one, Avalon decided as they waited for the mistress of the house to appear. She glanced at her cousin ruefully, wondering how long he would be willing to stay in such Arcadian surroundings. Well, they wouldn't be here long.

Then Megan Marshall, who appeared to be a few years younger than her husband, was walking slowly toward them, but there was no welcome on her face. She seemed mesmerized by the sight of Avalon, staring at her in a daze, almost as if she had just seen a ghost or wandered into a nightmare.

Avalon noted unconsciously the long blonde ponytail and big silver loops in the woman's ears, the casual, almost Bohemian clothes she wore, her eyes like green pools swirling with shock and alarm.

As the unnatural silence lengthened, Avalon began to feel like part of a painting, frozen in a time frame. How long, she wondered, would they all stand there like statues, waiting for Megan Marshall to speak?

CHAPTER
TWO

Finally Megan dragged her eyes away from Avalon and turned to her husband, saying in a strained voice:

"I'm sorry, Bob. I – was resting in the back and didn't hear you all come in." She turned to Avalon and Mac with a stiff smile. "Please – forgive me…"

She still seemed tongue-tied, struggling with what to say next. Avalon rescued her.

"We're the ones who should be apologizing, Mrs. Marshall…I'm sorry we've dropped in on you so unexpectedly. But my parents and I lived in this house when I was just a little girl, and we were passing by so close that I just couldn't resist seeing it again. I'm sorry if we've inconvenienced you…"

There was a puzzled frown between Megan's well-shaped eyebrows.

"Your parents?"

"Yes – Eric and Lora Evans. We lived here from the time I was six until I was ten, and then we moved to Chicago, which is where my family and Mac's still live. This is my cousin, Mac Evans – his father is my father's brother, you see…"

When Megan still looked blank, Mac explained:

"We're on our way to Natchez to see some of the old

antebellum houses there, and Avalon just thought she'd like to see this place again. We won't be here long..."

His voice, usually so robust and firm, trailed off uncertainly as Megan Marshall continued to stare at them as if in a stupor.

Finally she seemed to shake herself out of her shocked state.

"Oh, of course you're more than welcome to see the house. I was just – half asleep when you all came in, and – well, I'm – I'm sure I'll get back to normal once I wake up completely."

She smiled weakly and said to her husband:

"Why don't you take Mr. Evans into the summer room and get him a glass of tea, Bob? He looks as though he could use one."

When the two men had gone, Megan turned to Avalon and said somewhat timidly:

"What would you like to see first? Your old room?"

Avalon couldn't help noticing that the older woman's hands were trembling slightly as she started to lead the way up the spiral staircase. Her long, tapered fingers trailed tentatively along the highly-polished mahogany banister as they climbed the stairs together slowly.

"My husband and I have owned this house seven years now. How long ago did you say you and your family lived here?"

"We've been gone twelve years. I was ten when we left."

Megan's steps on the staircase stopped in mid-stride, and there was a short silence. When she spoke, her voice was low and pensive:

"So you're twenty-two."

Avalon heard her sigh deeply as they started climbing the stairs again.

"Here we are," she went on as they reached the landing on the second floor. "Where was your old room? At the end of the hall? I've always thought that would be the best place for a child, with that big oak tree just outside the window."

She started down the long hall, and Avalon followed. Along the carpeted hallway were several pieces of antique furniture and three large oil paintings in gilt frames, so well-lighted even in the afternoon that they glowed like vibrant jewels in fine gold settings. Avalon couldn't resist stopping to look at them.

She walked over to the first one, of a well-known Louisiana plantation house in what was called the "raised cottage" style. She could recall touring the house as a child, with Eric and Lora. She distinctly remembered disliking the dank smell of the ground level area, which was sometimes used for storage.

"It looks so *real*," she murmured to Megan, who had paused, seemingly surprised by her guest's interest in the oils. "Who painted this?" Avalon asked.

"A young man by the name of David Daniels. He carried the financial responsibility for his elderly mother until she passed away last year, and he still helps a sister who lives in Chicago now, so he owns a business in town. But he paints part-time and has won several prestigious awards. We're pretty proud of him around here."

"I know him!" Avalon exclaimed, turning to look at Megan. "He was only about sixteen when we moved away, but I knew him really well because he was madly in love with my Sunday school teacher, Johnna Herrington."

"He still is," Megan said wryly. "Those two have been crazy about each other for twelve years or more, but her parents keep talking her out of marrying him just because he's not from a wealthy family or famous...

"And ironically, he probably would be well-known if it weren't for them. They've done everything in their power to ruin his career. And they have the money and influence to do it. Do you remember them?"

Avalon nodded as she recalled what she'd known of the Herringtons as a child. They were extremely wealthy, as well as very proud, and they hadn't mingled much. She remembered how the kids at school had laughed at David for being in love with Johnna.

He had about the same chance of marrying a Herrington as a chimneysweep had of marrying the Queen of England, they joked. Avalon had been very young then, but she remembered thinking the same thing, although more kindly than some of the others.

Herrington Hall, where Johnna lived with her parents, was more like the Parthenon than a family home. Avalon had been inside many an antebellum mansion since her childhood days here, but she'd never seen anything quite like it.

The tour guide books described the central hall as being nearly a hundred feet in length, with hand-carved ceiling medallions, and connecting drawing rooms that were opened up for balls and other formal occasions. There were twenty-eight huge columns around the house, with eighteen-foot ceilings on the first floor, fifteen white Carrara marble fireplaces, enormous antique French crystal chandeliers, museum-quality furnishings, sixteen-foot pier mirrors, a famous unsupported "flying" staircase, and on and on.

As an adult, Avalon wondered what kind of egoism drove people to build such a pompous palace. She knew she could never be happy in such a place. She had such precious memories of the very ordinary house she was seeing again today...

She could still picture Lora Evans holding Avalon's little housecoat in front of the radiator so she'd have something warm to slip into on cold mornings. They hadn't even had central heating in this house back then.

But Lora had admired Johnna Herrington even as a teenager, often noting how different Johnna was from the rest of her elusive and exclusive family. Avalon also recalled that Lora had tried several times to get Johnna's parents to come to the old-fashioned box suppers that were held in the school building across the street from the church, saying it might make them more popular and happier, too. But they never came.

With these thoughts, she passed on to the next painting and stood staring at it as if in a dream. The painting was of an island with a Greek revival house on it. The house itself, although clearly very grand, was almost hidden by the dense and dark foliage that surrounded it like a jungle. But she could tell that it was white and had columns across the front.

Avalon felt her face growing flushed, and she lifted her hands to her cheeks and felt the heat there. Surely she would wake up in a moment and be free from this vise around her heart. It was pounding so violently, she could hear the blood buzzing in her ears.

Her eyes filmed over, and just before she fainted, she heard someone rasp out in a whisper so weak she barely recognized her own voice:

"Help me!"

CHAPTER
THREE

When Avalon opened her eyes, she was lying in a four-poster bed with a dim lamp glowing next to her on a small table.

It was a warm and comfortable atmosphere; but when she looked through the doorway into the hall, she could still see part of the painting that had taken her to the brink of intolerable terror.

She struggled to sit up. "Mrs. Marshall!" She was still hoarse and had to call a second time: "Megan!"

Immediately Megan Marshall was there, solicitous and serious. She sat down on the side of the bed.

"You poor thing!" she said. "I'm so sorry I wasn't right here when you woke up – I'd just stepped downstairs for a minute. You've been asleep for hours! I'm so thankful you're all right. What on earth happened to you?"

"I don't know," Avalon said, shaking her head in confusion. "I just suddenly felt – so strange – just overcome by sheer terror. I don't *know* why! I'm sorry to be such a bother."

Megan patted Avalon's arm comfortingly. "You're not a bother, dear girl. I'm just so sorry I did anything to cause you pain."

Avalon felt shy and embarrassed, but she had to say:

"I can still see it from here – that painting of David's. Could you shut that door for me, please?"

She leaned her head back against the pillow and closed her eyes.

"Of course!" Megan rose instantly and closed the door. She came back to sit beside Avalon again. "The painting? I had no idea it was the painting that made you faint! Have you seen it before – that island and house, I mean?"

"I don't know." Avalon was clearly agitated. "That's just it – I don't know!"

Her heart fluttered with the possibility of telling someone what she'd never shared with anyone before. She hardly knew this woman, but somehow she wanted to tell her what she'd never been able to tell anyone else in her entire life – even her adoptive mother.

Lora Evans knew that Avalon had had nightmares as a small child for several years after she'd been abandoned and adopted, and then a few times over the past twenty years. But she didn't know the details of the dreams, nor that they had started re-surfacing with a vengeance every time Avalon visited the South.

Now Avalon found herself telling Megan Marshall:

"That place in David Daniels's painting – I see it at the beginning of a nightmare I've had off and on since I was a small child. I had it again just last night. It's horrible! I see that island and the house first, but my dream changes, and – oh, I don't know!"

Suddenly unable to share more, her voice rose in pain and frustration.

Megan patted her hand gently. "It's all right. Don't even think about it right now. Just forget everything, OK? You need a good night's sleep, that's all."

"Not here," Avalon blurted abruptly, and then was sorry when Megan looked hurt. "I mean – I'd love to stay, but I just can't – not with that thing hanging in the hallway." She shook her head vigorously. "I just can't. I'm sorry."

She started to throw off the bedspread that Megan had used to cover her, and then, surprising herself as much as Megan, she heard herself asking:

"Do *you* know what that place is, Mrs. Marshall?"

Megan's lips parted, and her eyebrows rose in consternation.

"What on earth makes you think *I'd* know anything about it? I've never seen that place in my life! I don't even know what or where it is – it's just one of David's paintings that I happened to like. What made you think *I* might know?"

She sounded genuinely puzzled, and Avalon breathed a sigh of relief. But she still had to say:

"I thought you might know something about it, if it had anything to do with my past – because of the way you looked at me when you first saw me downstairs...don't you remember? You came down the hall and looked at me as if you'd just seen a ghost or something!"

Megan took a quick breath and looked away.

Avalon said quickly:

"Please don't deny it, Mrs. Marshall...Megan. I know there was *something*."

Avalon realized she was holding her breath. The older woman rose from where she was sitting on the bed and walked to the window. She stood in complete silence for a long minute or two, her back to Avalon.

Avalon could scarcely breathe. So there *had* been something! It hadn't been her imagination. She felt as if her whole life were about to change, and she wanted to jump up and run down the hallway – anything to escape hearing what this woman might say next. But she sat as if frozen, waiting.

Finally Megan turned around and looked at Avalon — a long, lingering, affectionate look that should have been a comfort to Avalon, but somehow wasn't.

"First of all, Avalon, let me tell you a story about – a – a friend of mine. This young woman fell in love with a wonderful young man – well, actually not terribly young – he was ten years older than she. It all happened when she was in England – on a trip her parents gave her as a high school graduation gift.

"He'd never married because – he said – he'd never found the right girl. He was looking for someone really special, and he thought he'd found her in – in my friend. They went everywhere together for months, and when he asked her to marry him, she said 'Yes'.

"But when she came home and told her parents she'd fallen in love with an Englishman, they refused to even hear about it, not only because he was older than she by ten years, but mostly, I think, because they didn't want to face the very real possibility that he might want to take her to England to live. They were really quite possessive.

"And so – my – my friend and her fiancé eloped! She had merely called him 'Lancelot' lightly as soon as she realized how her parents felt about him, so although they tried hard to find her – both of them – they were handicapped by not knowing his real name.

"I have no doubt they would have forced her into an annulment of the marriage, or even a divorce – whatever they could have managed to do legally. And so, to this day, they never mention my – my friend's name, and they refuse to let anyone else say her name in their presence.

"They put away all of their photographs of – of her, and she was officially disowned when they failed to find her. Today it's as if – she never lived at all. It's very unfair, and very sad."

Avalon had been waiting with bated breath for some revelation about her own past, but it never came, and she was bewildered.

"But what does all of this have to do with me? You still haven't told me why you looked at me so strangely when we first met!"

Now Megan moved away from the window and sat back down on the bed. She sighed deeply, as she had on the way upstairs, earlier.

"I don't know for sure, Avalon...that's why I'm so ambivalent about saying anything. But I *think* you must be – her child. You look so much like – like she did when she was about your age. Your coloring is similar, and even some of your mannerisms and expressions. And when your cousin mentioned your name, I may have looked normal, but I thought I was going to faint!"

"But *why?*"

"Because – my – my friend always loved English history and English literature – that was the main reason she wanted to tour England after high school graduation, and I think that's one of the reasons she wanted to marry an Englishman. She just loved England and everything connected to it...

"And when she was a little girl, she had adored the tales of King Arthur and his Knights of the Round Table – Sir Lancelot and Guinevere, Camelot and all the rest of it. That was why she called the man she married 'Lancelot'.

"She said she knew it sounded silly and childish, but she wouldn't tell *anyone* his real name, for fear her parents would be able to find them and force her to give him up.

"In high school she'd loved Lord Tennyson's poems *Idylls of the King*, and she planned to give her first baby girl – if she ever had one – a highly unusual name. In fact, in all these years, I've never known or heard of anyone by that name...until today.

"She was going to name her baby after the place in the fables, where King Arthur and his knights were supposed to go when they died."

Avalon said breathlessly:

"I know that myth! It's Celtic, isn't it? The place was an island. There were people a thousand years ago who actually thought the island in the fable was real – it was supposed to be a place of peace and happiness – an island paradise. They made expensive voyages searching for it. I saw a brand new novel about it the other day! It was called -- "

She found herself choking on the word.

Megan Marshall nodded and said:

"Yes...the name of the island was Avalon."

CHAPTER
FOUR

Avalon sat and stared at Megan for a minute or two without speaking, then said stoutly:

"Don't tell me anymore, please. I – don't think I want to know, after all."

An island named Avalon! And a baby girl named after the island...and that horrible island in her nightmare and in David's painting, that made her feel like she was dying. Oh, she couldn't bear it! She started to get out of bed, but Megan stopped her.

"Wait, Avalon...wouldn't you at least be willing to look at – her picture when – she was a few years younger than you are now? It would be just like looking at yourself – and at least you would *know*...please."

Avalon shook her head without hesitation.

"I'm sorry, Megan. My curiosity overcame me momentarily, but I really don't want to know anything else!"

Megan seemed deeply affected, distressed by the strange turn the visit had taken; but she didn't try to stop Avalon again. Instead, she led her to a little powder room where she could comb her hair and freshen her make-up.

Avalon was appalled by her appearance. Her delicate

features were usually like translucent ivory lit from within; but now, for the second time today, they were chalky white, her large and luminous eyes like ghastly cavities in a corpse. She gave up trying to restore a little color to her face when she dropped the lipstick twice.

When she and Megan went back downstairs, Avalon realized what Megan had meant when she said Avalon had been "sleeping for hours". Mac and Bob were sitting in the long room at the back of the house with empty plates and glasses in front of them, and it was already getting dark outside.

They both stood up when she walked into the room, and Mac walked over to give her a quick hug, then peered into her face.

"Hey, what happened? Are you OK?" He seemed startled by the change in her.

She nodded and smiled faintly.

"I will be. But we need to go."

She might as well have said: "Get me out of here – now!" Mac heard it in her voice, even if the others didn't.

Bob Marshall spoke up quickly:

"You're not going to drive on to Natchez tonight, are you? It's getting late, and you're not well, Avalon. I think it would be foolish for you to travel any farther tonight, don't you?" He turned to Mac.

"I agree," Mac said firmly, much to Avalon's surprise and chagrin. But she knew Mac: there was no point in arguing with him.

Megan said pleadingly:

"If you don't want to stay here with us, at least let me

call David Daniels and tell him you're here, Avalon. You don't have to discuss his painting, you know. He'll be so glad to see you after all these years, and it would ease my mind about you. *Please* let me call him..."

Avalon was amazed at her own docile acceptance of this suggestion, but she had to admit it was a relief not to have to stay in this house or get back on the road after her grueling experience. She still felt shaky and sick inside.

When David arrived at the Marshalls' about fifteen minutes later, he smothered Avalon in a bear hug and wrung Mac's hand as if he'd known him all of his life.

"You're going to stay with me on my houseboat," David said, grinning at Avalon. "I'll bet you've never even been on one, have you?"

She shook her head, intrigued in spite of herself. So it was settled. Avalon reminded Mac of their Bed & Breakfast reservations in Natchez for that night and the rest of the weekend, and he used the Marshalls' phone to call and cancel, apologizing profusely to their hostess for canceling two of her three rooms on such short notice.

Megan and Bob Marshall were obviously relieved. They followed the three younger people out to their cars and said good night, urging Avalon and Mac to come to church with David the next morning, so they could be sure Avalon was all right.

"I'll drive," Mac said as he slid behind the wheel of Avalon's convertible and started to put up the top, since the wind had risen. But Avalon protested, so he left it down.

By now the Southern sky was black overhead, but it

was a soft black, like velvet strewn with sparkling, starry diamonds. On both sides of the road, honeysuckle cascaded over the fences and sprayed them with its sweet perfume.

"Now – tell me what really happened to you back there," Mac said as they followed David's car in the darkness. "Megan said you passed out while you were looking at one of David's paintings."

Avalon shook her head.

"I can't explain it, Mac. I don't understand it myself. How can I explain it to you?"

Why couldn't she share her nightmare with Mac, when she'd shared it with Megan? She barely knew Megan Marshall, while Mac was her oldest and most trusted friend. But no: Mac would pursue the issue of her past relentlessly and possibly discover things she'd always had a deep dread of knowing.

Even now, when she closed her eyes, she could still see that white-columned mansion and the jungle-like foliage around it. She tried to shut it out by picturing the house she'd looked at right before that – the raised cottage with its stone paving under the first floor of the house – the dank smell of the dampness she recalled from that childhood tour – the sour smell and the darkness – suddenly the terror was creeping up on her again, and she swallowed hard, resisting panic.

"I can't talk about any of it, Mac," she said quickly. "I can't even *think* about it. Please don't mention it again. And don't say anything to David!"

"OK, OK," Mac said, shrugging in resignation. "Whatever you say."

They drove in silence for the next few minutes, until the tail lights they were following disappeared momentarily as David turned onto the road that led down to the river. Then they saw him drive his car under a double carport, and Mac pulled in next to him.

It seemed unusual not to see a house next to the carport, and Avalon turned her eyes toward the river, some distance away. She couldn't believe that after the alarms of the day, she was going to get to do something she'd always wanted to do: spend the night on a houseboat. It certainly looked large enough for the three of them, and then some.

Now Mac put the convertible top up, and they got their bags and followed David as he led them down to the water along a well-built and well-lighted pier.

"There she is," David said with a gesture toward the houseboat, a mixture of modesty and pride in his pleasant voice. "Home, sweet home. Welcome aboard!" He unlocked the front door and led them inside.

"Oh, David, I like it!" Avalon exclaimed with enthusiasm as she looked around and set her overnight bag down. She thought to herself, this man is full of surprises! The place was like a designer magazine cover: masculine, certainly, but with a tasteful flair she'd never have expected from any man other than an artist.

"But he *is* an artist," she reminded herself, recalling his painting with a sense of dread.

Mac, already yawning and stretching, lost no time in saying:

"We've had a long day, folks. Don't you think we ought to be turning in pretty soon?" It was plain to see he'd accepted David's offer of instant friendship and was responding with his own brand of directness.

Within half an hour, all three were in their rooms – Mac with sheets and quilts spread out on the big leather couch in the front room, David in his own bedroom, and Avalon in the little guest room next to the deck at the back of the houseboat.

She pulled one of the drapes aside and looked out at the water. The houseboat's deck with its railing and comfortable chairs made her wish she could go out for a few minutes to enjoy the silence and solitude of the river.

Well, why not?

She unlocked the heavy sliding glass door and pulled it back to step outside. The gentle movement of the river made little lapping sounds as the waves caressed the sides of the boat, rocking it gently, almost like a baby's cradle. The crickets sang in the woods as a blue heron sailed low across the water, moonlight on its wings.

Avalon sat down in one of the lounge chairs on the little deck and leaned her head back, closing her eyes. What a respite this was from the horrible day behind her! Had it really been just one day?

It had started in the wee hours of this morning with her nightmare of the island in full color, and ended with an actual, if somewhat surreal, painting of the place! She'd always hoped it was something she'd made up in her mind as a child, but it must exist, or David couldn't have painted it...

And even worse, somewhere in Megan Marshall's house there was apparently a photograph of the woman who had named her Avalon...her *mother.* But no! Lora Evans was her mother.

She and Mac would simply have to leave immediately after church tomorrow...they would go on to Natchez and then back to Chicago, and she would never come back here again as long as she lived!

When David walked out onto the deck from his room at the other end of the houseboat, she knew she would have to keep him from saying anything about his painting...

"I thought I might find you out here," he said congenially. "Sitting on this deck always soothes me. That's why I made sure there's a deck all the way around the houseboat – kind of like the columns all the way around Herrington Hall." He grinned at the irony of it.

"It *is* soothing," Avalon agreed and patted the chair beside her. "Come keep me company. But let's not talk about what happened to me today, OK? I don't want to have bad dreams tonight." She despised her own cowardice; but she couldn't bear the thought of finding out more than Megan had already told her.

"No, I won't talk about it if you don't want to," David promised as he sat down in the chair next to her, "except to say that I'm really glad you ended up staying the night – I can hardly wait for you to see Johnna again, and for her to see you. You were just a little girl when she saw you last, and she was a teenager. You two wouldn't know each other if you met on the sidewalk!"

Avalon smiled. "I'm sure that's true. I'm looking forward to seeing her, too. She was always my heroine, you know. She knew more about the Bible at sixteen than most people do at sixty! She was sweet, pretty, and smart...

"David—", Avalon went on hesitantly at first and then gained courage to ask: "Why haven't you and Johnna gotten married after all these years, if you still care for each other? Please forgive me if I'm being nosy, but I'd like to understand what the problem is, if you feel like sharing it with me..." She trailed off uncertainly.

"It's OK, I don't mind telling you. There's nothing mysterious about it. Her parents just don't think I'm good enough for her, that's all." He shrugged, but she heard the pain in his voice.

"But if Johnna thinks you're good enough – ", she started, but he stopped her.

"Johnna loves me – I believe that with all my heart, Avalon. She's told me a hundred times since we've been in our twenties and old enough to think about getting married, that as soon as her parents give their approval, she'll marry me in a flash...

"But she says she won't go against them in such a major way. She says she just *can't* do it against their will. I think there must be some reason she can't tell me about..."

"Would they disinherit her?" Avalon asked.

"Oh, it's not that. It wouldn't matter much if they did. Johnna's already a millionaire many times over, though you'd never know it to talk to her. Her paternal grandfather left her a fortune in his will – she was the only grandchild at home, and they were very close. So her parents can't hold that over her.

"Besides, you've never met a less money-minded person in your life. She's really amazing, Avalon. She has the sweetest, most humble spirit of anyone I've ever known. Sometimes I wonder how she can even be a member of that family – they're so materialistic, so totally over-the-top about grand appearances. Johnna is definitely the exception...

"No, Avalon, money has nothing to do with it. My business is doing well, and my art is beginning to pay off, too...Oops! I'm sorry! I didn't mean to mention my art...Megan told me you passed out while you were looking at one of my paintings.

"I guess you've seen that place in a nightmare you've had? I always knew you were adopted, but I never heard the circumstances or anything. But forgive me for even bringing it up – I know you don't want to dream about it again tonight."

But it was too late. Swiftly, like a vulture flying off the river straight into her face, the painting at the Marshalls' flew into Avalon's memory and hovered there like a black monster.

And for one desperate moment, she almost conquered her deep-seated dread of discovering her past, to demand of David: "What *is* that place in your painting? *Where* is it?"

But Avalon knew that even if she could bear the knowledge of what the island was, and where, she still wouldn't know why she not only saw it in that terrible dream: she literally *felt* it.

CHAPTER
FIVE

The next morning, David, Mac and Avalon were back on the deck having breakfast by eight-thirty. Avalon had slept soundly after a battle with her inner pictures of "David's house", as she'd begun to call it in her own mind. She'd finally prayed for peace and had fallen into an untroubled sleep almost immediately.

David scrambled a dozen eggs and toasted half a loaf of wheat bread that they ate with home-made jam and real butter. He and Mac drank coffee out of LSU mugs, and Avalon drank her tea from a pretty cup which she held up now and then to catch the morning sunlight as it glinted through the antique ruby glass.

The breeze off the river was as mild as a baby's breath, and the sunlight slanted through the trees to glisten on the water. David and Avalon knew from their years of living in Louisiana that later in the day the air would be heavy with heat and moisture, and they relished these early hours of gentle warmth.

It was Sunday, so after breakfast they parted to get ready for the morning service at the little country church where Avalon's father, Eric Evans, had been the pastor during the four years they'd lived in the Marshalls' house.

Avalon was looking forward to seeing the people she remembered from those four special years of her childhood. They weren't expecting her, nor were they likely to recognize her after twelve years. She thought it would be fun to surprise them...

And it was.

David went ahead in his own car, and as soon as Avalon and Mac pulled up in front of the small white church building, she could feel all of the years in Chicago falling away, and she was a little girl again, walking up those very same steps and through the front door, ready to be surrounded by love.

Avalon wasn't disappointed. When she was introduced from the pulpit as the former pastor's daughter, she heard gasps of surprise and pleasure go up all over the sanctuary. And as soon as the service was over, she was enveloped in hugs from all directions, some of the older folks even waiting in line to see her again.

One elderly lady said to Mac:

"I can't seem to get close enough to Avalon to give her a hug, so I'll just hug you instead."

And she did it, much to Mac's amusement and delight.

Avalon had taken piano lessons from Lora Evans, and there was the piano on which she'd practiced for hours on end, with the window behind it where the King snake had lain and listened in serpentine silence. She pointed it out to Mac, and he smiled.

It was wonderful to see Johnna again. At twenty-eight, she was at the peak of her beauty. Slender, and yet supple, with an abundance of chestnut-colored hair that fell in natural waves around her face, her features were perfect, with what could only be called "beautiful bones". She would still be beautiful as an old woman. It was rare to find perfection like that in such a small community.

She took Avalon to their old Sunday school room, transporting Avalon back to a spine-tingling time of excitement, when a circle of children could spend a glorious hour or two hearing and seeing and sometimes acting out the most dramatic stories on earth – doing crafts, playing games, singing songs – and topping it all off with cookies and punch or hot chocolate and popcorn. What a way for a kid to spend Sunday morning!

She couldn't resist giving Johnna a hug and saying, "Thank you for all the good times and the love you gave us. You were wonderful."

Tears sprang to Johnna's eyes, and Avalon realized for the first time how lonely it must have been for her all these years, coming to church alone, without her parents. But there was David…Avalon just wished there were some way she could help those two fulfill their hopes and dreams of marriage.

David had looked so handsome this morning, walking down the aisle to the front of the sanctuary as an usher. Avalon could picture him walking down the same aisle with Johnna on his arm as his bride.

But wait – David should be standing at the front, waiting for Johnna, watching as she walked down the aisle on her father's arm….Andrew Herrington's arm?

Somehow the picture faded when Avalon thought of Johnna's parents. It would take nothing short of a miracle.

The morning service and pleasant memories had made Avalon far less anxious to escape than she'd felt last night; so when David suggested that the four of them have lunch together at the seafood restaurant on the river, a mile or two down the road from the church, she gladly agreed.

Since the weather was perfect and the restaurant was filled to capacity, the hostess took them through the crowded dining room and seated them on the deck overlooking the water. The river wound peacefully past them like a silver ribbon pricked with diamonds, bordered by an emerald forest.

A young waitress took their orders for shrimp and catfish, hush puppies and cole slaw, and the ever-present Southern sweet tea; and while Mac and David were deep in conversation across the table, she and Johnna tried to catch up on the past twelve years.

Avalon was relieved to find that her positive childhood memories were still so accurate, and she was thrilled to learn how much they had in common as adults. She loved listening to Johnna's voice, which she remembered from Sundays, when Johnna told the Bible stories Avalon had heard all of her life.

Lora Evans was a well-educated, articulate and warm-hearted woman who could tell a story so well that Avalon remembered it all week long. But Johnna's voice was different: it had a timbre unlike anyone else's in Avalon's life – like a crystal goblet struck lightly, ringing like a sweet-toned bell.

She knew that too often when children grew up, they were disappointed to find that the adults they'd idolized as children weren't quite the paragons they'd thought them to be. She was glad Johnna was turning out to be even better than her memories.

Johnna told Avalon about her teaching position as an assistant professor of history at Northeast Louisiana State College in Monroe, and about her students, whom she apparently loved almost like brothers and sisters – which she'd never really had, she added wistfully.

And Avalon shared her feelings of being somewhat cut adrift following her recent graduation from the private college not far from her home in Evanston, a suburb just north of Chicago. She'd grown so close to the professors and other students that she already missed them like family, and she would miss going back this fall.

When the four of them finally stood up to leave the restaurant, Johnna insisted that Avalon come to Herrington Hall later that afternoon for tea, and Avalon surprised herself by accepting.

Johnna said she'd told her parents that Avalon was one of her favorite Sunday school students from the past who now lived in Chicago, and Valerie Herrington had said she would love to meet someone who lived in one of her favorite cities.

So after lunch, Avalon refreshed her memories of Orchestra Hall and the Opera House, the Art Museum and Water Tower Place, Michigan Avenue's "Magnificent Mile", the Gold Coast, Marshall Field's and Navy

Pier, and some of the other attractions Johnna's mother might enjoy recalling.

Later that afternoon, Avalon relished the drive from David's houseboat to Herrington Hall. The weather was still perfect, the sky a deep azure blue with wispy white clouds; and the broad avenue leading up to the Hall was lined on both sides by ancient, gnarled oak trees that seemed to reach out to her with friendly arms.

They formed an archway overhead and brought to her mind a line or two of one of her favorite poems, *Cannon's Point* – "and overhead, the oaks joined hands and bowed with grace to welcome friends". Well, she was certainly Johnna's friend! Johnna was wonderful.

The old trees were also festooned with gray moss "hanging like silver tears", she thought whimsically, recalling another line of the same poem. She wondered how many tears had been shed in the Hall itself during the past 108 years...

She'd recently picked up a tourist guide in Monroe and had read up on Herrington Hall, so she knew that the house had been built in 1858, and the family had never owned slaves or used slave labor. That was certainly a point in their favor, one Avalon had been surprised to learn, in light of all she'd heard about the notorious Herrington pride.

The builder of the family fortune, John Winston Herrington, had made most of his money in diamonds, having come from England in the early 1840's already owning several mines in different parts of the British Empire.

The current owner of Herrington Hall was Johnna's

father, Andrew Jared Herrington. He had married into an old Southern family that had become rich before the Civil War, in the days when "cotton was King", as Southerners liked to say. His wife, Valerie Anne Stanton, had simply exchanged one Greek revival mansion for a larger and grander one without skipping a beat.

Avalon wasn't surprised that Johnna had never felt free to bring her little Sunday school pupils here from the small country church where she worshiped. Her parents probably would have looked down their noses at them, and that might have been hurtful to the children. Johnna would rather have died than see anyone in her class hurt or embarrassed, and Avalon had always loved her for it.

She pulled into the long, circular driveway and turned off the motor, making a final check of her make-up before getting out of the car.

Johnna herself opened the huge double doors, and Avalon laughed as she hugged her and said:

"I'm not accustomed to being a guest in one of these houses, Johnna. I'm more used to paying at the front door for the privilege of taking a tour – although the ones I've seen don't begin to compare to this," she added quickly.

Johnna laughed with her as she closed the tall doors behind them and led Avalon into the house.

"Well, at least we have it all to ourselves for a little while. Mother and Daddy had an unexpected call from town, and they're closeted in the library for a little while. But they shouldn't be long. Let me show you my part of the house while we're waiting for them."

Avalon hardly knew enough to appreciate the richness of her surroundings as Johnna led her up the winding staircase to her bedroom. The stairs themselves were totally unsupported, and Avalon had seen only two other "flying" staircases similar to it: one in the Nathaniel Russell house in Charleston, South Carolina, and the other at Auburn in Natchez, Mississippi.

The chandeliers hanging from the eighteen-foot ceilings were like clusters of glittering stars, so huge she found herself avoiding walking under them. As they mounted the staircase, she caught glimpses of the long drawing rooms on the first floor, with their famous Louis XIV furnishings.

She knew that the Herringtons did a great deal of entertaining in these rooms, but surely Johnna's parents did their real living elsewhere! The place felt more like a museum than a home.

When they finally reached Johnna's bedroom on the second floor, Avalon gasped with pleasure. It was so strikingly different from the rest of the house! Simple almost to austerity, everything in the normal-sized room was white and antique: the half-tester bed with its canopy and prim white eyelet bedspread, a plain mahogany highboy in one corner and secretary with bookcase in the other, the severely simple fireplace with its white marble mantel.

Even the oriental rug in the center of the dark wood floor was nearly white. A comfortable-looking armchair with a skirted footstool was loaded with books, which Avalon could see from the doorway were volumes on

European history.

"Oh, Johnna, this is so refreshing – I love it!" Avalon said as she went farther into the room.

"Well, I told Mother when I got out of graduate school five years ago that if she wanted me to live at home, I had to have some personal space that I could really relax in and enjoy, and this is it."

She opened another door and showed Avalon the small private bath, then opened French windows and walked out onto a balcony at the back of the house. It overlooked the river in the distance.

Between the Hall and the river lay a beautifully shaped ornamental lake surrounded by twisted oaks dripping with Spanish moss, and weeping willows that drooped like melancholy maidens trailing their tresses in the water. Several large white swans floated slowly in the shadows.

"I love sitting here and reading and thinking about David in his houseboat on the river," Johnna said, smiling at the rapt expression on Avalon's face. "But we need to go back downstairs now. Mother and Daddy will be there soon."

When they reached the front drawing room, Johnna sat down on a settee and motioned to Avalon to sit next to her.

"Avalon, I want to prepare you for meeting my mother...you may have heard that she's reserved. But she's really not unfriendly – she's just extremely sentimental and vulnerable, and I think she withdraws in order to protect herself. Do you know what I mean?"

Avalon nodded, thinking of her own withdrawal

from a past that was apparently so painful she couldn't bear the memories in her conscious mind.

"Total self-control is the mark of a true lady, according to my mother. I've lived with her for twenty-eight years now and have never seen her 'lose her cool', as my students would say. I think it would take something truly earth-shattering to upset her *sang-froid*."

Avalon just smiled. She could sympathize with Valerie Herrington, if her reserve really were based on emotional vulnerability. But she was thankful to have a mother like Lora Evans – so spontaneous and open in her responses. Avalon had always agreed with Anne Elliot in Jane Austen's book, *Persuasion*, that it was hard to trust someone who never spoke an impulsive word!

Johnna had just opened her mouth to speak again when they both looked up to see an elegantly-dressed and immaculately-groomed older couple in the doorway of the drawing room, and Avalon knew she was finally seeing Johnna's parents.

They were in their early sixties and sophisticated in the extreme. Andrew Herrington was perfectly trim from head to toe, with the proud bearing of a man who was wealthy, influential and thoroughly self-confident. Valerie, posture-perfect and elegant even in casual clothes, was as slender as her daughter, and almost as beautiful.

Avalon hardly had time to worry about staring rudely before Mrs. Herrington's face turned a sickly gray, and she sagged weakly against her husband. Johnna rushed forward to help her father get her mother to the nearest chair, where the older woman leaned back

and closed her eyes, seeming to be almost fainting.
Johnna looked at her father with alarm.

"What's wrong with Mother?"

It was plain she'd never seen her mother like this!

Andrew Herrington's voice was restrained and icy,
but Avalon could see that he was very angry.

"What is this, Johnna, some kind of cruel joke?"

Johnna looked up at him, startled.

"What do you mean?" Her voice trembled.

Andrew turned to Avalon and said sternly:

"Who are you, young lady? Why are you here?"

Avalon was so surprised she could hardly speak, but
finally she was able to stammer:

"I – I'm Avalon Evans."

Then, thinking it might help to identify herself with
someone local, she added:

"I – lived here when I was a little girl, in Bob and
Megan Marshall's house..."

At the mention of the Marshalls, Valerie Herrington
groaned.

Avalon looked at Johnna in distress.

"What's wrong? What have I said?"

Andrew Herrington said harshly:

"I'll tell you what's wrong. Megan Marshall helped
our daughter to elope when she was only eighteen, with
a man we never saw or knew. That was twenty-five
years ago, and we've never seen her again.

"And what has upset my wife so much – "

He took his wife's hand gently and held it between
both of his own before going on, his voice not quite so
severe now:

"What has upset my wife so much is the fact that you ...you look enough like our Lindsay to be her daughter."

CHAPTER
SIX

Later, Avalon could never remember exactly what happened next. She only knew she had followed Johnna upstairs, with Valerie Herrington supported by her husband and younger daughter.

All three of the women were in such a state of shock that not a word was spoken as they climbed the long, spiraling staircase. But when they finally reached the door of the older woman's bedroom, Johnna said sweetly, but firmly:

"Daddy, I think you'd better let me handle this..."

And Andrew Herrington, scion of wealth and power, who could have bought half the state and influenced the other half with a word from his lips, simply nodded sadly and turned away to descend the stairs alone.

Johnna helped her mother to lie down on the bed and covered her gently with a light quilt. Then she turned to Avalon and said quietly:

"Do you know anything about this, Avalon? I've always known you were adopted..."

Avalon had emerged from her stupefaction to wonder worriedly how much she should tell Johnna. What would happen when she shared what Megan had told her? Should she share it at all? Why not ask Megan to say nothing, and just say she herself knew nothing, either? Oh, *why* hadn't she left before any of this happened?

But Avalon had been brought up to be honest even when it hurt, and she knew she couldn't honestly withhold what she knew, little as it was, even though she couldn't imagine the knowledge bringing anything but pain to all of them.

She took a deep breath and very softly told Johnna everything Megan had shared with her – the story about Megan's friend who had fallen in love with an Englishman while traveling in England after her graduation from high school, about his being ten years her senior, her never telling anyone his name for fear her parents would find them and force her to give him up...

She even told Johnna about Megan's friend's obsession with all things English and especially her childhood fascination with the stories of King Arthur and the fabled island of Avalon, and her plan to name her baby Avalon if she ever had a little girl...

"Megan said she almost fainted when she saw me for the first time," Avalon said, "because I looked so much like her friend, and also because of my name – so unusual!

"She – she wanted to show me a photograph of her friend, who she was convinced was my mother. She said it would be just like looking at myself."

"It would be!" said Valerie Herrington suddenly from her prone position on her bed, and Johnna and Avalon jumped with surprise.

Mrs. Herrington was raising herself feebly on her elbow in an effort to be more forceful.

"Mother, don't agitate yourself..."

"I'll agitate myself if I want to, Johnna! I've heard everything she's said – it's all true, and even her voice sounds like Lindsay's. This girl is Lindsay's daughter, and I don't mean to let her get away from me the way Lindsay did."

Avalon's heart nearly stopped beating as she faced the possible long-term ramifications of being Valerie and Andrew Herrington's granddaughter.

In a flash, she considered the feasibility of simply walking out of the room and out of the house. She knew Johnna wouldn't stop her. She and Mac could be packed and gone in less than half an hour, head for Chicago and never look back. Oh, *why, why* hadn't she done it sooner?

Then she saw the look on Johnna's sweet, beautiful face and knew she couldn't do it. Johnna was gazing at her as if she knew exactly what was passing through Avalon's mind, and her eyes were full of a pleading pity.

"Johnna, look in my top desk drawer – "

Valerie Herrington was sitting up on the side of her bed now.

"The right side, in the back, under my stationery. Bring me the picture there."

Avalon's feet were glued to the floor out of love for Johnna, but her heart was flying far away from this place, her mind racing to escape the inevitable.

Johnna retrieved the silver-framed photograph from the bottom of her mother's desk drawer and stood staring at it as if she would never stop. Then she turned slowly to look at Avalon.

She carefully laid the photograph on her mother's lap and crossed the room to throw her arms around Avalon, bursting into tears as she did. Avalon cried, too, not having seen the picture yet, but somehow knowing what Johnna must be feeling.

Avalon had never felt the need for any family she didn't have – she'd never missed the birth mother and father she'd never known. On the contrary, she'd wanted to forget they even existed!

But poor Johnna, without knowing why, had missed the sister she couldn't remember and was now feeling the sweetness of finding that unknown sister's child.

Avalon's heart was hurting and her brain about to burst with the new complications in her peaceful and happy life. But one good thing had come out of it: Johnna was her aunt.

They were both wiping their eyes and laughing at their mutual tears when Mrs. Herrington said:

"Come look at the picture, please..."

She was holding it out to Avalon, and Avalon took it in her hands and reluctantly dragged her eyes downward to see the woman there. She almost found herself unable to follow through: there would be no turning back, once she saw.

But she did look, and Megan Marshall and Valerie Herrington had been right: it *was* like looking at a picture of herself...

The eyes were the same shape exactly and the same shade of green; the hair was the same texture and color, even the same general style; the oval face, the pert and perfectly shaped nose; the full lips; the white, even teeth; the dimples on both sides of the soft mouth; even the smile. Avalon could almost believe someone had planted a photograph of her in this house.

But she knew better. She'd had the name Avalon before her parents ever saw her. And there was the island in David's painting. No one had made her have nightmares about it or faint when she saw it. Apparently it was a painfully real part of her past. She had told Johnna everything – except that.

She stood holding the picture of young Lindsay Herrington, knowing in her heart that this woman had been her mother – her "real" mother, as Mac would say – but she felt nothing. How strange! Perhaps she would feel something later, when she knew more...

Avalon gently handed the photograph back to Johnna's mother – *her* grandmother now, she supposed, though it all still seemed unreal, somehow.

"But, Johnna, I don't understand...had you never seen that photograph before?" Avalon asked.

"No, Avalon...I was only three when Lindsay ran away, and I can honestly say I don't remember her at all. There hasn't been a picture of her in this house for twenty-five years."

"No, Johnna," her mother corrected her. "It's only been twenty-two years. Your father and I looked for Lindsay for three whole years without stopping, before we finally gave up. We searched through all of England, even when the bombs were falling on London! We risked our lives to find our little girl."

She stopped, her pale face puckering.

"But we didn't even know her married name. Lindsay would only talk about 'Lancelot' – such an adolescent fantasy! She refused to tell us his name. We were so crushed...

"Finding her was our purpose in life for those three years! Johnna, you stayed here with Sarah so much that if she hadn't been black, I think you'd have believed *she* was your mother! She and Lindsay had been very close, so it broke her heart, too...

"Maybe I was wrong to do it, but I just couldn't bear to look at a picture of Lindsay after we finally gave up trying to find her. I just couldn't bear it! And it hurt me just as much to hear her name."

Johnna said softly to Avalon:

"I don't recall ever hearing Lindsay's name spoken in this house in all the years I was growing up, and I certainly never saw her picture. If I had, I'd have known who you were instantly when you came back this time as an adult.

"Even I myself practically forgot I'd ever had a sister, knowing so little of her story and everyone so unwilling to tell me anything about her – and also, everyone knew that she didn't want to be found.

"Even Megan Marshall never talked about Lindsay, knowing how hurtful the story would be for me, but mainly knowing how furious Mother and Daddy were with her for helping Lindsay to escape – "

Johnna's hand flew to her mouth.

"I mean, *elope!* Oh, Mother, I'm so sorry. That was a slip of the tongue. I didn't mean it!"

She was horrified by her Freudian slip.

Somehow Johnna's words sank into Avalon's consciousness, although they'd been inadvertent and embarrassing. Suddenly she realized that if she could only face her past, she could give Johnna a future. Her nightmare could be turned into Johnna's dream.

Valerie Herrington knew nothing about David's painting and the part it had apparently played in Avalon's – and therefore Lindsay's – past. Avalon knew something that her grandmother would give anything in the world to know…

When Valerie finally said, "Child, how much do you know about your past?", Avalon smiled and willingly answered:

"Well, first of all, let me tell you a little bit about my wonderful parents – and they will always be my parents."

She paused to let that sink in before going on:

"Their names are Eric and Lora Evans, and they are the two most precious people on earth to me."

She looked at Johnna for encouragement, knowing how much Johnna had loved them both when Eric Evans had been her pastor here twelve years ago.

Johnna smiled warmly, and Avalon went on:

"They never tried to deceive me about my adoption…I've always known. My mother has told me the story so many times. She has often said she believes God knew we needed each other and just made sure we ended up together. Somehow, I believe it, too.

"Anyway, they'd been married for about ten years and had just about given up on having a child of their own. Then one Sunday morning, someone – they never found out who it was – simply waited until the pastor and the people bowed their heads and closed their eyes to pray and chose that opportune moment to deposit a little girl – me – on the back pew of the church, and then walked out.

"They tell me I was dirty and disheveled, my little shoes were caked with mud, my hair was matted with grass and burrs, and I was so traumatized that I couldn't speak for nearly six months. I didn't even cry. By the time I could have told them anything, I must have forgotten everything."

Mrs. Herrington said indignantly:

"Didn't they try to find your mother?"

"Of course they did!"

Avalon had to hold her temper in check and remember that this poor woman was a mother who didn't know yet just how hard Eric and Lora Evans *had* tried to find Lindsay Herrington.

"My daddy and all of the men in that church got together and contacted the authorities of two states in every direction. They spent thousands of dollars of their own money putting advertisements in all the newspapers and on the radio, and they went to all the adoption agencies to see if anyone had tried to give up a child.

"They did this for six months, and there was nothing. No one had ever seen or heard of me. It was as if I had materialized out of nowhere."

Johnna asked curiously:

"How did they know your name?"

"Whoever left me there had pinned a little piece

of paper to my dress, dirty as it was, and it said, 'Her name is Avalon.' So, my parents – hoping that by keeping that name someone might know me somewhere down the road – have called me that ever since."

Avalon sighed as she finished her story. It was the first time she'd shared it in a long time. Then she realized that Valerie was weeping quietly, and for the first time, Avalon felt real pity for her. She went and sat down beside the older woman and patted her hand gently.

"I'm sorry," she said softly, meaning it.

Mrs. Herrington raised her head and dabbed her reddened eyes with a handkerchief as she said brokenly:

"Lindsay is probably dead. She must be. She was such a soft-hearted girl and would have loved her baby so much – she would never have allowed something like that to happen to you if she were alive...

"My baby girl is probably gone – or something has happened to her that I'm not sure I could bear knowing! But I *have* to know, or I'll die. And you have to help me find out!"

CHAPTER
SEVEN

Avalon was trying to decide how to tell her grandmother that she would help them find out about her mother, but only under certain conditions, when Johnna said excitedly:

"I just thought of something, Avalon."

Avalon raised her head and said distractedly:

"Yes, Johnna? What is it?"

"Where was your Dad pastoring at the time? I mean, when someone left you on the back pew of their church? That would certainly be a starting point, wouldn't it?"

She sounded so hopeful that Avalon hated to remind her:

"They advertised for my family for hundreds of miles in every direction, Johnna. If they didn't find anybody to claim me or even to identify me back then, so soon after the fact, what could we hope to find now? Someone could have had me in a car for days, driving clear across the country. We could have come from literally anywhere!...

"So I think the location of the church is really irrelevant at this point, but I can certainly tell you where it was. Actually, it's not that far from here – in St. Francisville, north of Baton Rouge."

"But if that's the case, why wouldn't *we* have seen the appeals? We were looking for Lindsay for three long years," Mrs. Herrington interrupted skeptically.

"Mother, please…" Johnna said gently.

"Well, first of all, this would have happened long after those three years, wouldn't it? If – if Lindsay –" Avalon couldn't bring herself to say, "my mother" yet. She wasn't sure she ever would.

"If Lindsay left home twenty-five years ago, that was in 1941, wasn't it? The doctors told my parents I was probably about two and a half when I was abandoned in the late summer of '46…

"That was five years after she eloped! You had stopped looking for Lindsay by then. And what would have made you think I was connected with her, anyway?

"In fact, I doubt that anyone who knew your family would even have thought of you in connection with something like that – an abandoned child! Especially one who was as neglected and traumatized as I was."

Mrs. Herrington winced.

"Yes…I…can see that. I guess you're right." She seemed to wilt.

Avalon struggled with herself for a moment, and then she said:

"However…there *is* something I haven't told you yet. I – I don't understand it, but I saw a painting of a place the other day – I – recognized it and I think I must have been there before I was abandoned, which means Lindsay was probably there, too. It's – a place in one of David Daniels's paintings…"

At the mention of David, Johnna's mother rose and

said acidly:

"We don't mention that young man in this house."

Avalon rose, too, and faced her new-found grandmother. She said formally:

"I'm going to have to mention him if you want to find out about your older daughter, Mrs. Herrington. In fact, you're going to have to do a great deal more than just mention him, or I won't go one step further with this. As far as I'm concerned, I didn't come here today, and I know nothing."

Mrs. Herrington looked at Avalon and realized fully that this young woman did not have any history with her, nor did she have the soft feelings toward her that had kept Johnna at home all these years. She looked hesitant and unhappy for a few more moments, but she finally sat back down.

"What do you mean I'm going to have to do a great deal more than mention him?"

"I mean you're going to have to let Johnna marry him."

There was a sudden dead silence. Avalon saw Johnna's lovely eyes widen with surprise. Then a slow smile began to spread across her face.

Avalon was amazed at how firmly and calmly she'd been able to speak the words. She added:

"If I ask David and Megan to say nothing about it, you'll never even know which painting had such an effect on me."

Johnna's mother was speechless with shock, so Avalon took advantage of it to say:

"I suggest we ask David about his painting only after

he knows that he and Johnna can be married."

She knew that the life-changing decision would be made now or never, so she simply shut her mouth and prayed.

No one could have been more surprised than Avalon when the older woman started to laugh softly, and at first Avalon was alarmed, afraid her grandmother was becoming hysterical under the strain.

But finally Valerie said, with a little sob at the end of her laughter:

"Well, I've hung onto one daughter because I'd lost the other one...I guess the least I can do is let Johnna go if I'm going to find out about Lindsay."

Then she turned toward Johnna and said with genuine feeling:

"I'm sorry, Johnna...I just *couldn't* let you go! It seemed that every time you were willing to stay at home with me, it satisfied something in me. I guess it reassured me that I wasn't a bad mother – that at least one of my girls loved me enough to stay home rather than marry a man I didn't want her to marry. I just couldn't bear to lose both of you...and especially you. You were the baby of my 'old age'."

She laughed at the irony of it. "At least, I felt old at thirty-six. But I was so young compared to now. I'm so sorry, Johnna. Can you ever forgive a foolish – and selfish – old woman?"

She held out her hand to her younger daughter with real sorrow on her face, and Johnna responded in a quick rush of joy and affection, kneeling down in front of her mother and hugging her.

"Do you really mean it, Mother?"

"I've held you back too long, Johnna. If I don't know how much you love me by now, I guess I never will."

"I knew something was wrong," Johnna said, wiping away happy tears as she spoke, "but I didn't know exactly what it was...so I never really understood. I only knew it would kill Mother if I left."

Avalon said, "Well, now that that's settled, I can tell you: David's painting is hanging in the Marshalls' upstairs hallway. At least, it was there until I – I fainted when I was looking at it. Then she took it down."

"You fainted!" Johnna exclaimed.

Avalon nodded, almost unable to believe that she was really talking about it at last, and without much discomfort.

"I can't tell you how horrible it made me feel. I haven't been able to talk about it, or even to think about it without just – oh, I don't know how to describe it! The problem is, I've seen that place in David's painting in a terrible nightmare I've had off and on all my life. The nightmare always starts with the island and house."

Johnna said: "Could you tell us just a little more about this painting of – David's?"

She smiled at Avalon like a fellow-conspirator as she spoke his name.

"Well, first of all, let me exonerate Megan. When she was telling me about my – about Lindsay, I asked her what she knew about that place in David's painting, and she says she doesn't know the first thing about it. And I believe her..."

"But what's *in* the painting, child?"

Valerie had bristled a little at Megan's name, but Avalon could tell she was making a concerted effort to be gracious, so she replied patiently:

"It's a painting of an island and a house. The island is very overgrown with vegetation, and the house is almost invisible because of it. It's a Greek revival mansion, though – you can see that much. And it's in the middle of the island – at least, you can see water on two sides, but it's impossible to tell how large the island really is."

They were all silent for a while. Then Johnna said:

"Have you said anything to David yet about his painting, to find out where this island is?"

Avalon shook her head.

"I haven't even been able to talk about it until today, Johnna. The feelings it gave me were so painful, I don't think I can say it strongly enough."

Avalon's grandmother moaned slightly and said:

"Oh, dear…that means something terrible must have happened."

Avalon started to speak, but Johnna motioned to her to stay silent. And in another moment or two, Mrs. Herrington said in a slightly stronger voice:

"I can't help it. I've got to know." She lifted her small chin and jutted it out a bit, and Johnna smiled.

Johnna's voice trembled a little when she said:

"I guess the next step is to call David and ask him about it…"

Avalon jumped in immediately.

"Exactly. He's the only one who can tell us about it.

I'll call him right now. Or – why don't *you* do it, Johnna? Maybe he'd like to just come on over and tell all of us about it in person..."

Out of long habit, Mrs. Herrington's lips thinned out into a tight line, but Avalon wasn't worried: those lips would smile at David Daniels yet.

Johnna left the room and went into the hallway to call David. Avalon saw that there was a phone on her grandmother's desk, but she was glad Johnna would have privacy in which to give David the good news.

When Johnna came back into the room a few minutes later, she was literally glowing.

"He's on his way," she announced joyfully, and for a moment Avalon thought she might twirl around and shout. She certainly wouldn't have blamed her.

Mrs. Herrington seemed to revert briefly to the efficient woman-of-the-world she would need to be as mother of the bride, and she also had to break the news to her husband.

Johnna helped her freshen her make-up after all the tears she'd shed, and they worked on her hair for a few minutes. Then she went downstairs, and the two girls were left alone in the room.

"I still can't believe it," Johnna said, and now she did twirl around, with a laugh.

Avalon chuckled.

"You know, I've always believed Romans 8:28, where Paul says that God works in all things for the good of those who love Him – but I don't think I've ever seen it illustrated quite as dramatically as this!"

Suddenly Johnna was serious again.

"Oh, Avalon, thank you. Thank you from the bottom of my heart, for not running away from all of this. I know you must have wanted to."

Avalon said soberly:

"I certainly thought about it. But I looked at your face, Johnna, and suddenly realized how I could turn my nightmare into your dream. That's how I thought of it at the time, in my own mind."

"Your nightmare into my dream...", Johnna said thoughtfully. "I do hope it doesn't turn into a *real* nightmare for you, Avalon...I'd feel so guilty."

"No, don't even think that, Johnna. The Lord knows everything that's happening to both of us right now. It's going to be all right, whatever happens...I'm sure of it."

According to Megan Marshall's story, Lindsay Herrington had been disinherited when she eloped, so at least Avalon didn't have to worry about any unpleasant financial complications, and she was thankful for that: it might have made her very unpopular with Johnna's parents.

When Valerie Herrington came back upstairs, Johnna's father was with her. Avalon was glad to see that he looked sober, but not severe. He actually looked at Avalon with a sort of abashed apology in his eyes.

She started to leave the room so they could discuss Johnna's and David's marriage privately; but Andrew Herrington stopped her by saying:

"Please stay, young lady...Avalon. I hardly know what to say or how to say it, but we – we see you as part of the family, and we want you to be in on this, if you don't mind..."

Avalon was surprised by her feelings of warmth toward this man who was her grandfather but who had been so cold and hard in their first encounter. "I've always loved Johnna, Mr. Herrington, and I'd love to be part of this. But I'd like to be sure Johnna doesn't mind..."

"Oh, Avalon. Of course I want you here! I want you to be in my wedding, too." Johnna hugged her quickly, still glowing.

Her father said, a little sadly: "Just how soon do you want this wedding to be, Johnna?"

Even Avalon was taken aback when Johnna said instantly: "Tomorrow!"

They all stared at her, incredulous. Mrs. Herrington recovered her voice first, though it sounded shaky as she said:

"But you have to have a wedding dress and veil, and a bouquet, and a trousseau for your honeymoon. And a reception. And invitations. We can't *do* all of that in a day!" She had turned pale at the thought.

Johnna smiled a slow, sweet, satisfied smile and said: "I've been putting it all together since I finished my graduate degree five years ago, and it's all there, ready. Except the reception and invitations, of course. And I can live without those. It's what David wants, too...we've waited so long."

It occurred to Avalon then that Johnna knew her parents very well indeed and was anxious to take immediate advantage of their softened hearts...

Tomorrow!

CHAPTER
EIGHT

They were all breathless and nearly paralyzed with amazement, but Johnna's father was finally able to say:

"Couldn't you wait at least until this weekend? You've got to have a marriage license, and I've got to get Collyn Edwards to take your diamond jewelry out of the safety deposit box at the bank in Monroe for your wedding, and that's not optional. You knew your grandfather, Johnna. He'd turn over in his grave or come back and haunt us if I let you be married without that!

"And there's a letter in that same box, too, that he said wasn't to be opened until your wedding day. You know the bank isn't open today, so I couldn't even get it until tomorrow, unless I call in a favor.

"In fact, I'll have to call in more than one favor to get you married legally on such short notice! Couldn't you give us at least until Friday or Saturday?"

He repeated his plea with such pathos that Avalon found herself hoping Johnna would give in. She could see that Johnna was battling mightily with her own desires, and then Valerie added her appeal:

"Please, Johnna…it would mean so much to me to have a little more time…just a few days?"

Finally, Johnna sighed and nodded.

"I'll – have to call David and tell him. Do you want me to ask him about this other matter of the painting?"

"Why not ask him to come and talk to me first, while your mother gets a little rest," Andrew said mildly. "And when the two of us have finished talking, he can tell Valerie and Avalon all about the painting while you're getting things done. Will that work?"

They all agreed, and an hour later, David Daniels disappeared into the library of Herrington Hall with Andrew Herrington, hoping to become his son-in-law. Valerie remained upstairs in her bedroom to rest.

The two younger women went to Johnna's room, where she pulled a huge box out from under her bed. The style of Johnna's wedding dress was far more elaborate than Avalon had expected, in light of the simplicity of her bedroom.

"I chose everything with David's artistic love of beauty in mind," she explained. "My choice would have been a simple sheath, a circlet of orange blossoms on my head and no diamond jewelry at all."

At the thought of the diamonds, she sighed. "Mother will insist I wear the diamonds my grandfather gave me for my wedding day, so everything else might as well match them, I suppose. David has always been afraid that if I ever married him, my parents would turn against me and not even come to our wedding...

"So I wanted to be sure it's all just as it would be if they were positively thrilled about the whole thing. Mother *will* be thrilled about my dress – oh! and my bouquet."

Johnna laid the dress down and reached for another box under the bed. Inside was the shell of an enormous bouquet exquisitely designed with tulle and lace and ribbon, with places already fixed for the insertion of fresh flowers. Avalon saw a thin white Bible at the base of it.

"When will you get your diamonds and the letter from your grandfather?" Avalon asked.

"Well, Sarah's son – you know Sarah Edwards, our housekeeper – her son Collyn is one of the vice-presidents at the bank Daddy uses in Monroe, so I imagine we'll get the safety-deposit box out tomorrow."

At that moment, Andrew Herrington knocked lightly on the door of her bedroom, and when she opened it, he said soberly:

"David is waiting for you downstairs in the library, Johnna."

Johnna looked at her father's face with some trepidation and scooted out the door past him quickly, nearly flying down the stairs.

As Andrew stood in the doorway, Avalon smiled shyly at him, thinking that she was actually beginning to like him, in spite of his serious self-control and habitual reticence.

Just before he turned away, she said bravely:

"You won't be sorry you gave your permission for Johnna to marry David, Mr. Herrington. He really is an exceptionally wonderful person."

He smiled back at her, seemingly somewhat shy himself, and Avalon realized as he went back downstairs that he hadn't said he *had* given them permission...

So when Johnna and David came back upstairs together, arm-in-arm, relaxed and radiant, Avalon breathed a sigh of relief. She'd been almost afraid that the Herringtons might change their minds unless the information they got from David about his mysterious painting made it worthwhile to give Johnna up.

But apparently that wasn't the case. Things seemed to be settled, regardless of the forthcoming explanation on which all their hopes were resting.

She waited where she was while David and Johnna went into Valerie Herrington's room, knowing it would be an emotional time for the three of them.

Finally, Johnna came back into her own bedroom, still smiling.

"Oh, Avalon, it's so wonderful! I still can hardly believe it all, myself. David says Daddy was so kind to him, and just now, Mother treated him as if she'd always wanted me to marry him. I feel as if I'm in a dream and will wake up any minute!"

She hugged herself rapturously.

"Go on down there, now, and listen to what David has to say about that painting. I didn't even ask him about it – we had so much to say. And I have so much to do! I'll have to take advantage of every minute between now and Friday night."

When Avalon walked into Valerie's bedroom, she was a little alarmed to see the painting of the island already in the room. She hadn't realized that David would actually bring it with him. She avoided looking at it and chose a chair from which she couldn't see it.

David had risen politely when Avalon came into the

room, but now he sat back down. Valerie Herrington was sitting in a comfortable armchair near her bed, with a troubled but hopeful expression on her face.

Avalon couldn't have described her own emotions at that moment. She deeply dreaded hearing what David might have to say about the island; and on the other hand, she wanted to get it over with as quickly as possible.

She was relieved when Valerie said calmly:

"Tell us everything you know, David. That's all I ask."

"Well," he said, "if I remember correctly, it was about six or seven years ago, when I was doing some research for a couple of paintings I'd been asked to do of Melrose and Oakland, two plantation houses just south of Natchitoches. I'd gone there for the week …

"One night I was having dinner at a local café, and the cook came out to see how I liked the steak − I'd asked to have it done a certain way − and we started talking about different places…

"He told me he'd worked at several of the big plantation houses, sometimes as a cook, but more often as a gardener, and he started to describe one of the places to me, when the owner of the café came over and told him to go back to the kitchen…

"Later, I was walking out to my car and saw that he was about to walk home from work − he didn't have a car, apparently, so naturally I offered him a ride. And on the way to his house, he told me about this island and the mansion that had been built on it…

"He said: 'I could be a rich man today if I had been

willing to stay there – if I'd been willing to do a spot of murder'…"

Valerie and Avalon both exclaimed: "Murder!"

Valerie had turned ashen, but David went on:

"He wouldn't tell me what it was all about, but I got the distinct impression that he'd been asked to do away with someone for a reward, and he had decided at the last minute not to go through with it…

"When we got to his house, I saw the pathetically poor place where he lived. I couldn't help but pity and appreciate the man for choosing to do the right thing, and I wanted to know more – mainly where this island was.

"But he really clammed up then, saying he himself might be done away with if he told me, as there was still a huge fortune involved in the situation. So I accepted his refusal to tell me where it was and succeeded in getting him to describe it to me in as much detail as possible…and this painting is the result."

David stopped speaking and sat in silence. At first, Avalon and Valerie just looked at him blankly.

Then Valerie said in a choked voice:

"Do you mean to say you still don't know where this island is?"

David shook his head sadly.

"I'm sorry. I tried, but I had no idea it would ever mean anything to Johnna or her family. How could I know that? And I don't think the old man would have told me any more than he did, anyway. He felt his life was at stake. He said no one on the island knew where he'd disappeared to – he had made sure of that. But he wasn't taking any chances."

"So could you find him again? I mean, you surely remember where this restaurant and this man's house are, don't you? It hasn't been all that long since you were there!" Avalon was surprised to realize that she was almost as desperate to know more as Valerie was.

David shook his head.

"He told me that night that his job was playing out and he would be moving on soon...he had no idea where."

Valerie looked as if she would cry, and Avalon felt like crying with her.

"Couldn't you at least try to find him and get more information from him, now that we know it matters? Surely he would have pity on a grieving mother like Valerie here."

"Avalon, you know how much I love Johnna and everyone connected to her. I'd do anything to help...but that man was getting on in years even back then and could very well be dead by now. I wouldn't know where to begin, anyway."

"Couldn't you go back to that restaurant and ask them if they know anything?"

"I already did that, after I dropped him off at his house. I was so curious, I wanted to at least know his last name. He had refused to tell me, but I thought he probably would have told his employer in order to get his paycheck."

The two women looked at him hopefully, but he shook his head again.

"It was no good. The café had hired him just as a day

laborer during a busy tourist event and paid him in cash. The only name they knew him by was the same one he told me: Joe...

"So that's all we have to go by...just 'Joe'."

CHAPTER NINE

Valerie Herrington seemed to sink into a sort of stupor when David finished. When it became apparent that there was no more information forthcoming, she stared at him desolately for a few more moments in silence, and then she began to weep quietly.

Avalon was deeply disappointed, too. She didn't quite know what she had expected; but in spite of her dread and horror of the place in the painting itself, and her life-long aversion to knowing anything about her origins, she had to admit to herself that she'd hoped David could tell them more, for Johnna's and Valerie's sake. But there was no more to know…

At least, there was no way of finding out more. They couldn't search the whole country or even the whole state of Louisiana for something that might not even exist except in the imagination of an old man.

But it couldn't be just old Joe's imagination! The place had to be real, or she wouldn't have seen it in her nightmares, and she wouldn't have passed out when she saw it in David's painting.

Avalon prayed for wisdom silently for a few more moments and then slipped to her knees in front of the weeping woman to say gently:

"Mrs. Herrington – Valerie – Grandmother..."

Valerie Herrington's head remained bowed until she heard the word "grandmother"; and then she raised it and looked into Avalon's face keenly.

The older woman's eyes were filled with a kind of hopeless despair that went to Avalon's heart, and her next words were unexpected, even to herself.

"I don't know how to do it, or even if it can be done. But if this place in David's painting is real, and if it can be found, I'll find it, with God's help...does that make it any easier to bear?"

Avalon smiled tentatively and was rewarded with a flicker of relief and affection on her grandmother's dejected face.

"I know I should just be thankful to have you, my dear...you look so very much like my Lindsay, and you *are* her baby girl – the one she named Avalon, after her ridiculous paradise island."

She wiped her wet eyes with a handkerchief.

"I *am* grateful we've found you – God knows. But being so close to knowing about Lindsay, and then not to know, after all! It's just too awful."

She started to cry again, and Avalon said, more firmly this time:

"I really believe my – my mother – would have wanted you to forget about her for a little while longer and focus instead on Johnna – her little baby sister. Don't you think so, too? Didn't she love her? I'm sure she did."

She smiled into her grandmother's face and was encouraged by Valerie's small nod.

"Can't we just let Lindsay rest a little longer and think about Johnna on her wedding day – her wedding weekend? She's been such a good, dutiful daughter all these years...she deserves that, don't you think?" Avalon spoke gently.

Valerie stifled a sob. "I know you're right, Avalon. *Avalon...*"

Her lips twisted into an ironic smile as she went on:

"I never thought I'd see the day I would say that name with any pleasure! When Lindsay talked about her paradise island and her 'Lancelot', I wanted to scream. Never in a million years would I have imagined that someday her own little baby girl would just wander into our lives one day..."

Her eyes welled up again, but this time she reached out to Avalon and held her close for a few moments, and Avalon was so moved she didn't even try to stop the tears.

By the time both of them had recovered from their emotions, David had left the room and had taken the offending painting with him.

Avalon was relieved. She hadn't made any reference to exactly *when* she would start trying to find the island in David's painting. She was perfectly sincere in her offer, but she still dreaded it and was thankful her grandmother didn't press her.

Now both women rose and walked together to Johnna's room to see if they could help. Johnna was literally surrounded by wedding and trousseau clothes, on the bed, the chairs, the closet – they were everywhere.

When she gleefully held up her beautiful things and showed them to her mother and her niece, Avalon could see that Valerie was happily enthralled, and she felt relieved.

Then Johnna surprised them both by holding out the most exquisite creation of all and informing them that it was for Avalon to wear at the wedding.

It was the color of the crepe myrtle around Megan's house and made of material as soft as clouds. And it was the most delicious concoction Avalon had ever seen. She hugged Johnna.

"Where on earth did you get this? And how did you know I adore this color? And this fabric! And how do you know it'll fit me, anyway?" she said laughingly, holding it out and then hugging it to her.

Johnna said softly:

"It was your mother's dress, Avalon. Sarah went to Lindsay's old trunks and got it out for you as soon as we told her everything that was happening. She says there's a whole gorgeous and elegant wardrobe and several furs in them – a little bit behind the fashions, of course, but she says Lindsay had an eye for classic designs, and most of her things will never be out of date. It's all yours, if you want it."

"There's her jewelry, too," Valerie spoke up quickly. "She had some beautiful pieces that she left behind... I'm not sure why, really. They were hers, but they were very expensive, and maybe she was afraid we would think her husband was marrying her for her money, I don't know...

"Anyway, they're still here, and they're yours, Avalon. In fact, I'm going to insist that you take them and consider them your inheritance from your mother. They're worth a fortune."

Sudden tears sprang to Avalon's eyes, and she couldn't speak for a moment or two. Then she said, so sincerely that neither of the other two women could doubt that she meant it:

"How can I bear to profit in any way from – my – my mother's pain and whatever she might have gone through for me and with me? I don't think I can..."

Johnna took her hand and made her sit down on the bed, then said soberly:

"Avalon, let's get something settled here and now, OK? You are Lindsay's daughter, the child of her dreams, the little baby girl she couldn't wait to name Avalon...

"We love you for yourself (you've always been one of my favorite people in the world, you know that!) but we love you now as part of our flesh and blood. We won't ask anything of you – "

Johnna looked at her mother momentarily, and Valerie nodded her agreement.

" – except to let us love you as a member of this family – and to accept the things we want to give you that are born out of that love....do you understand what I'm trying to say?"

Johnna's voice was gentle but persuasive, and Avalon found herself nodding her acquiescence.

"But not right now, Johnna, all right? I don't think I can handle any more tonight. Can I just take the dress I'm to wear in your wedding and deal with all of the rest later?"

"Of course!" Johnna said. "But you do have to take the jewelry that goes with the dress – it's *my* wedding, you know!" Her eyes sparkled.

She reached into a flat white box and drew out a dainty and tastefully designed necklace of rubies in a setting of antique gold. The rubies exactly matched the deep pink of the dress; and so did the ruby drop earrings and the matching bracelet that Johnna gave her next.

By the time Avalon left Herrington Hall, she felt a little like Cinderella – and hoped her coach wouldn't turn into a pumpkin before the wedding on Friday night!

The following few days were a blur of activity not only at the Hall, but around David's houseboat as well, with the groom in the house, and the maid of honor, and the best man. Avalon had been given her wedding clothes, but Mac and David had to go into Monroe to find their tuxedos and accoutrements.

Not only did David have to do a hundred things to get ready for his wedding, but he also had to take care of his business affairs in preparation for a two-week honeymoon in New Orleans, along the River Road, and in Natchez.

Avalon gave him the name of Whitehaven Bed & Breakfast in Natchez, a lovely old Victorian house with a verandah and widow's walk all around, less than a mile from the Mississippi, where she and Mac knew the owners, and he booked reservations for the Rose Room for several nights. Avalon told him to be sure to take Johnna to one of the outdoor restaurants at Natchez-under-the-Hill, down on the river.

Megan was floating on a cloud. She'd been so afraid that Avalon would simply walk out on the Herringtons if they discovered who she really was, and she was thrilled to the core by the mutual affection that seemed to be developing instead.

It not only gave her positive pleasure, she said; it also negated a great deal of the guilt she'd felt all these years for her part in helping Lindsay Herrington to elope, never to be seen or heard from again.

And when Avalon had come along, the regret and guilt had been twice as deep, because now she knew that another life had been affected by her actions.

She gave Avalon the photograph she'd tried to show her the day Avalon had passed out in front of David's painting, and this time Avalon was able to look at Lindsay's face without pain.

It gave her a warm feeling to wear the deep pink crepe dress Lindsay had chosen years ago. If only Lindsay could be here to see her wear it on Johnna's special day!

Avalon never knew just how they all managed it, but by seven-thirty Friday night, everything was ready for the wedding. The pastor and congregation of the little church had done everything in their power to make the place positively pristine, and the candlelit sanctuary, small and simple as it was, had the atmosphere of a storybook fantasy.

The pews were packed with people who could barely restrain their impatience to see the bride and groom they had loved for so many years, and Johnna's Sunday school class of junior boys were all lined up on two rows near the front of the sanctuary on the bride's side, shining with gleeful excitement.

Heads turned as Valerie was seated, almost as beautiful and certainly as elegant as the bride. And then Avalon as maid of honor was making her way slowly to the altar where David and Mac and the minister were already waiting.

There was a pregnant pause in the music, and suddenly everyone was standing and turning around to watch the bride as she came down the aisle. Her face glowed with health and happiness, and her throat glowed with the "family diamonds", as Valerie called them.

They were fabulous, without a doubt. She looked like a princess or an angel from Heaven. Avalon just hoped the letter from Johnna's grandfather had been as beautiful as the diamonds and had brought her even more pleasure...

It was an unusual and moving service, and when it was finally over, they all scattered to their cars. Andrew and Valerie had invited everyone to a reception at Herrington Hall, and as Avalon and Mac followed the others in her little convertible, she thought what a blessing it was that the wedding had been at night.

The sprawling oaks that lined both sides of the long avenue leading to the Hall had been skillfully strung with thousands of tiny white lights, and every chandelier in the huge house at the end of the avenue was lit to the limit.

If they had all thought Johnna looked like a princess or an angel straight out of Heaven at the wedding, they must surely think Herrington Hall was lit up like a palace or Heaven itself. It seemed Andrew and Valerie were trying to make up for all the years they had deprived Johnna of her big day. And Avalon thought perhaps they were thinking of Lindsay, too...

Mac had known Avalon so long and so well that when he'd learned she was really Johnna's niece and the Herringtons' granddaughter, he hadn't worried for a minute that it would change anything. He had simply told her that he was ready to head back to Chicago whenever she was, and he hoped it would be soon.

Now, as they pulled up to the front door of the white-columned mansion with all of its lights blazing and uniformed servants going back and forth to help Johnna and David take things into the house, Mac seemed to be having second thoughts.

"You're not going to let them talk you into staying or anything, are you, Avalon?"

He sounded a little worried, and Avalon laughed.

"You silly! Of course not. But I did promise Valerie I'd look for the island in David's painting. I didn't say *when* I'd do it, though. Don't worry, Mac. I'm as ready to go home as you are."

Several hours later, when the reception was over and most of the wedding guests had gone home, Johnna pulled Avalon aside and said she had something she needed to tell her.

She looked gorgeous in her going-away suit, and Avalon couldn't begin to imagine what could be important enough to delay leaving for the wedding trip to New Orleans. It was already nearly midnight.

Avalon followed her aunt curiously into the empty library, and Johnna closed the tall doors behind them. She stood with her back toward Avalon for several silent moments, and Avalon's heart nearly stopped. She knew Johnna well enough to know that something was dreadfully wrong. When Johnna finally turned around to face Avalon, her beautiful face was a mask of agony.

"What *is* it?" Avalon asked breathlessly, suddenly terrified.

"Oh, Avalon," Johnna burst into tears and threw herself into her new niece's arms. "It's Mother! Daddy just told me she has cancer – terminal cancer that will kill her in less than a year! And I just got married and am going off and leaving her! He should have told me sooner!"

She wept passionately, and Avalon's heart sank within her. She could hardly believe it. Poor Johnna! And poor Valerie... She was speechless and prayed silently for wisdom.

"Mother doesn't know it yet, Avalon," Johnna sobbed brokenly. "She felt bad on Wednesday and went to the doctor. We thought she was just exhausted from all of the wedding preparations...

"But Daddy said the doctor was suspicious and ran a lot of tests. He asked for the results right away and got them today. He told Daddy privately that she has a melanoma that will just race through her body, and he's never seen anyone live more than a year with that kind of cancer!

"Daddy didn't have the heart to tell her, with my wedding coming up, and he didn't tell me until just a few minutes ago because he said he knew I'd call the wedding off. He said he's felt sorry for me all these years, wanting to marry David and knowing how possessive Mother was and why..."

She sobbed without restraint, her head on Avalon's shoulder, and Avalon patted her back comfortingly.

"Oh, Johnna...I'm so sorry. I just can't believe it! Is there anything *I* can do?"

To Avalon's surprise, Johnna raised her tear-ravaged face and said passionately:

"Yes! There is! You can find Lindsay for her! You've just *got* to, Avalon, and as soon as possible! If any of *us* started searching for her – especially Daddy – Lindsay would just retreat farther, if she *is* alive somewhere.

"But if *you* do it – her own child – she just might come forward before it's too late for Mother. You're the only one who can do it! Will you try to find her? For me? And soon?"

She looked at Avalon with such desperation in her eyes that Avalon heard herself say:

"Of course I will, Johnna. But we don't even know if Lindsay is alive! We just need to pray that if she *is*, I can find her in time." And they did, then and there.

An hour later, Avalon had the satisfaction of seeing Johnna and David leave for their wedding trip with smiles on their faces. And when Valerie slipped her thin arm around Avalon's waist after the bride and groom were gone, Avalon put her arm around her grandmother's shoulders sympathetically. She could still hardly believe what Johnna had told her.

Valerie said plaintively:

"Avalon, dear, Megan Marshall has just told me that you're planning to start back to Chicago as early as tomorrow morning! I can't bear to think of your going away so soon...please say it isn't true."

The older woman's face was weary and full of distress, and Avalon could imagine how hard it had been for her to say goodbye to Johnna.

Avalon hugged her grandmother affectionately.

"I'm not sure exactly what time we'll get on the road, Valerie, but I promise I'll come and say goodbye first."

Andrew was standing nearby, and now he said soberly:

"I'm glad to hear you say that, Avalon, because there's something we need to tell you before you go back to Chicago. It won't take long, but it's crucial. We'll look forward to seeing you in the morning."

CHAPTER
TEN

Avalon spent that night in her old childhood room at the Marshalls', where in spite of her warm memories of the place, she tossed and turned, playing Andrew's words over and over in her mind: "There's something we need to tell you."

What on earth could it be? It couldn't be about Valerie's cancer, because Johnna had said Valerie still didn't know, and Andrew had said, "*We* have something to tell you..."

When Mac drove over from David's houseboat to pick Avalon up the next morning, she and Megan were still upstairs. Meg was holding some things that she wanted Avalon to take back to Chicago with her – David's painting of the island, and several more photographs of Lindsay.

"I know you don't like this painting, Avalon, but don't you think you should keep it with you so you can find this place someday?"

Megan looked so forlorn and lonely that Avalon hugged her and said:

"You've been so sweet to me, Megan – I hope I *can* find that island for your sake, as much as for the Herringtons'. You've carried your guilt and regret about

Lindsay Herrington for so many years! I wish you could just let it go and realize that she probably would have done what she did even if you hadn't helped her. Have you ever considered that?"

Megan smiled sadly and said:

"I know her grandfather encouraged her to elope, so I suppose you could be right. She might have done it anyway, without my help."

Avalon said: "One thing we all need to remember about this painting, going forward, is the very real possibility that if I do find that place, whatever I find out may be very painful. Especially to you...you were such good friends. Are you sure you really want to know what happened to her?"

Megan nodded soberly.

"I think it would help me put it to rest, if you know what I mean. Finding you has helped me so much, Avalon, because I know you've been happy in your life, in spite of being abandoned and adopted...

"I'm so thankful things have turned out all right for you. I don't think I could bear it if Lindsay's little girl had died or suffered long-term as a result of her mother's elopement."

In the end, Avalon left the painting of the island with Megan, assuring her it wouldn't be forgotten. She would come back for it just as soon as possible, when she was able to begin her search. Finally, she and Mac were on their way to Herrington Hall.

When they arrived and rang the front doorbell, they were surprised to see Andrew himself open the door to them. He welcomed them cordially, but Avalon couldn't help but recall the first time he'd ever seen her and how cold and angry he had been. Now she trembled at the thought of what he might be about to tell her.

He led her and Mac into the library, where Valerie was waiting for them. Valerie was gracious to Mac and more affectionate than ever to Avalon, embracing her as if she never wanted to let her go. Andrew motioned them toward the wingback chairs in front of the fireplace and then seated himself next to his wife on a settee.

Valerie said quickly, before anyone else could speak:

"Avalon, honey, I've asked Sarah to get your mother's trunks together for you to take back with you, and her jewelry cases, as well."

Avalon had anticipated this, but she still hardly knew what to say.

"That's very sweet of you, Valerie, but I'm afraid my little convertible wouldn't begin to hold any trunks. It's really very small. And I'd truly rather leave – my – my mother's jewelry here with you, at least for the time being, if you don't mind."

Valerie looked disappointed, but she seemed to accept this with a nod and a small smile.

Andrew said quickly: "Avalon, there's something you need to know before you and your cousin go back to Chicago."

He seemed ill-at-ease, and Avalon held her breath, fearful of more surprises. She began to pray silently.

"As you know," he went on, "there was a letter in the safety-deposit box along with the diamonds my father gave Johnna to be worn at her wedding."

Avalon's heart lurched. What in the world could that

letter contain that had anything to do with *her* – somebody Johnna's grandfather hadn't even known existed when he wrote it?

"In this letter, my father, Andrew Herrington, Sr. admits that he encouraged our daughter Lindsay – your mother – to elope."

This was no surprise, since Megan had just told Avalon the same thing less than fifteen minutes ago. She began to relax.

"He informs us that he is the one who told Lindsay not to take anything with her because he was afraid we would accuse her husband of marrying her for money.

"She was the heiress to a vast fortune through my father, as his eldest grandchild. She was always his favorite, and since she was fifteen by the time another grandchild – Johnna – came along, the two of them had been very close for many years...

"As my father's only child, I was given the family business, and it has provided more than amply for our needs. And, of course, we have a life interest in Herrington Hall.

"My father's philosophy was that as a man, I would be in a far better position to take care of myself than his granddaughters would be, and so he made special provisions for them in his will.

"When your mother left home to be married without our permission, we naturally took steps to stop anyone from being able to benefit from her fortune. My father informs us in his letter that he knew the man Lindsay was marrying to be a member of one of England's wealthiest families, so he knew she would not be in need of her inheritance, nor her wardrobe and jewelry...

"That's why, when my wife and I made the decision to eliminate any benefits to Lindsay from our own will, my father said nothing in protest because he knew that our decision would have no ill effect on Lindsay...

"And that's why he was willing to give in to our request that he change his will to benefit Johnna instead of Lindsay. Johnna was just three years old when your mother left home, and as she grew up, she and my father became as close as he and Lindsay had been."

Andrew paused, and Avalon took advantage of that pause to say, in a puzzled voice:

"I still don't understand what any of this has to do with me, sir..."

Andrew Herrington got up and strode to the fireplace, where he stood in silence for the next few moments with his hands behind his back, as if trying to decide exactly how to word what he had to say.

Finally, he continued:

"We've always assumed that my father's letter to be opened on the occasion of Johnna's wedding would simply contain a codicil to his will giving the remainder of the estate to Johnna and her husband...

"It was a codicil to his original will, all right, but he left Herrington Hall and the remainder of his estate to any progeny of Lindsay's who might turn up in the future...and that, my dear Avalon, appears to be you."

Avalon sat in shocked silence for several minutes, while the French clock on the fireplace mantel slowly ticked away the seconds. Had there been bitterness in Andrew's tone? Or was it just the irony of the unexpected? Avalon couldn't tell. At last she found her voice.

"Well, I hope you know I won't take a penny away from Johnna! She's the only reason I've stayed this long, and she's the main reason I'm going to look for Lindsay..."

Valerie looked up with a hurt expression, and Avalon hurried on to say:

"I don't mean that I don't care about your feelings, too, Valerie, because I do. But Johnna is the real reason I'm even willing to accept a role in this family!

"I *love* my family in Chicago! Eric and Lora Evans have been the light of my life for twenty years, and I'd rather die than do anything to hurt them!

"In fact," she went on in a low voice, "I think if I'd known when I decided to take this little side-trip that all of this was going to come to light, I'd have driven straight to Natchez without stopping at all."

Andrew interrupted briskly:

"Johnna's inheritance is almost limitless, so you can put your mind at ease about her. But leaving Johnna out of the matter entirely, as well as my own share of the family assets, you need to understand what kind of position this places you in, personally."

"What do you mean?" she asked quickly.

"I mean that this makes you a very wealthy young woman indeed. I don't know the exact amount of the remainder of my father's estate, but if I had to guess and place a figure on it, it would be somewhere in the neighborhood of two hundred million dollars."

This time, there could be no doubt in anyone's mind

that Andrew was bitter. The next few minutes were a bit of a blur in Avalon's later memories. She and Mac remained at the Hall just long enough for her to recover from Andrew's sudden, staggering announcement, the timing and delivery of which Mac considered to be in very poor taste, considering its effect on Avalon.

Avalon herself found that the thing that helped her stay serene in the face of a stunning shock was Valerie, sitting next to her on the settee, stroking her hand absently and speaking in a low voice of Lindsay.

Valerie had aged ten years since the night they'd discussed the painting of the island with David and had learned how little he knew about the place. But Avalon knew that Valerie's cancer was at least partly responsible for her haggard appearance. She wondered how long it would be before Valerie knew it, too.

She clung to Avalon, seemingly desperate to keep her close as long as possible, afraid that if she let her get away from her now, she would lose her forever, as she had lost Lindsay.

Once she had recovered her equilibrium, Avalon tried to assure her grandmother that she would be back, and if it were God's will, she would find that island in David's painting and learn what there was to know about her mother. Valerie hugged her one last time, then dissolved into tears and disappeared into the next room.

Avalon and Mac said an uncomfortable "Goodbye" to Andrew and made their way out to the car; and as Mac drove slowly down the long avenue between the old oaks, Avalon shared with him what Johnna had told her the night before, about Valerie's cancer.

"Well, I just hope Lindsay Herrington *is* alive some-where," Mac said softly.

"Oh, she just *has* to be, Mac! Doesn't it seem strange that I should care about that now? For the past twenty years, I haven't even wanted to admit I *had* a 'birth mother'! And now I feel I just *have* to find her. I'm just thankful I'll have financial resources for the search..."

"From what you've told me about Valerie's cancer, you'd better get started soon."

Avalon nodded. "I don't know how or where to start, Mac, but we should be back in Chicago by late tomorrow, and from that moment on, it becomes my top priority!"

How could she know that in three days her top priority would be saving her own life?

CHAPTER
ELEVEN

She and Mac were barely back in Chicago when Avalon realized she was being followed. The man was razor-thin, his face sullen and bitter; and when his dark eyes fastened on her, as they were now, it was like having cold, heavy stones thrown at her.

He'd been on the subway every time she'd gone downtown these past two weeks. He always found a seat as close to her as possible and glared at her with naked hostility. He followed her from her station to the street every time she got off the train; but that was all he'd done – so far.

Avalon was accustomed to men's stares. But not men like this, and not stares like his. She couldn't imagine why anyone would be following her, especially someone who looked like a throw-back to Al Capone. He struck such an alien, jarring note in her pleasant, gentle world.

Even at twenty-two, she was so close to Lora and Eric that it would have been natural for her to tell them instantly when anything was wrong. But she had put them on a plane to Israel almost as soon as she and Mac had returned, using part of her newly inherited fortune to give them a trip they'd wanted to take for many years.

They'd agreed instantly that her first priority had to be the search for her mother and the island. Lora wanted Avalon to start out that very day, saying: "I know how I would feel if you just disappeared one day, and I didn't see you for twenty-five years – especially if I were dying of cancer!" They hoped she would feel freer to start immediately, with them out of the way.

But then the strange man had started following her, and Avalon couldn't risk being followed out of town, traveling alone. Her friends all worked, and Mac wouldn't have any more vacation days for a while.

The elevated train finally plunged into the subway, and Avalon watched anxiously as they sped past the stations, one after another. As soon as she saw the sign for her stop, she rose quickly and walked to the doors, deliberately ignoring the stranger.

But he was right behind her, and she could almost feel his bold, belligerent eyes boring into the back of her neck. She took a deep breath and prayed silently for protection.

Then she stepped out onto the subway platform, striding swiftly toward the stairs that would take her to the street. She didn't dare use the escalator and be compelled to remain stationery, even surrounded by people.

Rapidly threading her way through the crowd on the stairs, she reached the busy street in less than a minute and stopped to look behind her. The man had disappeared, and Avalon breathed a sigh of relief.

Now she had to decide whether or not to tell Mac. She was meeting him a little later for dinner at an Indian restaurant in Old Town, after she did a few errands in the Loop.

When she got to Piper's Alley and made her way past the intriguing little shops, stopping to browse here and there, she thought how much she loved Old Town itself, despite the fact that it was beginning to degenerate into a haunt of hippies.

How odd that during all her years in Chicago, she'd never known *anyone* who felt the way these people apparently did, and yet the media focused on them as if they represented every college student in America!

At the restaurant, she quickly found a table toward the back and settled herself to wait for Mac. He had taken Avalon's car to work today; but even so, he was late arriving.

And by the time he showed up at their table, Avalon had decided to keep the matter of the stranger on the train to herself. After all, what could Mac do about him, anyway?

Now, as the two of them looked over their menus, chatting casually, she gasped and grabbed Mac's hand, nearly knocking his water glass over.

"Oh, Mac, there he is!"

He calmly steadied the glass and said: "Who? Where?"

Avalon nodded toward the door. The man who had been following her was standing there looking around as if in search of someone. His thin face was like a chopping block, dented and scored by – what? Just life? Bitterness? Or worse?

The hostess walked over to him and apparently asked

if he wanted to be seated, because the man shook his head and turned around to walk out of the restaurant – but not before he stopped and stared straight at Avalon and Mac sitting at their table, even though it was in a somewhat shadowy spot.

The malevolence in his eyes was palpable, and Avalon shivered.

"Oh, Mac, who *is* he?"

"*You're* asking *me?* How would I know? I've never seen the guy before in my life. Have you?" He turned and looked at her suspiciously.

She nodded guiltily. "I wanted to tell you about him...I really did. But I didn't think there was anything you could do about him, anyway. He – he hasn't really done anything wrong – he just glares at me and follows me off the train."

"Just 'glares at you and follows you off the train'. Good grief, Avalon, are you *crazy?* This is Chicago, not Columbia! How long has this been going on?"

"I saw him for the first time almost as soon as we got back from Louisiana. And he's been on my train every time I've taken it downtown. He gets off at my stop and follows me to the street. But he never even speaks to me! I mean, what could you do about him, anyway? He hasn't *done* anything."

"Well, he has something in mind, or he wouldn't be harassing you this way. That look he gave us just now was downright menacing."

"But why on earth *would* anyone be following me? A man like that, especially? He looks like a – a mobster. What on earth have *I* done?"

Mac appeared to have a niggling thought at the back of his mind which gradually made its way to the front and finally came out as:

"You've become a very wealthy young woman, that's what."

Avalon looked at him as if he'd suddenly gone mad. Then she burst into laughter.

"You're not serious!"

Mac said, as seriously as she'd ever heard him speak:

"Avalon, you're a very rich girl now. I know it doesn't make much difference to you or me, or to Uncle Eric and Aunt Lora — all of us know that the important things in life are still what they've always been, and they don't have very much to do with money.

"But believe me, not everybody in this world feels that way. You are now in possession of more money than most people on this planet will ever see or dream of having...and certainly enough money for some people to kill for."

Avalon had stopped laughing as soon as she realized that Mac was serious. And now she said as soberly as he could have wished:

"Mac...you can't be seriously suggesting that somebody would *kill* me for my new inheritance. That's just crazy! Who? And why? Nobody even knows about it yet except you and me, and Mother and Daddy – "

"And Andrew and Valerie Herrington...not to mention Johnna and David Daniels, and now David's sister, Leah – "

He was clearly implying that her birth family, her newly - discovered blood relatives, might be trying to get rid of her.

"Oh, for Pete's sake, Mac!" Avalon was almost angry and sounded it.

"Andrew and Valerie are my grandparents! They loved my birth mother dearly and were glad to find out I was Lindsay's daughter.

"They didn't have to tell me about that codicil to Andrew Sr.'s will, you know. They could have trashed it or left it in the safety-deposit box. Besides, they're filthy rich without a penny of the money he left me.

"And so is Aunt Johnna – and now David, as her husband. Besides, Johnna cared about me long before we found out her sister was my mother. She loved me when I was just a little girl in her Sunday school class twelve years ago, and I've known David just as long. I'd trust both of them with my life!

"And Leah Daniels? Please. Mac, that girl has lived on next to nothing for so long she wouldn't know what to do with a lot of money! Not only that, she's David's sister. Do you really think he and Johnna would let Leah go without anything she might want and couldn't afford? Honestly! Everybody we know has everything they need and more. Why on earth would they want what I have?"

Mac just looked at her and shook his head stubbornly.

"All I can say is, you need to be very careful from now on. No more trips on the El alone, OK? I mean it."

Avalon sighed, letting go of her sudden indignation.

"Look, I know you care about me, Mac, and that's why you're saying these things. I understand that, and I appreciate it. I really do. And that man who was here just now does scare me a little...but I still refuse to start suspecting everybody of being after my money!

"Besides, that man who's been following me doesn't look like the kind of person any of the people you just named would have anything to do with. Now, does he?"

Mac admitted it grudgingly, and when their food came, he seemed determined to make up for nearly spoiling their meal. He regaled Avalon with all sorts of amusing anecdotes of his work at the engineering firm near the Time-Life building, and when they got back to the car, he said amiably:

"I really am sorry for being so pessimistic, Avalon. Maybe I just have a suspicious mind. Tell you what – I'm always the one not wanting to drive with the top down on your little car, and I know how much you love it...

"So let's put it down and enjoy the drive back to Evanston, OK? But go slowly, so you don't mess up my 'do'." He pretended to smooth his dark hair, grinning.

Avalon just shook her head with a wry smile and pressed the button to let the top down, accepting his offer quickly.

In winter, the wind swept off Lake Michigan with howling shrieks and icy claws like a wild, hungry predator, and old timers called it "The Hawk". She could remember holding onto street signs a few times to keep from being blown down on icy sidewalks when the wind whipped its way into downtown Chicago. The summer breeze was a sweet-faced, cooing dove in comparison, and they might as well take advantage of its mild softness while they could.

Avalon relaxed and drove slowly in the far right lane, basking in the warm sunshine and the pleasure she always felt on Lakeshore Drive. On her left, the early evening traffic flowed smoothly; and on her right, the blue waters of Lake Michigan were a halcyon reflection of soft, summer skies. The wavelets with their little whitecaps were gentle, for a change.

There was a charming collage of people on the beaches at this hour, playing volleyball, flying kites or throwing frisbees for their dogs to catch with their teeth. People sat on benches, feeding the gulls and pigeons who considered Chicago "home" just as surely as did their human benefactors.

As they drove farther north, Avalon saw others taking advantage of the last hours of daylight in Lincoln Park, some jogging alone, some as couples, and even as whole families. Some were riding bicycles, their dogs trailing behind them on leashes. A few old men fished from the rocks next to the lake.

She was loving it all, wishing every day could be like this, wondering why anyone would ever want to live anywhere else, when a panel truck suddenly swerved into her lane, forcing Avalon to hit her brakes hard and veer sharply to the right to avoid an impact.

But the brakes didn't work, and the car kept veering, at a point where Lakeshore Drive opened into Lincoln Park, with its joggers and bikers, and the dogs she loved so much and pitied for their helplessness.

The thought of hitting one of the dogs was almost more horrible to her than the thought of hitting a human being – at least the humans knew to get out of the way! Thank the Lord she'd been driving so slowly!

Her heart in her throat, she laid on the horn to let everybody know that the car was out of control. And she prayed.

She was still praying when they jumped the curb and slammed into a concrete water fountain, stopping the car cold, along with its driver and her passenger.

CHAPTER

TWELVE

"Your brakes didn't work because the line had been cut so the brake fluid would leak out. It's as simple as that."

Mac spoke almost harshly. He was sitting on Leah Daniels's sofa a mile or so from the accident that had left him and Avalon without wheels and with severe headaches and soreness.

One of the joggers who'd been about to drink from the water fountain they struck had sprinted across Lakeshore Drive to the nearest phone and called the police, who came and heard their story, then secured a wrecker to tow the car away.

The jogger also called the phone number they gave him for David Daniels's sister Leah, and she came for them immediately, taking them to her studio apartment in nearby Uptown.

Avalon and Mac were momentarily stunned and bruised by the impact, but the poor little convertible was a total loss. Avalon shed a few tears when it was towed away so ignominiously, and Mac reminded her that, if she wished, they could call any dealer in Chicago and have a new one there in a few minutes. She could easily afford that now. Avalon just gave him a sorrowful look and said nothing.

Now she was resting on Leah's Murphy bed which was let down from the wall as soon as Leah unlocked her apartment and invited them inside. Avalon still could hardly believe what had happened, and she certainly didn't want to believe it had happened for the reason Mac was suggesting.

But Mac knew cars, and both he and the driver of the wrecker looked under the car and said they could clearly see that the brake line had been cut. The policeman said they would have it checked out by a mechanic just for the record, but he went ahead and wrote it into his accident report.

Now Mac was inexorable on the subject.

"I hope this convinces you I'm not some kind of nut-case when I say somebody out there wants you dead. That guy we saw at the restaurant in Old Town probably did it – either before or after we saw him."

Avalon had already described the accident and the strange man to Leah privately; and she wanted to get Mac out of the apartment before he started going on about all of the people who might want to see Avalon dead, since Leah herself had been one of the names he'd mentioned at dinner.

Not that Avalon really believed Mac would name names – she didn't; but by now she was so weary of the whole subject, she just wanted to close her eyes and rest.

Mac declined Leah's offer to take him home in her car, saying he would walk to the Lawrence Avenue station and take the El back to Evanston.

When he was gone, Avalon sighed and said:

"Oh, Leah...I'm so glad Mother and Daddy aren't here right now to hear about this. Promise me you won't mention it to anybody at church tomorrow, OK? I don't want my folks' trip spoiled by worrying about me. They were so happy the last time I talked to them."

"Where are they now?" Leah asked from the next room, a bright but minuscule kitchenette with everything cleverly arranged in a space about the size of a large walk-in closet.

A tiny table and two chairs filled a nook in front of the bow window that overlooked Lakeshore Drive and, beyond it, Lincoln Park and Lake Michigan. Leah seemed as happy as a clam with the arrangement, and Avalon didn't wonder at it. She herself would enjoy a place like this.

She could hear Leah rattling dishes and knew there would soon be strong, sweet tea and cinnamon toast to go with it. It was Leah's cure for everything from heartache to headache, she'd once told Avalon. When Leah came back into the room with a smile and a tray, Avalon sat up in the bed and answered her question.

"They were in Egypt and headed to Iraq the next day. Daddy said he knows Babylon is just a pile of dusty ruins, but he still wants to see it, and it's less than an hour from Baghdad.

"He said they had ten glorious days in the Holy Land, and now they're about to head east to see where Abraham started out and the villages that are still named after Abraham's grandfather and great-grandfather.

"And of course, they want to see the Tigris and Euphrates, and the area that so many archeologists have pinpointed as the probable site of the Garden of Eden. Naturally, Daddy's loving every minute of it."

Both of the young women smiled. They admired Eric Evans's passion for the historical reliability of the Scriptures, Avalon having lived with it for twenty years, and Leah for about two weeks.

David Daniels had told Avalon that his sister Leah was living in Chicago now, and Avalon called her as soon as she and Mac got back from their trip to the South.

Leah was thrilled to know that her old pastor from Louisiana was now at a church in a suburb of Chicago. She'd always been fond of the Evanses and immediately started coming to their church in Evanston.

She'd been living in Chicago for nearly two years, she told Avalon, and had a studio where she did her sculpting during the day. She'd had some success, selling several pieces of her art to wealthy collectors, with other pieces on display in galleries across Chicago.

"When will your folks be back, Avalon?" Leah asked on her way back to the kitchen with the tray, after they'd finished their tea and toast.

"Another week to ten days, I think. I wanted them to take in some European capitals on this trip, but I don't think they're going to do it right now...maybe later. Daddy hates to be away from the church that long. I can hardly wait for them to get back, especially since I can't leave anyway, with this weird man following me everywhere!"

The following day was Sunday, and Eric Evans's substitute was a man from India, a former Hindu of the highest Brahmin caste, now a Christian, who told the church about the little baby girls in India who were left on the street to die just because they were female.

He and his wife wanted to start a shelter for them, and when the service was over, Avalon took the small, dark-skinned man into the church office and handed him a check for five million dollars.

She spent the next week caught up in the most exciting and significant project of her life, and although her new attorney thought she was insane to spend her money in this way, she was smiling like the Cheshire cat in *Alice in Wonderland*. Almost before she knew it, her parents were coming home.

Leah offered to drive her to the airport, since Avalon's little convertible was still out of commission.

"It's a good thing you're driving, Leah – I'm so excited," she said happily when Leah picked her up in front of the parsonage. "This is the longest my parents and I have ever been away from each other, and you wouldn't believe how much I've missed them."

Leah gave her a sad smile and said:

"Oh, yes, I would, Avalon. When our mother died last year, I thought I couldn't bear it. She was my biggest supporter – a 'fan club' of one! We never really knew our Dad, you know. David has been a wonderful brother, but I would never have had the courage to become a sculptor – nor would David have become a painter – if not for our mother's encouragement."

After a few moments of shared silence, Avalon said:

"I can't help but wonder what would have happened to me if Mother and Daddy hadn't adopted me. I positively tremble to think where I might be today."

"Whoever left you at their church that day did you a big favor, that's for sure," Leah said strongly. "Not only did you end up with parents who dearly love you, which is a wonderful thing and something to be thankful for – but you ended up with two exceptional human beings: intelligent, sensitive, compassionate, wise – just beautiful people, period. The people you were born to couldn't possibly have been any better."

Avalon agreed with her wholeheartedly, and they talked desultorily the rest of the way to O'Hare. Leah let Avalon out at the front doors and drove on to park her car.

As soon as Avalon was inside, she checked the flight screen and noted the number of the gate where Eric's and Lora's flight would arrive. Then she stepped up to the airline's reservations counter and asked if they were sure Flight #479 would be on time.

The clerk behind the counter was still checking the screen for last-minute information when an official-looking man walked over to Avalon and said:

"Did I hear you ask about Flight #479, Miss?"

Avalon smiled at him as she replied:

"Yes, my parents are coming in on that flight, and it's supposed to be here around 5:30. I was just checking to see if it's going to be on time. They've been gone for several weeks, and I'm pretty anxious to see them."

"Ah," he said, nodding. "I understand. Well, I need to tell you, the airline is asking everyone who's waiting for that flight to join us in a room where we have some refreshments for you while you wait. We've just heard that it's....uh, going to be quite a bit behind schedule. Would you mind coming with me?"

He started to put his hand under her elbow to show her the way, but Avalon pulled away from him.

"I'm waiting for a friend – she's parking her car right now, and I can't leave until she gets here. Can't you just tell me where this room is? I'm sure we can find it on our own."

The man's face changed ever so slightly as he said:

"I think you'd better come with me now, if you don't mind, Miss...it's important, and I really can't explain here. One of our other workers can let your friend know where to find you."

He walked over to the counter and called a young woman over, leaning toward her and saying something Avalon couldn't hear. Then he walked back to Avalon and said:

"Your friend will be told where to meet you as soon as she gets here – what is her name?"

Avalon hesitated momentarily, then said:

"Leah...Leah Daniels."

The man nodded and spoke again to the girl behind the counter. Then he put his hand under Avalon's elbow once more, and this time she didn't resist.

As they walked down the long concourse toward the gate where her parents' flight was to arrive, Avalon had a strange feeling and wondered if it were just the discomfort of having a stranger touching her. The man had insisted on holding her elbow as they walked, and not wanting to be rude or unkind, she had allowed him to do so.

But when he stopped in front of a door across from the waiting room for Flight #479 and started to open it for her to walk in, her feelings ran rampant, and she knew without any doubt that something was very wrong.

She turned to him and said firmly:

"I'm not going in there with you. What is this? What's going on?"

But she did go into the room. And it was there that Leah found her fifteen minutes later, sobbing her heart out along with many others, over the news that Flight #479 had gone down about halfway between New York and Chicago.

The airline had simply been stalling for time until they knew for sure, and now they did know: there were no survivors.

CHAPTER
THIRTEEN

Avalon was numb for days after her parents' death. Her friends and Mac's family and the church folks all tried to comfort her, but they were suffering, too. Eric and Lora Evans had been extraordinary people, and they would be painfully missed by many people besides their adopted daughter.

She wondered what she'd have done without Mac and Leah to help her make funeral arrangements and take care of all the business details that death demands and that are all the more difficult for that very reason.

Her only relief during those dark days was seeing Mac and Leah learning to lean on each other as they encouraged Avalon to lean on them both. She loved them and was glad they were beginning to care for each other. And she knew they both loved her like a sister and would do anything in the world to help her.

But no one in this world could take her parents' place. She realized that any child, especially an only child, must feel the same dismal despair she felt at the loss of beloved parents. But she thought that perhaps she felt a little more than many children might, simply because her life had been such a nightmare before they adopted her, and she'd been so desperately in need when she came into their lives.

They had wanted a child so long that they'd given her all the love they'd been storing up for the ten years of their childless marriage. She felt sure there would never be anyone else like them in her life, who would love her as much as they had.

The funeral was beautiful, despite Avalon's intense grief and the sudden shock the double disaster had been for everyone. Mac's father, Eric Evans's older brother, for whose sake Avalon's family had moved to a suburb of Chicago when he became ill, had almost had a fatal heart attack when he heard the news.

But he had survived and had managed his brother's affairs to a marvel, with Mac's help. Of course there was no problem about money; Avalon would have covered everything if her parents' savings had not. But they had been extremely self-disciplined people all of their lives and left not one penny of debt anywhere.

And Avalon knew in her heart of hearts that they were with the Lord whom they had both loved and served for so long, and they were safer and happier now than they ever could have been on earth.

But it was still a sad and bereft young woman who walked through the parsonage the day after the funeral and tried to decide what to do next, where to go.

The church's Board of Trustees was so kind, insisting that she stay in the parsonage as long as she liked. It had been her home for the past twelve years, and it would take them some time to secure a new pastor, they said. The candidates could stay with people in the congregation when they came to try out.

But Avalon had enjoyed too many hours of life and laughter in that house with Eric and Lora for her to be able to stay there long without them.

She started packing the day following the funeral, going through her mother's things and choosing the items that meant the most to her, as keepsakes. She asked Mac to come and do the same with her father's clothes and personal belongings, knowing Mac would know what to do with them better than she would.

But she went through her father's personal library herself, choosing many of the volumes they had read together or he'd read to her as she was growing up. There were all of C. S. Lewis's books, beginning with *The Chronicles of Narnia* when she was about eight or nine, and going through Lewis's science fiction trilogy, a few years later.

The paperback copies of *Out of the Silent Planet*, *Perelandra* and *That Hideous Strength* were about to fall apart, they'd been read so often; but Avalon packed them away carefully, unwilling to throw away the memories contained in their tattered pages.

There were Lewis's signature classics: *Mere Christianity*, *The Problem of Pain*, *The Abolition of Man*, *The Great Divorce*, *Miracles*, *A Grief Observed* and *The Screwtape Letters*. She and Eric had discussed all of them endlessly.

Once everything was organized and packed, Mac came and took the boxes away to be stored at his family's home in Barrington. He took many of Eric's personal items to the Salvation Army store and the Pacific Garden Mission in downtown Chicago, recalling that his uncle had always had a soft spot for the city's street people.

Avalon spent one more night in the house and then called Leah: could she come and stay with her in her apartment for a few days? She just couldn't bear the thought of another night alone in that house where she'd been so happy.

Leah said "Yes" instantly and was pulling up in front of the Evanston parsonage half an hour later. Her studio apartment was small, but her sofa was a daybed, and she would absolutely love having Avalon's company, she said.

As Avalon locked the front door of the parsonage behind her, she reached out and touched the well-polished brass knocker for the last time, and then the dark green ivy curling above the doorjamb overhead. Oh, how could she bear to walk away forever from this house with all of its memories?

But they were gone, those two precious people...and the Lord whose love they had exemplified so beautifully would be with her. He always had been, but Avalon knew that she would value His presence and companionship even more in the days ahead.

"You know, Leah, I'm thankful for one thing," she said as they drove through the streets of Evanston toward Uptown and Leah's apartment.

"I never told Mother and Daddy about the accident Mac and I had in my little car, and about the brake line being cut. I'm so glad I didn't. They had a wonderful, worry-free last month on this earth, seeing things and places they had wanted to see all of their lives, and they sounded so happy!"

Suddenly overcome by her memory of the sound of Lora's voice on the phone the last time they'd talked, she burst into tears. Leah wisely remained silent, simply reaching over and covering Avalon's hand with her own for a moment or two. They were quiet the rest of the way, and Avalon made a conscious effort to control her emotions for Leah's sake.

Leah found a parking place on the street in front of her apartment building and helped Avalon carry her suitcases inside. She checked her mailbox in the lobby, and then the two girls took the antiquated elevator up to the eighth floor.

"My neighbors love curry, as you can tell," Leah said with a wry grin as she unlocked her apartment and walked in, setting Avalon's bags down inside the door. "Most of them are engineers and other professionals from India. That smell always makes me hungry for Indian food, so I end up eating it more often than I would otherwise."

"Speaking of Indian food," Avalon said, "I haven't eaten any since Mac and I were in Old Town the day of our accident. Have you had any lately?"

"Do you want to go somewhere to eat, Avalon? I just didn't know if you'd be hungry..."

"Well, I am, believe it or not...and you've just made me hungry for Indian food. Or rather, your neighbors have. Is there an Indian restaurant near here?"

"There is one, but it's not very good, I'm afraid...but I know of one in the Loop that's really fantastic. And we can take the El, so we won't have to worry about finding a parking place. Want to?"

"Sounds good to me. I'm with you."

Leah locked her apartment again, and she and Avalon set out to walk the few blocks to the elevated train station at Lawrence Avenue, where they climbed the stairs to the platform and stood watching for the green-and-white cars that made life easier for some people and survivable for many others. When the train finally came, they found seats together and chatted amiably all the way downtown.

It was early afternoon, so the train wasn't crowded, and Avalon caught herself looking around for the strange man who'd been following her. She hadn't seen him since that day in Old Town, just minutes before their accident on Lakeshore Drive. She was infinitely more conscious of danger now, painfully alert.

But the man with the cold, stony eyes in the chopping block face was nowhere to be seen, and she relaxed.

They got off the subway at Marshall Field's, and as she and Leah went through the big doors of the bargain basement, Avalon said with a smile:

"This is my shopping turf, you know, Leah. I buy most of my clothes here."

Leah laughed. "You probably won't be doing that very much longer, though, will you?"

Avalon grew serious suddenly and said:

"You know, I think I probably will. You can find some incredible bargains here if you look for them – really good clothes for a fraction of their original cost. It's actually fun!...

"I'm not sure I would enjoy walking into Saks or Neiman Marcus or Bloomingdale's or even upstairs here at Marshall Field's and just buying the first thing I liked without looking at the price tag. What challenge is there in that?"

She smiled at her friend conspiratorially, and Leah realized afresh just how rare an upbringing Avalon Evans had enjoyed.

"Maybe we can come back down here after we eat," Avalon said as they made their way to street level and walked a block or two to the Indian restaurant Leah had recommended.

"Sure, why not?" Leah said agreeably.

When they finished their meal, they went outside and walked at a leisurely pace back to Marshall Field's, where they spent the next hour searching the racks in the bargain basement for clothes that Avalon could use on her trip to Louisiana.

Leah found a few things she liked, too, so the shopping spree was as successful as the meal. They were both laughing and enjoying themselves thoroughly as they sauntered back to the subway with their packages.

It was rush hour now, so the station was crowded, and commuters were pouring down the escalators and stairs like sardines eager to be packed into metal cans.

The two young women stood as close to the edge of the platform as they dared, hoping to get into one of the cars when the train pulled in. The doors stayed open for such a short time, and the crowd surged around them, everyone naturally wanting to get home as soon as possible.

People were polite as a rule, so Avalon was surprised when someone bumped her hard, causing her to fall against Leah.

And before she could catch herself, she was pushed again – this time, so forcefully that before she knew what was happening, she was falling off the platform onto the tracks – just as the train came roaring into the tunnel.

CHAPTER
FOURTEEN

Avalon's screams filled the subway as she started to fall, but the roar and clatter of the speeding train plunging through the darkness drowned out her cries of terror.

In the blink of an eye, a couple of men standing next to her grabbed her from behind and pulled her back to safety – a split second before the train came hurtling over the spot where Avalon would have been mangled.

The horrified crowd around them buzzed with relief and congratulations before they got on the train. With tears in her eyes, her heart hammering like a piston, Avalon profusely thanked the two men who had literally saved her life. And when they saw that she was going to be all right, they, too, were gone.

Suddenly she heard Leah shrieking next to her:

"Stop that man! Stop him! Stop him!"

Leah was nearly jumping up and down in her excitement, screaming and pointing to a thin, wiry man with a stoop and a narrow, ugly face, who was moving at a dead run toward the stairs to the street.

Leah kept screaming "Stop him! Stop him!" and pointing, until a policeman standing nearby finally drew his gun and started running for the stairs.

Leah pulled Avalon along with her as she ran, but Avalon could hardly stand up, her legs were still so weak from her brush with death, so Leah finally let go of her and kept running, keeping the man in sight and yelling at the policeman to do whatever it took to keep him from getting away.

And she succeeded. Avalon thought with admiration that no one would have guessed her relentless friend to be a quiet sculptor accustomed to a life of refinement, at least professionally. She was a hideous harridan until the man was caught and being questioned at the nearby police station.

Avalon followed as quickly as her limp legs would carry her and saw at a distance the scuffle that ended successfully for Leah and the law.

Now they were sitting in a waiting room at the police station, and Avalon had allowed Leah to call Mac. Avalon didn't want him there, knowing he would scold and harass her mercilessly due to his concern for her, and she dreaded hearing his "I told you so."

Then Officer McDonald, the young officer who had been questioning the strange man, came over to her with a photograph in his hand. When he showed it to her and asked, "Do you have any idea how he got this, Miss?" Avalon found that she was glad Mac was on his way.

The photograph was of her. The worst of it was that it was a snapshot of her walking out of her own home, the parsonage in Evanston.

She turned it over and read her name and address, a description of her car and the license plate number, her approximate height and weight, hair and eye color – and an amount: $3,000. It had all been done neatly on a typewriter. She was shocked and sickened.

As soon as Mac got there, Officer McDonald called the three of them into a private room and closed the door behind him.

"First of all, we owe you our thanks, young lady," he said to Leah. "The man you spotted for us is a hit man who's been on the loose for a while now. His name is Manny Byrd. His friends on the inside call him 'The Buzzard' because he finishes off his victims so thoroughly."

He turned and looked at Avalon.

"You must be walking on the right side of the street, ma'am – that's all I can say."

Mac said: "Do you mean this guy is escaped from prison?"

The officer had the grace to look sheepish when he replied, "No. He – broke parole."

Mac was ruddy-complexioned to begin with, but now his skin was suffused with a brick-red color as he blurted:

"A hired killer out on parole? You've got to be kidding!" He was furious.

"I wish I were, Mr. Evans, believe me. This guy has a good lawyer – the best. Do you think we like it any more than you do? We don't! We just keep making arrests and pray that some of them stick."

The young officer was embarrassed but defensive, and Avalon said gently:

"It's all right, Mac. The guy didn't get away with anything, and he's in custody now. I'm safe."

Mac calmed down long enough to say:

"Is that right, Officer McDonald? *Is* she safe now? Is this creep going to stay in jail this time? Or does she need to keep watching her back?"

Officer McDonald shook his head and sounded serious when he said:

"I don't think we need to worry about that this time...Miss Evans." He looked at Avalon. "He not only had a picture of you in his possession, but he also had the money on him for the hit: $3,000 in cash."

Avalon's skin crawled with a sudden memory of being pushed hard on the subway platform. How horrible that someone had been *paid* to do that!

"Can we – may we listen to the interrogation, officer? I'd like to hear what this man has to say about his – his mission to – to kill me. I still can hardly believe it's true, but I think I need to understand what's behind all of this, if my life is at stake."

He agreed and gained permission for Avalon and Mac and Leah to sit behind the two-way mirror and listen to the second interrogating officer's questions and Manny Byrd's replies.

When he was asked: "Who hired you to kill Miss Evans, Byrd?" the wiry little man just shook his dark head and shrugged.

"Nobody, man. I just found that picture in my mail-box one day, with all that stuff on the back. How do I know why it was there? I don't know what makes you think I was hired to bump her off, anyway. I never killed nobody."

"No, of course you didn't, Manny. That's why your

friends call you The Buzzard, because you're stupid and unsuccessful and they know you just take the other guys' pickings after they finish the kill..."

Thus goaded, Manny Byrd sat up straighter and said:

"Aw, you think you're such a smart cop. OK, so somebody out there thought I could do a job for 'em. That don't mean I took the job. I'm on parole, man. I'm stayin' clean for my mama!"

He leered, showing the gaps in his tobacco-stained teeth. His mouth moved into the shape of a smile, but his eyes reminded Avalon of the empty, black windows in the old gutted hotel Al Capone had used many years ago, on South Michigan Avenue. The windows of that architectural carcass surely had all kinds of repulsive, loathsome things behind them.

There could be no doubt now, that Manny Byrd had sabotaged her little convertible by cutting the brake line the day she and Mac saw him in Old Town...

And to think how close he had come to succeeding in pushing her off the subway platform to die under the wheels of the oncoming train, just a few minutes ago! It almost took her breath away, just thinking about it.

She took another look at the back of the snapshot of herself coming out of the parsonage in Evanston. For the first time, she noticed one word typed at the very bottom of the photograph, which she had failed to see earlier. It said simply: "Accident".

So he was supposed to make it look like an accident, was he? Well, this awful man had very nearly succeeded in that. She and Mac could have been killed on Lakeshore Drive the other day, and if her little car had been just slightly more damaged by the collision, no one could have determined for sure that the brake line had been cut.

And if she *had* fallen from the platform today and been crushed under the train, who could say with any certainty that it hadn't been just a tragic accident, the result of pushy rush-hour crowds in the subway?

But *who*? That was the question that haunted Avalon now. Who would want to do such a thing to her? And *why*? Mac was so sure it had something to do with her new fortune.

But there was no one involved in Avalon's life who even needed her money! She had reminded Mac that Andrew and Valerie, Johnna and David, and even Leah, potentially, as David's sister, were all as rich as Croesus without ever touching a penny of her new inheritance.

And besides that, she simply couldn't – wouldn't! – believe it of any of them! So she kept coming back to those two questions: who, and why?

As the interrogation continued, Avalon listened avidly to Manny Byrd's answers, trying to learn something that would help her understand what was happening. Once, the interrogating officer asked him:

"Where did you get that $3,000, Byrd? We know you haven't been working at anything legitimate. Where'd it come from, if it wasn't payment for a hit?"

Manny blew a big breath through his loose lips, making him sound just like a horse. He dropped his head and seemed to be trying to decide how to respond in the way that would get him into the least trouble.

Finally, he raised his eyes and said:

"It was in th' envelope with that picture of the girl. I was plannin' to turn it in so you guys could trace the bills. You got the picture now, too, so you can trace that typewriter.

"That cop that brought me here knows I was runnin' in the direction of this station lickety-split when he knocked me down. Looks to me like you guys punish people who try to do you a favor!"

He smirked at the officer.

Mac snorted angrily and said to Officer McDonald, who was sitting next to them in the little observation room:

"He's not going to get away with that, is he? That's preposterous!"

Officer McDonald raised his hand and said instantly:

"Don't worry, Mr. Evans, he's not getting away with anything. We believe he was trying to kill your – cousin, is it? – and we know the money was his payment for doing it. We will be tracing the bills and the typewriter, certainly, but Manny Byrd isn't going to get any of the credit for that, I assure you."

He turned to Avalon and said kindly:

"I think you can sleep in peace tonight, Miss Evans. Unless somebody has hired more than one killer to do away with you, your worries are over. This guy's not going to be back on the street for a long time."

Avalon pressed charges, and when it was all over, Mac offered to take her and Leah back to Leah's apartment, and they invited him to stay and have a late-night snack with them to celebrate Byrd's capture and Avalon's safety.

While Leah was in her tiny kitchen fixing the food, Mac said to Avalon:

"I still don't like it. That cop can't promise you anything. He doesn't know how long that creep will be in custody – how can he? Byrd hadn't even called his lawyer yet when we left, and Officer McDonald said he has 'one of the best', which just means the guy is good at getting crooks off the hook."

"But he told us Manny Byrd broke parole! You know they'll send him back!" Avalon protested.

"Well, I still think you and Leah ought to move in with Mom and Dad at our place, where I can keep an eye on you and know you're safe. How about it?"

When Avalon passed along Mac's invitation to Leah, she could see Leah struggling with her spirit of independence against the very real temptation to spend more time with Mac and get better acquainted with his parents.

"Why don't you go on, Avalon?" she said shyly. "You're the one who's in danger. Nothing is going to happen to me here, and I have my work..."

"Oh, please come with me, Leah...I would enjoy it so much more with you there. And look what might have happened today if you hadn't been with me!

"Why, you were the one who saw Manny Byrd and actually helped the police catch him. My life would still be in danger if you hadn't been with me. Have you thought about that?"

Avalon hoped Leah would say "Yes". Avalon liked this petite, dark-haired girl far more than anyone Mac had ever dated, and she wanted the two of them to have this extra time together.

And it was true that Leah had saved her life from any future efforts of Manny Byrd's, just as surely as those two men on the subway platform had saved it today.

Finally, Leah agreed to go, and she packed a small bag. Avalon's suitcases were still sitting unopened beside the front door, so Mac helped her carry them down to his car.

It was a long way from Uptown to Barrington – in more ways than just miles. Avalon had been to Mac's house more times than she could count and had always taken it for granted. She was able to enjoy the ambiance of the place whenever she was there, without being the least bit envious of Mac.

Leah's eyes, on the other hand, widened with surprise and artistic appreciation when Mac turned off the street and drove through large ornate gates up a long, winding drive bordered on both sides by sculptured shrubs. Old-fashioned gas lamps shone all along the way.

At the end of the drive, on a high point of the grounds, stood a classic Edwardian-style mansion built in the early 1940's. Well-manicured lawns spread away from the house, all surrounded by a tall brick wall. Amber lights glowed in nearly every window and gave the place a warm, welcoming atmosphere in spite of its grandeur.

Mac drove all the way around the house and pulled his car into one of the empty spaces in the four-car garage. Then he opened the car doors for Leah and Avalon and helped them carry their luggage up the stairs of the back porch into the house.

The two rooms that Mac's mother had chosen for them were upstairs, and both were large and comfortable. The rooms were connected by a door, but each had its own private bath.

Avalon and Leah were both so worn out and weary from the stress and strain of the day that they welcomed the chance to say an early "Goodnight" to Mac and his parents and get a good night's sleep.

When Leah turned out her light in the next room, Avalon got up and closed the connecting door so her night light wouldn't keep her friend awake.

Then she lay peacefully in the big Eastlake bed, just thanking the Lord for sparing her life that day, and also thanking Him for the fact that Manny Byrd had been arrested, and she was safe.

And she felt safe. So it was strange that she should have the dream that night. It was the first time she'd had it in Chicago since she was a child.

Soon after Avalon drifted off to sleep, she felt herself being held tightly in someone's arms as he rowed a small boat. She twisted herself around and looked back at the island and house that they were rowing away from, and she screamed in her sleep. But it was a silent scream, so no one heard it.

Then the dream changed, and she was being carried through the woods – dark, ominous woods with no moonlight, and she could hear alarming noises from animals nearby.

She had been told often enough that there were wild

hogs and snakes, bobcats and even wolves, and sometimes alligators in the water near the edge of the woods, and she *must* stay away from them!

Avalon was tossing and turning in her sleep, struggling to wake up and escape from the nightmare, but she couldn't. She felt the very real terror of a tiny girl left all alone in the utter darkness of a late night in deep woods that she had always been warned to stay out of, especially because of snakes.

Then she saw one, and her panic was complete. It was coiled in a huge pile, brown and rough-looking, and she was sure it would uncoil itself and crawl toward her! She screamed again, but this time Leah heard her and came running from the room next door to see what was wrong.

And Avalon almost wished she hadn't, because just before Leah shook her to wake her up from the nightmare, Avalon had heard her mother's voice for the first time – her birth mother, Lindsay's – and heard her say, in a voice as sweet as an angel's:

"I love you, little Avalon. Never forget that!"

CHAPTER
FIFTEEN

The next day was Sunday, and as Avalon dressed for church in the morning, the strongest memory that kept coming back to her from the nightmare she'd had the night before was the sound of her mother's voice as she'd said so sweetly: "I love you, little Avalon. Never forget that!" There had been no doubt in her mind that it was Lindsay's voice.

But when had Lindsay said it? That was the mystery. There were people who could recall incidents from their babyhood when they were as young as one or two. But Avalon had absolutely no memory of Lindsay Herrington whatsoever.

She'd seen a photograph of her, so she knew what she had looked like. But how could she possibly know how her mother's voice had sounded? Had she ever really heard Lindsay say those words, or was the whole thing – nightmare and all – just a product of an admittedly active imagination?

It was strange…until Lora Evans had died, Avalon simply couldn't think of Lindsay Herrington as her mother. But it was different now, and she realized that the difference was her own emotional need for a mother, period.

Avalon and Lora had been so close for twenty years that she didn't think she would or could ever be that close to anyone again...

But to have a biological mother...the mother who had actually given birth to her...going through the "valley of the shadow of death" for her, as she'd sometimes heard the birth process called...*that* would be a gift most precious and welcome at this lonely time in her life. And it would mean the world to her grandmother Valerie.

When she and Leah went downstairs, Avalon insisted that Leah ride in the front seat with Mac on the way to church. Mac and his parents had attended the church in Evanston for many years, and they weren't going to walk away just because Charles's younger brother Eric was no longer the pastor.

She knew it was going to be hard this first time, seeing everyone there except Eric in the pulpit and Lora at the piano. But these people had loved her since she was ten years old, and she didn't dread the hugs and kind words she knew everyone would have for her.

Right now, though, she didn't want to think about anything except last night and the dream – or rather, the nightmare – she'd had. So she wanted to sit in the back seat of the car alone and think.

When they got to the church, everything was just as Avalon had thought it would be, and she got through the service and all of the expressions of sympathy even more easily than she had expected. There was a general sense of loss and sadness among the congregation, which was very natural under the circumstances.

But the visiting minister's sermon entitled "Life Goes On!" was anything but callous. It was an enlivening reminder that life goes on in Heaven for those who walked with Christ in their lives here on earth, just as surely as it goes on here for those who are left until later.

Avalon found her heart strangely warmed and comforted. For the first time since their death, she could actually visualize her parents there – more alive than ever, happy and at peace.

And when the service was over and she and Leah were leaving the sanctuary, she thought perhaps the nightmare of her parents' death and the nightmare she'd had last night were about to be softened by a dream. Later on, much later on, Avalon was amazed at her own ability to even notice anyone so soon after losing her parents. But perhaps that loss in itself was the reason...

Standing at the back door of the vestibule, shaking the minister's hand, was the best-looking young man Avalon had ever seen in her twenty-two years: at least six foot, built like a linebacker, his blond hair lightened by the same sun that had bronzed the rest of him.

Dressed impeccably in a dark gray two-piece suit and a gray-and-blue silk tie, he looked like a Greek god, or perhaps even more like a young Siegfried.

She caught her breath, dazzled. She had always prided herself on being impervious to good looks, per se. A man had to be a great deal more than handsome to appeal to her. But in this case, she was attracted in spite of herself.

Leah had stopped to speak to Mac for a moment, so

Avalon was still staring unconsciously when the young man turned around slowly and looked straight into her eyes with a completely natural smile, as if he'd felt her eyes on him and was glad she was there.

He walked over to where she was standing and said quietly:

"Avalon? I've just heard about your parents, and I want you to know how very sorry I am. I met your Dad several times downtown at the Pacific Garden Mission when he spoke there, and I was doing some volunteer work...."

"He was a fine man, and I know a lot of people will miss him deeply – I can only imagine how much you'll miss him, as his daughter. He – told me a little bit about you, you see, and I happen to know how much he thought of you and loved you."

His deep blue eyes seemed to add silently: "Now that I've met you, I can understand why."

Avalon found herself stammering, something she hardly ever did except under duress.

"I – I'm sorry, but you seem to have the advantage of me – you know my name, but I don't know yours...."

This young man was so completely different from anyone she'd ever dated seriously, that she suddenly felt unsophisticated and artless. The service this morning had also helped her to realize that her parents were really gone forever, and she felt a kind of aloneness in the world.

"Lawrence Masters. Didn't your Dad ever mention me to you at all?"

He sounded like a hopeful little boy at that moment,

and Avalon was sorry to have to say:

"No, I'm afraid he didn't, Mr. Masters."

"Oh, please!" he laughed. "Call me Lawrence. You'll make me feel like an old man if you call me 'Mr.'!" His smile was guileless and engaging, and Avalon thought she had never seen such white teeth. Maybe it was just the tan....

That was the beginning, and the next several Sundays he sat in the pew with her and Leah, and of course, Mac. She and Leah were still staying at her Uncle Charles's house in Barrington, which seemed to suit everybody involved.

Leah and Mac were beginning to go just about everywhere together, and they always insisted that Avalon come with them, but she was starting to feel like a fifth wheel.

So when Lawrence asked her after church one Sunday to go to lunch with him somewhere in downtown Chicago, she said "Yes" without hesitation. But she knew that Mac and Leah would enjoy going, too, so she asked if he'd mind if they came along.

Lawrence was more than agreeable. He suggested they try Gino's Pizza, and so the four of them were soon walking down the steps that led below street-level and sitting across a table from each other beside a graffiti-covered wall – one of the hallmarks of the place that made it famous.

After they placed their orders, Lawrence said playfully:

"OK, folks, what are we going to write on this wall for posterity?" He held up a crayon as if waiting for their instructions.

Mac laughed and said: "How about this? 'The Buzzard is caged – celebrate!'"

Lawrence looked at Mac blankly.

"What? 'The Buzzard is caged'? What on earth does *that* mean?"

Mac began to explain what had been happening to Avalon, starting with the accident caused by someone's tampering with her brake line, and ending with her nearly being pushed off the subway platform by a hired killer named Manny Byrd, whose nickname in prison was 'The Buzzard'.

Avalon felt embarrassed as she listened, especially when Lawrence's blue eyes widened to the extent that he looked utterly incredulous, and she wondered if he even believed the things Mac was telling him.

She knew they sounded melodramatic – almost made up, like a movie or a television show – but they were certainly true, and it would hurt her if Lawrence thought Mac was dramatizing or exaggerating.

But the first words out of Lawrence's mouth after Mac finished speaking dispelled that fear completely. His face and voice registered only natural horror at the situation, and he said fervently:

"That must have been terrifying! It's hard to believe things like that can really happen to someone like Avalon – even in a city like Chicago. That's horrible!"

He turned to Avalon suddenly and reached for her hand.

"You know, you really shouldn't be going anywhere by yourself after this. Who knows how long that killer will really be off the streets? Didn't you say he's been turned loose before?"

His distress was deep and real, and if Avalon had been wondering about his feelings for her, she couldn't wonder any longer. He was looking at her like someone who cared intensely.

Mac said: "Well, the cops took the $3,000 he'd been paid up front, so it's not likely he'd risk his neck to try to make the hit for nothing, even if he does manage to get out again."

"Yes, but don't those thugs have reputations to uphold, as hit men? If he fails to complete a job, won't he 'lose face' with the other goons in town? That might make him dangerous, even without the money. I don't like it at all, Avalon. I'm worried about you. What precautions are you taking to protect yourself?"

"Well, I'm leaving for Louisiana right away, which should help." It was the first time she had announced her intention so definitely, and Mac and Leah looked at her with surprise. Lawrence looked shocked.

"Louisiana! Why? What's in Louisiana?" Then, as if afraid he was being a bit blatant with his curiosity, he said apologetically: "I'm sorry...it's really none of my business – I'm just concerned about you."

"It's all right. There's no reason why you shouldn't know about it." She went on, saying to Mac and Leah: "I've been meaning to tell you – now that there's no one following me, I'm going as soon as possible, to look for the island in David's painting and see if I can find my mother...my birth mother, that is."

Lawrence looked even more at sea, so Avalon turned

to him and explained:

"My parents adopted me when I was about two and a half, after I was abandoned – left on the back seat of the church they were pastoring in a little town in Louisiana called St. Francisville.

"I was in pretty bad shape. I couldn't talk for six months after that, and by the time I could speak, I guess I'd forgotten everything that had happened to me before that time.

"But now that my adoptive parents are both gone, I find I'm beginning to have a great desire to find my birth mother. I'm not sure you can understand that..."

"Yes, I can," Lawrence said quickly. "My mother died last year. I never knew I could miss someone so much. Her death left me in a much better financial position than I've ever been in before in my life, but if I could have her alive again, I'd gladly be a beggar."

"I'm sorry...I had no idea. Well, then, maybe you can understand..."

Avalon was touched by his obvious attachment to his deceased mother.

"But I don't understand about this island you said you're going to look for," he went on. "What does that have to do with it? Or is that something I shouldn't be asking?"

Avalon explained the situation to him, and his response was to ask:

"But won't that be dangerous? I mean, if you were in bad shape when you were abandoned, wouldn't it be risky to go back to that place – if that's where somebody abused you? I don't think that's at all wise, do you?"

Avalon smiled and said:

"Well, it was twenty years ago, and besides, I have no choice. My grandmother is dying of cancer, and she's frantic to know what happened to my mother before she dies...

"She and my grandfather wouldn't let my mother marry the man of her choice, so they eloped, and my grandparents never saw her again. I know my grandmother feels very guilty about it and wants desperately to ask for my mother's forgiveness."

Lawrence seemed more confused than ever.

"Your grandmother?"

Avalon nodded. "Yes, Valerie Herrington. When she saw me, she knew instantly that I was Lindsay's daughter – I think I look enough like my mother to be her twin. You should see our pictures side by side – it's almost uncanny...

"Anyway, I'm going, and soon. If anybody wants to come with me, you're welcome! My dear little car has been officially declared irreparable, so I'm going to take my cousin Mac's advice and do what he wanted me to do the day we had our wreck."

"And what is that?" Lawrence was all curiosity.

"I'm going to get a new car – another convertible, but with a back seat this time, so I can take somebody with me besides Mac, for a change." She made a face at Mac. "Well, are you satisfied now?"

"I will be when you tell me it's a Jaguar or a Ferrari, or better yet, maybe even a Lamborghini."

Lawrence smiled at Avalon as if to defend her against Mac's sarcasm.

"I'm sure she'll look just as beautiful in a Chevy or a Ford," he said gallantly.

Avalon blushed as she said sheepishly:

"I'm afraid Mac is closer to the truth, Lawrence. My attorney told me I should make my car one of my investments, so I ordered a Maserati. Just for you, Mac. Now are you satisfied?"

Mac started laughing when he saw the look on Lawrence's face: he was staring at Avalon as if he thought she'd lost her mind.

"Why shouldn't she have one?" Mac said happily. "The girl has just inherited two hundred million dollars from her great-grandfather, Andrew Herrington, Sr. I think I'll go to Louisiana with you, Avalon, if your invitation is for real. By the way, the new car *is* silver, I hope?"

Avalon smiled and said it was, and she and Mac and Leah all began to talk excitedly at once, so none of them noticed that Lawrence wasn't joining in the conversation.

He looked a little green around the gills, and he sat silently, apparently so stunned he couldn't speak.

CHAPTER
SIXTEEN

Avalon thought Lawrence would call her that week, after their lunch together on Sunday, but he didn't. And the following Sunday morning, he wasn't at church, either.

She looked all around the sanctuary for him, thinking he might have decided to sit someplace else for a change. But he was nowhere to be seen. Her heart sank a little when she realized he simply wasn't there.

She remembered now how quiet he'd been after they'd talked about her new car and the trip to Louisiana. She had thought perhaps he was just worried and preoccupied about her safety or wondering how long she would be gone.

But his absence from church this morning put a new light on things. She began to wonder if it had anything to do with what Mac had blurted out at Gino's last Sunday, about the two hundred million dollars she had recently inherited.

It *was* an obscene amount of money to mention so blatantly. It hadn't been very genteel of Mac, but Mac had never claimed to be genteel.

He was actually enjoying the thought of Avalon's riches far more than she was, and he hadn't been exactly discreet about it.

Had it offended Lawrence's sensibilities? She tried hard to put the whole thing out of her mind as she started making plans for her trip.

The Maserati was delivered early Monday morning, and Mac managed to come home for lunch and put about forty miles on it – "just checking it out for you", he explained with a grin.

Avalon enjoyed watching him have such a good time, like a kid with a new toy. Well, she supposed a new silver Maserati convertible would qualify as a "big boy's toy" in anybody's book.

She thought Mac was probably relishing her new financial status more than he normally would have, due to Charles Evans's portfolio having gone through some drastic changes lately, with some of his investments taking a nosedive.

Avalon had even heard her aunt and uncle discussing the distinct possibility of having to give up their house in Barrington. Giving up an elegant estate wouldn't have meant much to Avalon and her parents, but it would mean a great deal to Mac and his.

He and Leah were getting more and more serious every day, and Avalon hoped they would both decide to go to Louisiana with her when she left in a week or so. Avalon had talked to Johnna several times about coming to see her while she was there, and Leah had talked to David.

Avalon thought how wonderful it would be if Mac and Leah married each other. Leah's brother David was married to Avalon's Aunt Johnna, and Mac was

Avalon's cousin – well, by adoption, anyway. They would all be just one big, happy family.

That afternoon, Avalon received a surprising phone call.

"It's an Officer McDonald, dear," Mac's mother Elaine said in her soft, subdued voice as she handed the phone to Avalon.

Elaine Evans knew all about Avalon's brush with death at the subway station near Marshall Field's downtown, but she still considered calls from the police somehow shameful. Avalon just smiled and took the phone from her aunt.

"Miss Evans?" said the familiar voice of the officer who had assured her that Manny Byrd would not be on the street again anytime soon.

"Yes, Officer McDonald. How are you? This is a pleasant surprise."

"Yes, well, it – I – Miss Evans, I hardly know how to tell you what I'm calling about. I don't think I've ever had to do it before, and I've been on the force for nearly ten years now." He sounded tense and irritable.

Avalon's stomach tightened in preparation for bad news.

"I'm sure you remember that I told you there wasn't any reason to worry about Manny Byrd for a long time to come."

"Yes, I do remember that. Has anything changed? Is that why you're calling?"

Avalon dreaded hearing what he had to tell her, but she was trying to make it easier for him.

"Yes, that *is* why I'm calling. I just wanted to let you

know that something has happened that you need to know about. Manny's lawyer managed to get his parole reinstated, and he was on the street again as of a week ago this past Saturday."

Avalon felt her heart lurch sickeningly. "More than a week ago! Is there some reason you've waited this long to call me?" She deliberately kept her voice as steady and mild as possible, but she could feel her knees weakening and her fingertips growing cold.

"Yes, because we had a very good tail on him, and we weren't worried about him. And then we were waiting for a definite I.D."

"Identification? Of what? I don't understand."

"Well, we had Manny under observation when he met somebody on the Michigan Avenue Bridge at about 2:30 in the morning, this past Friday. It certainly appeared to be by appointment.

"The two of them just stood there talking for a few minutes, but then there was a struggle and apparently a knife attack which killed Manny, and his assailant pushed his body over the bridge into the river.

"The tail was too far away to apprehend the attacker, and if the Chicago River ran the way most rivers do, we might never have seen Manny again....

"But we were able to recover the body this afternoon, and if we hadn't been sure it was Manny by any other means, we'd have known it by the fact that he had your photograph on him again, just like before. But no money."

Avalon sat down unsteadily on the little chair beside the phone, appalled that a hired killer had spent nearly a week on the street looking for her when she'd felt so safe!

She was still sitting there stunned after Officer MacDonald hung up, when the phone rang again. This time it was Lawrence, and Avalon almost burst into tears at the sound of his voice.

It had been so long since she'd heard it; and the relief she felt in knowing that he still cared enough about her to call almost matched the relief she felt in knowing that Manny Byrd was dead.

Lawrence was furious when she told him what she'd just learned from the police.

"How could they let a man like that just walk out? I don't understand that at all. It's crazy! No wonder the murder rate in Chicago is so high! I know one thing, Avalon Evans. You're going to be under constant surveillance from now on by me – Manny Byrd or no Manny Byrd. Beginning tonight. Will you come to dinner with me?"

He picked her up two hours later. She'd taken a quick shower and put on a new outfit – one she'd bought in the bargain basement at Marshall Field's with Leah that awful day when she'd almost been killed in the subway. Somehow it made her feel stronger, to wear it as a reminder that the danger was over now.

Lawrence met Mac's parents and saw Avalon's new car; then they drove out of the estate and into downtown Chicago. Somehow, she didn't want to ask him why he hadn't been at church this past Sunday and why he'd waited so long to call her.

And she didn't have to. As soon as they were seated

at the table he'd reserved for two at J. J. Biggs on Dearborn Avenue, a gorgeous old nineteenth century mansion that had been converted into an elegant and expensive restaurant, he told her.

"I've almost gone crazy without you, Avalon...I really wanted to let you go and never see you again, but I just couldn't. When Mac said what he did that day at Gino's, about your inheriting all that money, I just sort of lost it.

"I'm a poor man, Avalon. I've never had much of anything. When my mother died, she left me all she had, but it wasn't much, even though it was more than I'd ever had before..."

The waiter came then to take their orders, and after Lawrence had ordered for both of them, he went on quietly:

"When I got out of high school, there simply weren't any funds for college. Most of my adult life, I've worked full-time just to help keep the wolf away from the door, and I've never made much money.

"I did some volunteer work, which is where I met your dad. But I have to say, as articulate as he was, he couldn't describe you adequately. When I saw you for real that first Sunday, I just fell in love with you..."

Avalon opened her mouth to protest – this was going a little too fast – but Lawrence was like a runaway freight train that gathers momentum as it goes.

"And then that Sunday when Mac told me you were an heiress to millions!" He lowered his voice discreetly as he spoke the word. "I just felt like I would ruin your life if I stayed around. You deserve so much better! So much more. I don't mind telling you, it made me uncomfortable....

"For one thing, I didn't want to risk repeating the pattern my parents set. You see, my mother was born to money, and her family literally disowned her when she married my father. That disenfranchisement affected their marriage adversely all the years they were married, and it finally led to divorce. My mother never really got over it...

"Plus, I've always been extremely independent, and I struggled with how I would really feel about being married to someone with a lot more money than I could ever earn or provide for her. That's why I didn't call last week and didn't show up at church this past Sunday....

"But the bottom line is that I've fallen in love with you. And I can't stop loving you just because you've suddenly become an heiress. So here I am. Here *we* are."

He reached over and took her hand gently in his, looking into her eyes as he spoke the last few words. She felt herself warming under his fervent gaze and fought the feeling.

She had broken off a disappointing engagement just a year ago and didn't want to get seriously involved again so soon. But she didn't want him to just walk away, either.

So when he reached into his coat pocket and took out a small jewelry box that could only be a ring, she put her hand out gently and stopped him.

"Not now, Lawrence. It's sweet of you, but I just can't. I like you, but that's just too serious a move. Even if I felt what I should feel for you, I'm still too fragile from losing my parents, and from all these other things that have been happening to me lately...I'm just not ready for that now. We haven't really known each other very long, you know..."

She looked at him appealingly. He was hurt and disappointed, but he put the little box back into his pocket and nodded dismally.

"I think I understand how you feel, Avalon. I probably shouldn't have panicked and spoken to you tonight...so soon. I know it seems sudden to you, but as you know now, I loved you before I ever laid eyes on you, so it doesn't seem sudden to me...

"But as long as I know you care about me a little, and as long as I know there's hope for the future, I can wait...I *will* wait. Forever, if I have to."

They were somehow able to finish their dinner and the rest of the evening without too much discomfort, and when he dropped her off at the front door, he kissed her for the first time, a lingering, tender kiss that Avalon was still feeling as she climbed the stairs to her bedroom.

She knew the moment she saw Leah at the top of the staircase that Mac had proposed tonight, too. Leah's face was shining with bliss as she threw her arms around Avalon with a little squeal of happiness.

"Oh, Avalon! I'm *so* excited! Mac asked me to marry him today, and of course I said 'Yes'! Can you believe it? We're going to be family, you and I! Isn't it wonderful?"

She twirled around rapturously, and Avalon was reminded of the way Johnna had twirled around when her parents had finally given their blessing to her marrying David.

Avalon hugged Leah with delight and said:

"I can't think of anything in the world that will make me happier! It's just what I've been hoping and praying for. Have you set a date yet?"

Leah said breathlessly:

"We wanted to talk to you first, about your trip to Louisiana. We want to go with you, you know, to help you find the island and maybe your mother, and see Johnna and David, too...

"We thought we might just wait until we all get back from the trip to have the wedding. Johnna and David will come up for it, and of course we want you to be in it, and Lawrence, if you want him to be..."

Avalon looked solemn and sat down in a chair on the landing.

"I'm not sure I do, Leah...he was about to ask me to marry him tonight. He told me he loves me, and he had a ring he wanted to give me, but I stopped him."

Leah looked at her in surprise. "You stopped him? But why?"

"Oh, Leah, it was too sudden," Avalon said soberly. "That's such a serious step, and I'm just not sure enough about him, or about how I feel. You know about the engagement I broke off a year ago, and how unpleasant that was. It hasn't been very long since Mother and Daddy died, and I just haven't known Lawrence long enough..." Her voice broke, and Leah was instantly contrite.

"I'm sorry, Avalon...I do understand. I guess it really wasn't very smart or even kind of Lawrence to

spring this on you so suddenly, and so soon after –
everything."

Avalon took advantage of the "everything" to say:

"And you know, as if losing Mother and Daddy
weren't enough, that terrible man who's been after
me...did you know he got out again and was looking for
me for nearly a week, and I didn't even know it?"

Leah was as shocked as she herself had been, and
Avalon shared all that had happened since Manny
Byrd's lawyer had secured his release. When she finally
told Leah that Manny was dead, Leah was so relieved,
she almost cried.

She insisted that Avalon tell Mac, too, and she went
to get him. The three of them discussed the whole
situation around the kitchen table and made plans
together then and there for the trip to Louisiana. Mac
thought Avalon should use the time in Louisiana to give
herself some emotional space, and she agreed.

When Lawrence called her the next morning and
told her he'd been thinking about her all night and
couldn't bear the thought of her leaving for Louisiana
without him, she reminded him that he was welcome to
come along.

He thought it might look bad if they took a long trip
together without being married, but Avalon informed
him that Mac and Leah were going, too.

He was elated by the news that Mac and Leah were
engaged. That would be fun, he said; and he hoped their
happiness might make Avalon reconsider becoming
engaged herself...

When Mac drove the new Maserati out of his driveway in Barrington a week later, Leah's left hand was sporting a contemporary emerald-cut diamond in a yellow gold setting.

The ring Lawrence wanted to give Avalon was a gorgeous marquise diamond set in white gold. The diamond itself was at least two carats, and it was surrounded by twelve large, and what appeared to be very fine, emeralds.

Lawrence insisted that she take the ring, even when she told him plainly that she couldn't make the commitment he wanted her to make – not now, and maybe not ever, she hurried on to say.

Avalon knew her weakness: she felt sorry for the men who fell in love with her and hated to hurt them. That weakness had led her into one engagement that had taken her far too close to the altar for comfort.

She didn't want to fall into that error again, exacerbated by the loneliness brought on by her parents' death and a desire for the security of masculine protection in light of all the danger she'd faced recently.

When he adamantly refused to keep the ring, Avalon agreed to place it deep in her overnight case – "but only for safe-keeping", she said firmly. He offered it to her with his whole heart in his eyes, telling her it had been his mother's, and Avalon was very touched.

But she didn't wear the ring.

CHAPTER
SEVENTEEN

The trip was a dream. Mac insisted on driving Avalon's new car, since he would certainly never own one like that, he said. Avalon was more than willing to let him. So he and Leah sat in the front, and Avalon sat in back.

On the way downtown to pick up Lawrence, Mac said: "We couldn't have more perfect weather for this trip if we'd ordered it ourselves! Just look at this sunshine – it's bright, and warm enough to drive with the top down, but not hot enough to give us a sunburn. Man! The South doesn't have a thing on Chicago."

He glanced into the rear-view mirror to watch Avalon's face as he said it, knowing she was slowly opening her mind to the idea of spending more time in Louisiana. As much as Mac liked the South, he didn't much like that idea.

She scrunched up her nose at him and said with a tongue-in-cheek smile:

"It *is* gorgeous. Of course, it's August – it might not be quite so sunny and warm in January – or February."

As someone who had lived both north and south of the Mason-Dixon line, she'd always said there were only two things wrong with the North and two things wrong

with the South. The two things wrong with the South
were July and August, and the two things wrong with
the North were January and February!

Leah spoke up quickly, still unaccustomed to the
friendly sparring these two cousins engaged in with such
delight.

"What I love is the smell of all this new car leather.
Isn't it delicious? That is one heavenly fragrance. In my
book, the only thing that competes is a wood fire."

The smell of new leather did permeate the air, and
Mac had seen to it that her car was as spotless as it had
been the day it rolled off the showroom floor. The deep
silver paint glistened like mercury in the sunlight, and
the seats were as soft as marshmellows. Luxury features
were too numerous to fathom on this "maiden voyage",
as Mac liked to call it, but he was determined to master
and utilize as many as he could.

A few soft, white clouds drifted across the sky, which
was a deep blue endless heaven above them. The
summer wind was just a mild breeze that caressed their
bare arms and blew their hair gently around their faces.

Avalon was already excited about the trip; and as
they drove downtown, her spirits rose even higher with
a sense of freedom she hadn't felt since she'd first seen
Manny Byrd.

The fact that he was dead, coupled with the soothing
presence of these friends who she knew cared about her
deeply, gave her a feeling of security she hadn't known
for weeks. She wasn't in love with Lawrence – not yet,
anyway – but she was glad he was going with them.

They were going to take Route 66, starting at Lakeshore Drive just north of Buckingham Fountain. Lawrence's apartment was in the Loop, so they picked him up there. He was waiting for them at the street with his luggage, which Avalon couldn't help but notice was just one small, somewhat shabby, bag.

She hoped the trip wasn't going to put him in an awkward position financially. Offering to pay his expenses would probably be seen as an insult. She remembered his spirit of independence and respected it.

"Has anyone had breakfast yet?" was Lawrence's first question once his bag was in the trunk and he was in the back seat with Avalon.

He was wearing a white knit short-sleeved shirt and blue jeans, and when he flashed his white smile at her, reaching for her hand, Avalon thought what a good commercial he would make for almost anything.

"Toast and tea at about seven this morning, is all," Mac replied. "Think you can last 'til we get to Joliet? We'll feel like we're out of Chicago by then, at least." They all agreed, and the car rolled southwestward across the city.

"It's funny, isn't it," Avalon said as they pulled into Joliet, the first town that didn't feel quite so much like a suburb of Chicago, "I don't think I'd want to live in a small town again, but I love going through them on a trip. Don't you?"

She turned to Lawrence, smiling, and was surprised to see an expression she didn't understand on his handsome face. He had obviously been in a brown study of some sort, and apparently his thoughts had not all been pleasant.

He jerked himself out of his reverie to reply:

"Hmmm? Were you saying something about small towns? I would be happy never to set foot in one again."

There was an edge to his voice that Avalon had never heard before, and she realized with a shock that in the whole time she'd known him, she had never heard Lawrence talk about his childhood or where he'd grown up.

She knew his mother had died recently, but where? He had never volunteered any information, and the subject simply hadn't been raised. His accent was much like everyone else's around her, and she'd always just assumed he was from Chicago. Now she wondered.

He seemed to anticipate her curiosity, because he said quickly:

"Of course, any town seems small compared to Chicago, doesn't it? Joliet isn't exactly small-town America, is it?"

"Well, it may not be small," Mac said, "but it has all the features we love about Route 66 – speaking of which, how's that diner for breakfast?"

Mac pointed to a silver boxcar-shaped diner with a bright orange neon sign blinking even in broad daylight. It looked like something out of the early 'fifties.

"Fine with me," Lawrence said. "It's about time for 'second breakfast', wouldn't you say? Or maybe even 'elevenses'." He smiled and glanced at his watch.

The diner did serve breakfast all day. Over long, crisp strips of lean bacon and perfectly fried eggs, with a stack of buttered toast and several kinds of fresh fruit to choose from, they chatted cozily about the drive ahead.

"We can easily make it to Memphis tonight," Mac said with confidence. "It's less than five hundred miles from here. Even driving slowly enough to leave the top down a while longer, we should be there by ten tonight. Is that OK with everybody?"

They all agreed, and Lawrence went on to say:

"Speaking of Memphis and other southern cities – one of the guys I work with took a trip to Atlanta earlier this summer, and when he got back, he was really raving about how 'advanced' the South was. Said they even had freeways and skyscrapers...

"He couldn't believe it! I almost said, 'Yeah, they wear shoes down there, too, believe it or not!' But I held my tongue. Some people's ignorance about the South is worse than ignorance – it's arrogance."

The hard edge in his voice was back, and Avalon wondered: why was Lawrence defensive of the South? Had he ever lived there? If so, why hadn't he told her, knowing that her new family lived there, and that that's where they were headed?

Mac said: "I can top that. One of the women in my office came back from Mardi Gras in New Orleans this past Spring saying she'd never seen so many funeral homes in her life. She thought every white mansion with columns across the front was a funeral home! Can you believe it?"

They all laughed, and Lawrence asked:

"Where are we headed first when we get there? To find your island, I mean," he said, turning to Avalon.

She shrugged.

"We're not sure. We haven't really decided *where* to

go first. The only thing we have to go on is the name of the town where the old man was working at the time — the one who described the island and house to David. The old man's description was all David had to go by when he painted the place.

"We don't know the old man's last name or where to find him, and in fact, he could be dead by now. David said he appeared to be in his sixties when they met, and that was nine years ago. David thought it was only six or seven, but when he checked his travel records, it was longer ago than he'd thought."

"So why are we going to that town at all?" Lawrence asked with a puzzled frown. "What more do you hope to learn there, if the old man is gone?"

Avalon shrugged again.

"We're going there first because we don't know what else to do. Got any bright ideas?"

She had been almost teasing, but Lawrence surprised her by saying:

"Well, you might start by going back to the town where you were abandoned, and look for islands in that area. Doesn't that make more sense?"

Avalon thought about it for a few moments, then said:

"You know, it might. I – I've never wanted to go back there, simply because I didn't want to know about my past. I wanted with all of my heart to just forget what had happened before my parents adopted me.

"We left St. Francisville when I was about six, for my Dad to pastor the little country church near Columbia, and we never went back to the church they were pastoring when I was abandoned. They loved the people in St. Francisville, but I guess they didn't want to put me through the pain of those memories."

"But things are different now, aren't they?" Lawrence asked gently.

Avalon nodded sadly.

"Yes, things are very different now...Mother and Daddy are gone, and I have a whole new family who needs my help...help in laying a very painful past to rest." She lapsed into silence, and they all finished their meal in quiet conversation.

Once they were back on the road with blue skies and sunshine, she was able to shake the sadness from her mind and enjoy the picture-postcard weather, the breeze in her hair and face, and the pleasure of being with friends.

And once she began to imagine herself walking into the church that had tried so hard at their own expense to find her birth parents twenty years ago, she realized that for the first time in her life, she didn't feel an aversion to it.

They followed Route 66 all the way to St. Louis and stopped at just about every little souvenir shop along the way, buying postcards and curios for everybody back in Chicago. They stopped for coffee and snacks so often that Mac finally accused Avalon of trying to give equal patronage to every business along Route 66.

When Mac stopped for gas, they all got out and walked around while the service station attendants pumped gas, checked the oil and water, aired the tires and cleaned the windshield. The young men working at the station seemed to enjoy servicing the Maserati, so Mac didn't rush them.

Back in the car, he drove slowly; and even when the sun finally started its descent into the hotter hours of the mid-afternoon, they left the top down on the convertible and simply put on more sunscreen, sunglasses and scarves.

With her head leaning back against the soft seat of her new car, next to an extremely handsome man who was obviously in love with her, her favorite cousin driving happily with his new, lovable fiancée beside him, Avalon felt she was in a kind of paradise.

They quoted the Burma Shave signs along the side of the road in unison and sang along with Elvis and the Beatles on the radio. Avalon shouted with laughter when Mac tried to imitate Elvis by singing "Love Me Tender" to Leah with his collar turned up and his dark hair deliberately rumpled.

For the next few hours, she was able to forget about Manny Byrd and whoever had paid him to kill her. She forgot her nightmares about the island and mansion, the old ruins and the man who had left her there on a dark night. She was even able to forget her sweet parents and the sickening sense of loss she'd felt when they died in the plane crash.

By the time they got to Memphis that night, they were happy but tired. Mac pulled into the first nice motel he saw and parked in the well-lighted driveway in front of the office. While he got out and went inside to ask about rooms, the others sat in the convertible and talked.

"I hope he tells them one room is for the guys and one for the girls. I'd hate for them to think we were...well...you know!" Leah said, blushing.

"I wouldn't worry about it if I were you," Lawrence said.

Mac came back out to the car and said:

"They have two non-smoking rooms, each with two double beds, on the ground floor, away from the highway. Am I good, or what?" He grinned.

He got back in the car and drove around the motel to their rooms.

Leah said shyly: "You did tell them one room was for the guys, and the other for the girls, didn't you?"

"No, I told them we were on our honeymoon," Mac teased.

Leah made a face and swatted him on the arm playfully.

"No, actually," Mac went on, "I did tell them one was for the guys and one for you girls; but the funny thing is, they saw all of you sitting out here in the driveway and thought you and I – " he turned to Leah, "were brother and sister. And they thought Avalon and Lawrence were brother and sister, too. Can you beat that? Strange, huh?"

Lawrence just shook his head with a grin, but Avalon felt a small shock go through her at the thought. She glanced at Lawrence and then away again quickly, thinking:

"He does look enough like me to be my brother! We're both tall and blonde. His eyes are blue, and mine are green, but our features are very similar. Our noses are alike, and he has dimples in the same places I do. It's funny, I've noticed it before but didn't realize what I was noticing! How strange that people who've never seen either one of us before noticed it, too."

Later, when the two young women were settled in their room and getting ready to go to bed, Avalon said hesitantly:

"Leah, have you noticed that Lawrence never talks about his past? His background, I mean – where he was from before he moved to Chicago, and that kind of thing…?"

Leah was removing her makeup at the moment, but she stopped what she was doing and thought about it.

"No, I guess I never gave it much thought…does that bother you?" She resumed her facial.

"I'm not sure," Avalon said softly, almost to herself. "I just wonder about it, that's all. I never thought much about it, really, until tonight – when those people thought we were brothers and sisters – you and Mac, and Lawrence and I, I mean."

Leah looked at her in horror.

"Avalon! You don't think Lawrence is your brother! That's horrible!"

"No, no, of course not. I don't! It *would* be horrible."

For more reasons than one, she thought silently. *Who would have more motive than a brother to get rid of a sister who had just inherited every penny of their mother's money? But Lawrence had said he was in better shape financially after his mother's death, so apparently he had already received his inheritance…*

She shook herself free of the distressing thoughts that

had been running through her mind and laughed at herself.

"It's ridiculous to even think of it," she said to Leah. "Those people were just teasing us, but even if there is some similarity, it's pure coincidence. You and Mac certainly aren't brother and sister, and you look as much alike as Lawrence and I do."

"I think you're just tired," Leah said kindly. "I know I am. Things will look different in the morning, after a good night's sleep." She crawled under her covers and turned out her light, said "Goodnight" and was soon sleeping peacefully.

Avalon lay awake for a long time in the darkness, thinking. She couldn't really believe that Lawrence was related to her in any way, and surely not as her brother!

But she decided she would see in the morning if she could get him to tell her just a little more about his background – and especially about his mother.

CHAPTER

EIGHTEEN

The next morning, everything looked different to Avalon. She chided herself for even thinking such terrible things about Lawrence. As if he would tell his own sister he was in love with her and wanted to marry her, knowing their relationship! She must be in worse shape emotionally after her parents' death than she had realized, even to imagine something so preposterous.

After breakfast, the foursome regretfully said goodbye to Route 66 and started planning the rest of the trip. They would take Highway 61 through Mississippi until they could join Highway 65 in southern Arkansas, then stay on that into northeast Louisiana. Everybody agreed they'd had their fill of sunshine yesterday, so Mac left the top up on the convertible.

"My hair is beginning to feel like a thatched roof," Avalon moaned as she reached up to touch it. "And I'm already so sunburned I can hardly crack a smile this morning."

But she promptly proceeded to make a liar of herself by smiling at Lawrence, who sat beside her in the back seat once again. Lawrence's hair was sun-bleached, and Avalon's was not – at least, not yet – but they were both blonde; and although Lawrence was bronzed by the sun, he'd told her that his own complexion was normally as light as hers.

When they finally left Memphis's morning traffic behind and could relax, she asked casually:

"Lawrence, how did you manage to get such a beautiful tan? You must have had a nice, long vacation somewhere earlier this summer."

She was surprised when he changed the subject quickly, looking uncomfortable. It seemed to Avalon that he tried to appear not to have heard her question at all.

"Where did you say we were going first, when we get to Louisiana?" he asked animatedly, turning to her with a smile.

At first, she hardly knew how to respond: then she said simply,

"Why...Herrington Hall, of course...I'm sorry, I thought you knew that. David and Johnna will be there. You'll have a chance to meet Leah's brother and my aunt Johnna, and my grandparents."

"Isn't David the artist? The one who painted the island?"

"Yes...that's right. Why?"

"Oh, nothing...I just want to keep the players in this drama straight in my mind." He reached for her hand and pressed it affectionately, smiling.

They were silent for a minute or two. Then Lawrence said:

"Wouldn't it be fun to surprise him with the news that you found the island? I mean, we could do our looking first – before we stop and see David and your aunt. I suspect that once we get to that town…St. Francisville, wasn't it?…we'll be close enough to find the place on our own. Wouldn't it be great to surprise them?"

At first Avalon was so taken aback by Lawrence's suggestion that she couldn't seem to absorb it: but once the door was open in her mind, the idea began to look attractive. It *would* be gratifying to know what the situation was, when she finally went back to Herrington Hall.

It might actually be easier on her grandparents and Johnna not to be thinking about it every minute over the next few days, worrying about Avalon and wondering what kind of news she would be bringing back to the Hall. Perhaps it would be better just to walk in one day when it was a *fait accompli* and say: "We found it."

She didn't say anything to Mac or Leah about a possible change in plans until they were almost to Greenville, Mississippi and their link with Highway 65, which would take them within a few miles of their destination. She knew they were eager to see David and Johnna; but the more she thought about it, the more she liked the idea of finding the island first.

There was just one problem: the painting. She'd left it with Megan Marshall, and the painting would be helpful – perhaps even necessary – in finding and identifying the island and the house.

She said so to Lawrence in a low voice, just as they were coming into Greenville. They only had about a hundred miles to go, she said, so they would be at Herrington Hall in a couple of hours.

"Who did you say has this painting?" Lawrence asked, after Avalon explained how important it was.

"Megan Marshall. Her house isn't far from Herrington Hall, but I doubt we'd see anyone from there. And I know Megan wouldn't tell anyone what we're doing, if I ask her to keep quiet about it until we get back."

"Well, why don't we just swing by there and pick it up? I don't have a problem with doing that, do you?"

"I just hope she's at home...she's certainly not expecting us this afternoon. But the folks at the Hall are...I'm not sure how Leah's going to feel about not stopping to see David first. She's crazy about her brother and hasn't seen him in quite a while. She'll hate disappointing him."

"It's your trip, isn't it? And your car? Besides, why can't we drop Mac and Leah off to see her brother, while you and I go to pick up the painting? Or, better yet, they could drop us off at your friend's house and go on to the Hall and then come back for us. Wouldn't that work?"

Avalon thought about it briefly and decided it would. But she hadn't quite liked the way Lawrence had dismissed Leah's feelings with his "It's your trip, isn't it?"

When she broached the subject to Leah a few miles later, there didn't seem to be any problem. As long as Leah got to see David, it was all right, she said. They hadn't planned to stay at the Hall long today, anyway.

She and Mac were planning to drive to Monroe a few days from now and spend some time with Johnna and David while Avalon and Lawrence continued to search for the island; so she didn't mind waiting for the longer visit. Mac, however, was quiet for a long time after that, and Avalon wondered what on earth he was thinking.

They pulled into the Marshalls' driveway an hour and a half later, and Avalon was thankful to see a car parked there. When she rang the doorbell and Megan answered, the older woman's obvious joy at seeing her was touching.

They hugged each other like long-lost friends, and Megan's eyes sparkled with sisterly speculation when Avalon introduced Lawrence to her. Then Meg walked out to the car and talked to Mac and Leah for a few minutes, while Avalon and Lawrence waited in rockers on her front porch.

After Mac and Leah pulled away, Megan came back onto the porch and said with a teasing smile:

"I love your new car, Avalon. I think Mac does, too, though – he may never come back for you!"

Avalon blushed.

"Oh, Mac is like a little boy with a new toy, Meg. You do know why I had to get a new car, don't you?"

Avalon suddenly realized that Megan might not know about her accident in Chicago, and it was almost certain she didn't know about Manny Byrd and the attempts on her life. So she told her.

Megan was shocked.

"Oh, Avalon...how dreadful! Thank the Lord the man is dead, though I'd hate to be in his shoes on Judgment Day! Mercy! That poor soul. It's hard to understand what drives people to do things like that....just Satan, I guess. We live such a sheltered life here."

Avalon thought to herself that this little country crossroads was certainly quieter and less violent than Chicago, but Satan was always working everywhere. There was just greater anonymity, more temptations and more people who ignored God, in a huge city.

They all went inside the house then, and Megan brought the painting to Avalon. It was the first time Lawrence had ever seen it, and he seemed fascinated. He examined it closely.

"Did you say this artist – David – painted this from memory? Why can't *he* tell us where the island is?"

"Oh, no, Lawrence...David never saw the place himself. He just got the description from an old man in Natchitoches named Joe something or other – David was never able to learn his last name.

"The old man moved on right after that, and David says he might even be dead by now – he thinks Joe must have been close to seventy when they met nine years ago. Remember?"

Lawrence was peering intently at David's painting, apparently trying to memorize details that would help them in their search. He answered her question distractedly.

"Hmmm? Oh – sure...I just wasn't thinking. I remember now." He turned around with a smile.

Megan led them into the kitchen, where she set out and filled two large stem glasses with iced tea. Avalon expected Lawrence to exclaim over the sweetness of

Megan's "syrup", as Mac always called Southern tea, but he drank it in a sort of contemplative silence.

"Has Lawrence ever seen your mother's photograph, Avalon? Lindsay's, I mean...."

"No, I don't think so, Megan. I'd love for him to see her, though. You still have one here, don't you? Why don't you get it?"

Meg went upstairs immediately and came back down with an 8 x 10 photograph of Lindsay Herrington in a silver frame. When she showed it to Lawrence, his eyes widened with amazement.

"This is your mother, Avalon?" he sounded as surprised as Avalon herself had been the first time she'd seen a photograph of Lindsay.

"It looks like you! Exactly like you. And it's not just the blonde hair...it's the face itself. Your features are identical!" He seemed staggered by the similarity.

Avalon was a little taken aback by his intensity, but she laughed.

"I guess that's why my grandparents knew me instantly," she said.

"Yes....I can see why, now. It's...it's almost scary..." Lawrence seemed to be thinking deeply, his thoughts a million miles away. It gave Avalon an uncomfortable sensation. Why should it matter to him?

Mac and Leah came back for them less than an hour later, and they all left the Marshalls' house promising Meg to keep her and Bob posted on their progress. Avalon put the painting in the trunk of her car, wrapping it carefully to protect it. She also kept the picture of Lindsay.

Leah was full of David and Johnna – how wonderful they looked, and how happy they were. She kept everybody entertained all the way to St. Francisville with tales of their honeymoon in New Orleans and along the River Road and in Natchez. When they were finally pulling into St. Francisville a couple of hours later, she said:

"Oh, by the way, Johnna said they stopped to take pictures at just about every little town and plantation house on both sides of the Mississippi between New Orleans and Baton Rouge...

"And there was one place – somewhere near a little town called White Castle – where she said they actually saw an island, but no house. It was in a lake that we might call a swamp, I guess. They tried to explain where it was, in relation to the town...

"Anyway, they were so excited! She said they asked one of the locals about the place, and he said they call it Imitation Island, because somebody back in the 1890's tried to rebuild on the ruins of an old antebellum mansion and ended up with something they could have named the town after – you know, White Castle.

"Of course, the town is really named after Notto-way, the antebellum house that's *literally* a 'white castle'. What do you think? Should we check it out?"

Avalon and Lawrence were flabbergasted that Leah had kept this intriguing information to herself throughout the trip. They assaulted her with questions she couldn't answer.

Mac, however, had made careful notes about the place in question, but now he said firmly:

"I think it would be wise to forget all about it tonight. Let's get a good night's sleep and go to church in the morning, and then we can head to White Castle and Nottoway after lunch. That'll be soon enough, after all these years...

"And don't let it keep you awake tonight, Avalon. We don't really know any more now than we did before – it's just a remote possibility, that's all. I don't want you to get your hopes up and then be disappointed. OK?" He turned around and looked at her, waiting for a commitment.

"OK, OK...I'll try," she said resignedly, knowing she would think about it all night, anyway.

But she didn't. That night they ate in a quaint, picturesque restaurant just off Ferdinand Street in St. Francisville's historic district, and Avalon had an experience there that simply superimposed itself on her imagination about the island. It even came close to re-replacing her interest in it altogether.

It happened almost as soon as the four of them sat down at a table in one corner of the room, near a beautiful fireplace on which stood at least a dozen antique candlesticks of different designs and sizes.

The effect was charming; and in fact, there were antiques and fireplaces in every cozy room of the restaurant, which was in an antebellum house renovated for that purpose.

Avalon was gazing all around the room with delight, about to compare the ambiance to that of J. J. Biggs in Chicago, when she noticed a man at a nearby table, gaping at them as if transfixed. When she caught his eye, he turned away quickly, seemingly chagrined to be caught staring so rudely.

On second look, she saw that he was what she supposed most people would call handsome, as well as being well-dressed and meticulously groomed. His thick, dark hair and mustache were the precise opposite of Lawrence's Nordic blondeness; but there was a pleasant peacefulness about him, a sort of confident contentment, that evinced itself in his perfect posture and calm bearing – in spite of having just been caught in a social *faux pas*.

Turning her attention back to the others and the menu, Avalon tried to recall and analyze the expression she had surprised in the man's eyes. Had it been bewilderment? Dismay? She couldn't quite pin it down, but there had definitely been something unfathomable in that look.

The man left the restaurant soon afterward, and Avalon put him out of her mind for the remainder of the meal. It was excellent – she suspected there was a New Orleans *chef de cuisine* in the kitchen, even though they were still more than a hundred miles north of that city. Of course, Baton Rouge had chefs just as capable. Either way, it was a memorable meal.

But it wasn't the gourmet meal or the old-world charm of Antiques & Ambrosia that lingered in Avalon's mind when she climbed into bed that night at their motel on the highway. It was the dark-haired man who had stared at them so strangely.

She wondered: could the expression in his eyes have been one of *recognition?* But if so, of whom? She herself had been the one to catch his eye and cause him to turn away, apparently with embarrassment. But he hadn't been looking at her, she was sure of that. Or had he?

As Avalon drifted off to sleep, she realized that even if she never knew the answers, the stranger had at least made it possible for her to obey Mac's insistent injunction to forget about their search, at least for tonight.

She hadn't thought of the mysterious island once.

CHAPTER
NINETEEN

Avalon wasn't the only one who had a difficult time getting up the next morning. They were truly in the deep South now, and it wasn't early June this time, but August.

The little motel where they'd stayed didn't boast about their air-conditioning, and she thought it was a good thing – someone might have sued them for false advertising if they had. She understood now why most visitors to St. Francisville stayed at one of the many elegant guest houses in the area.

But everyone showed up for breakfast in the café next door, except Lawrence. Mac said he'd begged off for the morning, complaining that he had a splitting headache, something Avalon had never heard him do before.

She wondered if it might be because they were going to a church other than the one back home, where Lawrence felt comfortable. He'd gone to church with her almost every Sunday since they'd met, but there were times when she thought perhaps it hadn't been a life-long habit.

She saw to it that Mac took him some breakfast and told Mac to say they would miss him and hoped he'd be better soon.

Avalon was amazed at her own serenity as they drove back down the main street of town toward the church where she had been clandestinely deposited on the back pew twenty years ago.

After they adopted her, Eric and Lora had pastored here for four more years, until Avalon was six, and then they'd moved to the little country church near Columbia.

She thought that even though she'd been only six when they left St. Francisville, she might remember a few of the folks who'd been so intensely involved in the effort to find her birth family. They'd spent thousands of dollars and hundreds of hours in the fruitless search. Surely some of them would still remember.

The parking lot was full when they arrived, and they had a little trouble finding a spot. As she and Mac and Leah got out of the car and made their way toward the church, Avalon looked around eagerly for a familiar face among the folks chatting outside the front door, although she realized that everyone would look much older now.

But the faces, although friendly, were those of strangers; and when they walked through the front door, Avalon was astounded at the increased size of the crowd milling about in the narthex. She was glad to see it. This church had always been consistently supportive of Eric and Lora, and exceptionally kind to Avalon herself.

A smiling usher approached and welcomed them, handing each of them a copy of this morning's worship folder. Then he led them down a long, carpeted aisle to a pew that was still half empty.

Mac and Leah went in first and sat down. Just before Avalon entered the pew, she turned to the elderly usher and said quietly:

"Excuse me...my name is Avalon Evans. My Dad was Eric Evans, and he was the pastor of this church sixteen years ago. Do you know if any of the folks who might remember him are still here?"

Avalon had been hoping to see a familiar face, thinking someone might be glad to see her; but she was touched and gratified by the dramatic response she got from the old usher.

His mouth dropped open, and he grabbed her hand and shook it as if he'd never let it go. Then he threw his arms around her and patted her on the back.

"Avalon! Little Avalon...I can't believe it! My, but you've grown up to be a beauty. I can't believe my eyes! What are you doing here? Are you going to stay a while?"

They were blocking the aisle, and people were flowing around them like a river around two rocks. Finally, the old man took her by the elbow and led her to the front of the sanctuary, where he called over two older women and told them who she was. The dramatic scene was enacted all over again, and Avalon was simply inundated with questions.

Then it was time for the service to start, and the little knot of old friends unraveled itself to go their separate ways – the two ladies to children's church in the fellowship hall, the old usher to the back of the sanctuary, and Avalon to the pew where Mac and Leah sat waiting for her.

The sanctuary was nearly full, and Avalon realized that she'd forgotten how large and beautiful it was. She had grown to love the little classic white country church near Columbia so much during her childhood that she had almost forgotten this one...

But how could she have forgotten those gorgeous stained glass windows along both sides of the sanctuary? The window on her right showed Jesus cradling a little lamb in His arms, with the lamb's mother looking up at Him trustfully.

The window on her left depicted Him with small children gathered all around. Avalon felt tears prick her eyes as she thought what a difference He had made in her own life as a little child, beginning with this very church.

Looking around during one of the opening songs, she realized that a large percentage of the congregation was under forty. She could hardly wait to see the pastor. He must be doing something right.

She didn't have to wait long. Only the chairman and worship leader had been on the platform during the early part of the service, but when it was time for the morning message, the pastor made his way up the steps and took his place behind the pulpit.

Avalon thought she must be seeing things when she realized who it was: the same man who had been caught staring at them so oddly last night!

Was it possible? She found herself staring at him as rudely now as he had stared at them last night. And as she stared, she knew she'd been mistaken about him.

For one thing, he was younger than she'd thought last night in the restaurant's dim lighting. She had assumed he was in his late thirties or maybe even his early forties – he'd looked so mature and thoughtful. But she saw now that he couldn't be over thirty-five, and was perhaps even younger.

And somehow she knew he hadn't been staring rudely. The look she had tried so hard to analyze last night had probably been one of concern. How she knew this, was a mystery even to her; but seeing his facial expressions this morning as he preached made it as clear as if he had told her himself.

It was hard to concentrate on what he was saying – she kept seeing him as he'd looked last night; but she could tell he was an excellent speaker. She looked at the bulletin and saw that the title of the sermon was "Let Go and Let God".

Wasn't that what she was doing? Letting go of her fear of the past – or perhaps it was really fear of the future – and letting God lead her to her mother, if that were His will...

After the service, Avalon was in a quandary: should she make it a point to shake his hand? She'd heard him say he was preaching this morning because the church's Senior Pastor was on vacation in Florida with his family.

The question was decided for her by Mac, who nudged her as they were leaving their pew and showed her the names of the pastors listed on the back of the bulletin.

The Associate's name was Cameron Evans. She was

surprised, to say the least, but Evans wasn't such an uncommon name. It did make her determined to meet him, however; and after Mac and Leah had shaken his hand and walked away a few feet, Avalon found herself face to face with him.

In the stark sunlight of the glass-enclosed narthex, his face looked even younger than it had in the pulpit. She'd been thinking of him as an older man, but here he was probably not even ten years her senior. For some reason, this made her more nervous about meeting him.

She wasn't sure he had recognized Mac and Leah from last night, but there was no doubt that he knew her. His eyes widened with pleasure as he shook her hand warmly and said:

"I'm so glad you came to church this morning! You must have thought I was very rude last night, staring at all of you the way I did. I hope you forgave me. I didn't know who you were last night, but of course I do now, and I'm thrilled to finally be meeting you...you see, my dad is a distant cousin of your Dad's – Eric, I mean. I guess that makes us cousins – sort of, anyway. Of course I know you're adopted...

"And I'm so sorry about your Mother and Dad. I remember him from when I was just a little kid but never saw him after you folks moved away from here. But the people here adored him and your Mother. I know they must have been very special. I'm just so sorry. Do you have any idea yet what you'll do now that they're gone? Or is it too soon to ask?"

"Not at all...I'm trying to find my birth parents right now...mainly my mother, since her parents haven't seen her for twenty-five years and are very anxious to know what happened to her after she left home. My mother – Lora, I mean – thought I should try to find Lindsay Herrington for my grandmother's sake."

Cameron Evans looked a bit puzzled, and Avalon realized she was explaining things badly.

"It's a long story, I'm afraid," she said apologetically.

She could see several people out of the corner of her eye standing nearby, obviously waiting to shake Cameron's hand, so she said:

"Maybe I can explain more later. I don't want to monopolize you."

She smiled as she moved away.

"Don't run off just yet," he said quietly, as he turned to shake someone else's hand.

Avalon joined Mac and Leah outside the front doors of the church, where they were chatting with several people they'd just met. Mac said:

"Ready to go to lunch?"

Avalon hesitated to say anything about Cameron in front of the church folks, but she did say:

"I'll be ready shortly, but right now I need to run back in for just a minute."

She turned toward the doors before Mac could stop her and went back inside, looking for the ladies' lounge as she did so. It was halfway down the lobby, and just before she started into it, she heard Cameron's voice behind her.

"Avalon – wait! I wanted to ask if you and your friends would like to have lunch with me somewhere in town. I'd really like to hear your plans now that your folks are gone and you're sort of – on your own."

He looked so eager and hopeful that she said:

"Oh, I'd like that – why don't you go ask my cousin and his fiancée? They're waiting for me out front."

When she came out of the restroom, she could see through the glass doors that Cameron was already talking to Mac and Leah, and everybody seemed to be enjoying the conversation.

She joined them in time to hear Cameron suggest that they have lunch together at the restaurant where they'd all been last night.

Mac shrugged, and Leah said that was fine with her, so Cameron turned to Avalon.

"Is that all right with you, Avalon?"

He smiled into her eyes warmly.

"Fine! I loved the place. Maybe I'll take a look around today and check out some of the other rooms. I adore places like that! I especially loved the name – Antiques & Ambrosia. That's perfect for a town like St. Francisville."

They were all walking together out to her car in the parking lot when Cameron said:

"Oh, by the way – wasn't there someone else with you last night? I thought there were four of you at the restaurant."

Avalon realized then that she had forgotten about Lawrence completely! How could she have done that? She felt guilty, almost as if she'd done something wrong. She blushed and said:

"Yes, there was – he had a headache this morning

and wasn't able to come with us, but I'm sure he must feel better by now." She turned to Mac. "Shouldn't we run by the motel and see if Lawrence is well enough to come eat with us?"

Cameron Evans seemed to sense Avalon's discomfort, because he said quickly:

"Maybe I should take my car, too. That way you won't have to bring me back here to the church after lunch." He didn't wait for an answer but started toward his own car, looking back to wave and say: "See you there!"

Avalon was relieved without quite understanding why; and when they reached the motel, Lawrence was up and dressed.

But when Mac told him they were going back to the same restaurant where they'd been last night and were having lunch with the young associate pastor, Lawrence said he still wasn't quite up to par, and he'd appreciate their coming back for him when they were ready to leave town.

He had already asked the motel for a late check-out, he said, so another hour or so wouldn't matter. He would eat later.

Avalon and Leah and Mac reached Antiques & Ambrosia first and went inside to wait for Cameron. When he walked through the front door, they were amazed at the friendliness and deference shown him by everyone there.

The host shook his hand like a long-lost friend, calling him "Brother Evans", and several people already seated at tables called and waved to him, one or two reaching out to shake his hand as the group made their way to the table. The young black waiter who came to bring their water called him "Mister Cam" and then almost ran his legs off waiting on them.

Once they were seated at their table, Avalon looked around, not only in admiration of the elegant décor and beautiful antiques which gave the place its delightful atmosphere, but in wonder at the fact that the stranger who'd been such an enigma last night from across the room was sitting right here next to her today. Amazing!

When the waiter had taken their orders, Cameron leaned toward Avalon and said quietly:

"I'm sorry your other friend couldn't make it, Avalon. What did you say his name was?"

"Lawrence….Lawrence Masters. I think you'd have enjoyed meeting him. We've – we've only known each other a couple of months. He met my dad at the Pacific Garden Mission in Chicago and came to church after Mother and Daddy died…to meet me. He said Daddy talked about me so much that he just sort of – fell in love with me."

She felt shy, saying it. She didn't know why she felt compelled to let Cameron Evans know the situation. His dark eyes were riveted on hers as she spoke.

When she said – "He wanted to give me a ring, but I told him I wasn't ready for that…at least, not yet" – then, at that moment, his eyes looked the way they had looked last night, across the room. They were filled with something she didn't understand – couldn't quite put her finger on.

Was it consternation? Compassion? Concern? There

was that word again...*concern*, and she was sure that's what it had been last night. But why?

She felt a strong urge to ask, though she didn't know quite how to word the question; but Mac interrupted their tete-a-tete just then to ask Cameron about the plantations in the area. Then their food came, and the moment for confidences had passed.

"Isn't this where Audubon did some of his famous paintings of birds, Mr. Evans? At one of the plantation houses around here?" Leah asked between bites of crawfish bisque.

"Oh, please call me Cam...we have so many Evanses around this table, it might be confusing."

They all laughed. It seemed odd to Avalon that she'd never heard of Cameron Evans before today – or of his being in St. Francisville. But he'd said the two branches of the Evans family had never been close.

And it had been sixteen years since she and her parents had lived here. That was a long time in the life of someone as young as he was: animated and smiling, he didn't look thirty.

Cam answered Leah by telling them that John James Audubon had come to Oakley House near St. Francisville in 1821 and taught art to the young lady of the house, Eliza Pirrie...

And there were other plantations – Greenwood, Cottage Plantation, The Myrtles, Butler-Greenwood, Catalpa, Rosedown – why not stay and see at least a few of them? What was their hurry, anyway?

Avalon told him about her mission to find the island that was part of her life-long nightmare and, if possible, learn what had happened to her biological mother while her grandmother, who was dying of cancer, was still alive.

She tried to describe her mother's elopement and the reason for it, and her grandmother's need to get her daughter's forgiveness, if Lindsay were still alive.

"But where will you begin? It sounds a little like looking for a needle in a haystack, to me."

They mentioned White Castle and the nearby island that David and Johnna had spotted while on their honeymoon.

"Is that where you're going today, then? Right after lunch?" He seemed abruptly alert, anxious to know for certain where they were headed, and Avalon didn't mind his knowing.

When they finished their meal, Mac paid the check and walked back to the table to leave a generous tip for their waiter. Leah was a few feet away, examining a lighted China cabinet full of antique figurines, when Cameron said to Avalon quietly:

"I want you to take my phone number, Avalon, and please – keep it near you – *on* you, in fact."

He handed her a small piece of paper with a phone number on it. "And I want you to call me if you need help at any point. I mean that with all my heart. Any time, day or night. OK?" He looked intently into her face and waited for her to respond.

Now was the time to ask:

"Why? And why did you look at us the way you did last night? If it's concern I see in your eyes, what are you concerned *about*?"

But now that she had the opportunity, it was hard to say it. Everything she had imagined could be just that – her imagination. It had all been so nebulous – all except his insistence now that she take his phone number and keep it with her. But he was almost family, and a kind, caring man, which would explain it.

In spite of all that, Avalon said quickly and quietly:

"Why do you think I might need this, Mr. Evans? Cameron, I mean."

His voice was quiet, too, but far more intense than hers.

"I don't really know for sure, Avalon. I just – well, it's only a possibility, and I hesitate to say anything definite. I don't really feel free to go into details, in case I'm wrong. And I could be – I hope I am. But I *am* a little concerned, and I'd like the satisfaction of knowing that you have my number in case you need it...

"Please – it may be important. Keep it with you at all times. Will you do that for me? I know it's asking a lot, since you don't really know me, but it'll mean a great deal to my peace of mind if I know you're taking this seriously."

Mac and Leah walked up just then, and Avalon simply nodded. She was grateful for Cam's concern, but she didn't really know any more now than she had before.

And although Avalon was a far-sighted and perceptive young woman, still it was difficult for her to imagine, as she slipped the little folded piece of paper into her purse, under what circumstances she might ever need to use it.

CHAPTER
TWENTY

By the time she and Lawrence, Leah and Mac reached White Castle a couple of hours later, Avalon had almost forgotten about Cameron Evans's warning.

The ferry ride across the Mississippi River at St. Francisville and the drive south through New Roads along False River were so peaceful and beautiful, with the wide expanse of clear water on their left glistening in the summer sunshine, bordered by huge trees and flowering foliage all along the way.

The terrain was literally teeming with life, and it was easy to see why: the horrendous humidity in the air all around them was a relentless reminder, and they gratefully left the top up on the convertible for the air-conditioning.

Long, leisurely drives along winding roads had always been one of Avalon's favorite things to do, and she could feel her sense of glee slipping over into sheer exuberance as they passed one plantation house after another, some of them set far back from the road, their wide lawns dotted with enormous old trees draped with Spanish moss.

There were long avenues of oaks leading to some of the old houses, and several of the largest ones didn't seem to be occupied. Avalon and Leah agreed that the ones in a state of semi-ruin, with their sense of melancholy, were far more romantic and appealing than the others, and they asked Mac to stop at several of them.

Lawrence had recovered from his headache and entertained them most of the way by imitating a Cajun accent, which he did remarkably well. When Avalon asked where he'd learned how to do that, he said he'd had a friend in the army who was from Ville Platte, about an hour west of St. Francisville.

"He was the only Southerner in our barracks, and we gave him kind of a hard time – but we all liked him, and he knew it. I spent Thanksgiving with him and his family one year, and I'll never forget what he did one day – you won't believe it...

"Louisiana's almost like two separate states, you know, with a lot of Cajuns in the south, most of them Catholic...

"Anyway, one day we were riding around, and some guy pulled right out in front of us – almost made us have a wreck. My friend leaned out of his car and yelled at the guy: 'You – you *Baptist*!' Apparently, that was the worst insult he could think of!"

They laughed.

"Speaking of religion," Lawrence went on, "tell me more about this fellow who went to lunch with you today – the one from the church. Did you say he's a cousin of yours, Avalon?"

"Well...sort of. He's not blood kin, of course, since I was adopted. But he said his dad was a distant cousin of my Dad's – that is, my adoptive dad, Eric."

It occurred to Avalon then for the first time that she had given very little thought to her biological father – only to Lindsay. But the man Lindsay had called 'Lancelot' had to be somewhere in this world, unless he was already dead. Perhaps they both were...

"It seems to me you've become rich almost overnight, Avalon, and not just in a monetary sense, but in relationships, too," Mac said. "Before Uncle Eric and Aunt Lora died, they were your only family – except for me and my parents, of course.

"But now you have an aunt – Johnna; and an uncle by marriage – David; a set of grandparents – Andrew and Valerie Herrington – and possibly a mother and father. You might even have siblings, who knows?

"It's kind of bizarre, isn't it? If all of that hadn't started just a few weeks before your folks were killed in that plane crash, you really would have felt alone in the world, don't you think?"

How could she explain that she still felt "alone in the world" without her dearest friends on earth – Lora and Eric – in spite of the new family she had recently acquired so dramatically?

Of course she had adored Johnna since she'd been a little girl in her Sunday school class all those years ago; and she already felt a real fondness for Valerie and even Andrew, and certainly for David. But it would take time for that love to take root in her heart and grow.

And it hadn't been exactly astute of Mac to remind her that she had discovered her birth family just a few weeks before her adoptive parents had been killed.

Or had it been? Put conversely, that meant Eric and Lora Evans had died in a plane crash just a few weeks *after* Avalon had discovered her relationship to the Herringtons.

Her adoptive parents' sudden death had set her adrift emotionally, making it far more desirable on her part to find her birth mother, the project that was so important to Valerie Herrington. Mac certainly had a way of making her look at things differently, and it wasn't always comfortable.

She made some non-committal comment in response to Mac's statement and then turned to Lawrence to say:

"You didn't eat anything before we left St. Francisville. Aren't you hungry?"

"A little. But I'm far more interested in finding this island David and Johnna were talking about. Maybe we should stop at a store or a gas station when we get to White Castle and ask somebody about it."

About that time, they passed Nottoway, the gigantic and beautiful antebellum mansion famous for its phenomenal size and unique combination of Greek revival and Italianate architecture. Everybody in the car gazed in fascination.

Avalon laughed and said:

"Now, *there's* a house to rival Herrington Hall!"

Lawrence and Mac whistled in amazed admiration as they drove slowly past the place.

"How many square feet do you suppose are in that place?" Mac asked.

"53,000," Leah informed him solemnly. "Built in 1859. *That's* the 'white castle' that really gave this town its name – not the one on the island."

Mac, reminded of their purpose, said: "Let's go on into town and find a service station and ask about the island. Maybe somebody will be able to direct us to it, whether it's the island in David's painting or not."

Avalon agreed, and Mac pulled into the first place he saw. He got out and walked into the small store, while the others remained in the car. When he came back out, he was smiling.

"I guess he had some success," Lawrence said. "Hope so, anyway."

Avalon felt nervous for the first time since they'd left St. Francisville. She mentioned it, and Lawrence laughed at her, blaming it on the caffeine in the tea she'd brought with her from Antiques & Ambrosia in a large styrofoam cup.

She smiled, but she knew the tea wasn't the culprit. She felt around surreptitiously in her purse for the little slip of paper that had Cameron Evans' phone number on it.

She hadn't given it much thought until now; but it was there, and she breathed a sigh of relief. For some reason which she had not quite analyzed, she hadn't mentioned it to anyone – not even to Leah and Mac.

When Mac got back into the car, he said:

"Well, the guy in there said he's never heard of any island around here, but there are a lot of old houses – some of them in pretty bad shape, he said...

"He suggested we ask somebody else before we try to find it, since he's only lived here for fifteen years, so he's still a newcomer." Mac chuckled. "We're definitely in a small Southern town now."

"It is small," Lawrence agreed. "I think I noticed on the sign that the population is under two thousand."

"It's bigger than St. Francisville," Avalon informed him.

"Really?" Lawrence sounded surprised. "I guess I didn't pay much attention, since I wasn't feeling so hot. Anyway, the size of this place ought to make our search easier, don't you think?"

Two informants later, they were on their way with specific directions to the only island in the area. The woman who told them about it said she'd heard there was a big, old house on it – built on the ruins of one that fell apart after the Civil War.

She thought it had been completed in the late 1800's, lived in for about fifteen years and then deserted for many years. She'd heard that someone had refurbished it back in the 1940's, but she didn't know anything about the people.

That was all she could tell them, but it was enough. At least it had to be the place Johnna and David had told them about, whether it was the island in David's painting or not.

Apparently David hadn't recognized it. But perhaps that was to be expected, since he'd painted it from someone else's description, and that description was based on an older man's memory of many years ago.

Mac had been given a pencil-drawn map of the area and the way to the island, so he asked Avalon to drive while he studied the directions. They made their way down a series of narrow roads that had been well-used in past centuries.

The exposed roots of enormous, gnarled trees on both sides seemed to reach out to them as they passed, and Avalon thought they seemed alive almost in a human way. She wondered what stories these ancient specimens could tell, if only they could speak!

And then they were at the end of the road, and Imitation Island was there, in front of them. She supposed that's what they should call it, since they'd never heard any other name.

It was less than a quarter of a mile from shore, and they could see it clearly – at least, the part of it that was visible from here. Nothing about it looked familiar to her, and she was more relieved than she had imagined possible.

"I've never seen this place before in my life," she said to the others.

"You sound glad of that," Mac said almost reproachfully. "If that's the case, we're at a dead-end."

"We've just started," Lawrence reminded him. "We only left Chicago a couple of days ago, remember? I think it's almost miraculous we found any kind of an island in that length of time, don't you?"

Avalon agreed.

Leah said, "Yes, but David and Johnna drove along the Mississippi all the way from New Orleans to Natchez and explored all around the little towns along the way, and this was the only island they mentioned seeing anywhere. I'm disappointed." She turned to Avalon. "Are you sure you haven't ever seen this place or been here?"

Avalon looked out across the water again, doing her best to imagine something she simply didn't see.

"I'm sorry," she said, shaking her head.

"Well, this state is literally full of lakes and rivers and bayous and swamps, and there must be scores of little islands like this. It certainly doesn't have to be anywhere near the Mississippi River," Leah said.

Avalon had almost forgotten that Leah and David had lived in Louisiana all of their lives, until Leah's recent move to Chicago. Leah should know.

"Maybe we should at least get out and walk around a bit, now that we're here," Lawrence suggested, opening the door of the car and suiting his actions to his words. He came around and opened Avalon's door for her.

"We might get a better view of the island from outside of the car, too," he said.

They had driven to the end of the road and were surrounded on all sides by old woods, virgin timber by the looks of it. It was broad daylight, but the brilliant sunshine filtered very thinly through the thick tangle of trees and vines overhead.

The part of the island that they could see looked fresh and open by comparison, but there were probably plenty of water moccasins around, Avalon thought to herself, and an alligator or two. She shivered.

"How can you be cold in this heat?" Lawrence asked, putting his arm around her shoulders with a smile.

"Oh, I don't know," she answered. "I just thought about all the snakes and alligators down here. I've been in Chicago so long I almost forgot about them – up there, our wild animals are human." She smiled at her own quip.

Lawrence laughed. "I imagine these woods used to be full of wild animals, but I doubt there are many left now. I don't think you have anything to fear."

Mac and Leah had gotten out when Avalon and Lawrence did, and Mac walked to the very edge of the water and looked all around.

"I don't see any sign of human habitation over there, and if you're sure you've never seen the place before, Avalon..."

She shrugged. "We knew it was a long shot, anyway. It's the very first island we've checked out, so I guess we're not doing too badly. As Lawrence said, we just started two days ago. I guess we just chalk it up to experience and keep looking."

She hesitated and then went on: "I have to admit, I'm not really very disappointed."

"Well, we're wasting a lot of time and energy if you don't really want to find that island, Avalon," Mac said almost severely.

"I do, and I don't," she responded defensively. "I'm just slightly ambivalent about it. Can't you understand that?"

Leah looked alarmed, and Avalon walked back to the car rapidly and got in. She didn't know what she felt. She did want to find her mother, if Lindsay were still alive. She really did.

But the thought of actually seeing the place that had caused her to pass out, and meeting the mother who had

allowed her to be abused and abandoned, almost made
her feel weak in the knees. Wasn't that normal? Mac
should be more understanding.

"Well, I'm not sure where to go from here," Mac
said, walking back to the car with Leah and Lawrence.

Everyone was silent as they drove slowly back
through the woods along the narrow road. They were
about a mile away from the island when Leah said
suddenly:

"Wait! Look there...in the woods...do you see? It's
an old plantation house. Oh, let's stop and see it, can
we?"

She turned to Mac, touching his arm appealingly. It
wasn't the first time on this trip she'd made him stop
along the way to check out some old house. Avalon
appreciated her efforts to take everyone's mind off the
disappointment of the island.

But apparently Mac wasn't in the mood for it. It took
him a minute or two to finally slow down and pull off to
the side of the road.

"I don't see anything, Leah," he said grumpily,
peering into the woods.

"I think I did," Lawrence said, getting out of the car
and opening Leah's door, then coming around to open
Avalon's, helping her out of the car.

Leah was running ahead, but Mac moved at his own
sober pace, a few steps behind Lawrence and Avalon.
Leah had disappeared ahead of them.

Avalon nearly jumped out of her skin when a
peacock stepped into their path and squawked loudly,
his tail spread wide, the brilliant blues and greens irides-

cent in the sunlight. She closed her eyes and put her hand to her heart, laughing with relief.

They went a few more steps, and she looked up to see Leah standing beside an old white plantation house that had obviously fallen into ruin many years before. The roof had caved in, and the columns that had stood around the verandah were crumbling now. They were fluted, with ornate Corinthian capitals, elegant and expensive in their day.

There were wide steps up to the porch and the first floor of the house, but there wasn't much left of the floor. It was really just a ruin...hardly worth stopping to see.

She climbed the steps with Leah and walked around cautiously, looking at what had probably been the drawing room and a library. It was hard to imagine a family living here.

The elements had destroyed so much through the years. The house was like a Southern belle who'd been beautiful once but had become an old hag through the natural processes of time. It was sad to see.

Avalon walked out onto the verandah and looked around. Apparently there had been a verandah all the way around the house at one time. She walked on around to the very back and stopped to look out into the woods behind the house. The brush and trees had taken over the back yard, and flowering shrubs almost covered the verandah itself.

She looked down and saw something lying at her feet. It was a coil of rope, rotted by the elements. How many years would it take to do that?, she wondered idly.

And then she knew.

She looked up at the nearest column, with its jagged top like a broken tooth. Then she looked down at the pile of brown coiled rope again and realized: this was the "snake" that had so terrified a tiny two-and-a-half year old girl, who screamed in horror because she'd been so sure it would uncoil and crawl toward her in the darkness.

It had taken twenty years to rot that rope.

She had found the place in her nightmare, and it was real.

CHAPTER
TWENTY-ONE

"But I'm confused," Mac said when Avalon shouted for him to come and see what she had found. "I thought the *island* was in your nightmare – the island that was in David's painting. Wasn't that what made you faint? We're certainly not on an island here."

Avalon had leaned against the wall behind her for support when she realized what she was seeing, and now she was sitting down with her back against it, her arms across her knees and her head resting on her arms.

"I know that, Mac," she said softly. She felt sick inside.

"Well, what do we do now?" Mac asked more gently, mollified by her visible distress. "Where do we go from here? What do you want to do?"

"I don't know," she said, lifting her head momentarily to look at him.

She put her head back down, trying hard not to remember all of the terror she'd felt when the man had left her at the dark ruins, at the foot of the broken column – that column standing a few feet from where she sat at this moment, broken and crumbling.

But it was the *column* that was broken and crumbling at this moment, not she, Avalon reminded herself.

Hadn't the Lord gotten her out of that fix? And look what He'd done for her since! Why couldn't she just trust Him in this?

She held her hand out for Mac to help her to her feet, and after he pulled her up, she brushed herself off.

"If it were up to me, we would probably stop right now and just head back to Chicago. But we're not doing this for me – at least, not mainly for me. We've got to keep going for Valerie and Johnna...especially Valerie.

"They want so much to know about Lindsay. And we might need to keep looking for Lindsay for her own sake, if she's still alive. Who knows? At this point, I have to believe the Lord led us here, or we would never have found this place in a million years, since Leah just happened to see it. At least now we know my nightmares weren't a product of my imagination."

"But what connection does this place have to the island in the painting? I never even knew you had nightmares – certainly not about a place like this! You never told me."

"I know, Mac...I'm sorry. It wasn't something I wanted to share. Mother didn't even know about them. I had terrible dreams when I was first abandoned, but they gradually became more and more intermittent.

"And then I had another one a few years ago, when Mother and Daddy and I drove down to New Orleans along the River Road, and then again when you and I were on our way to Natchez this past June. I wanted to tell you, but I was so afraid of finding out more than I wanted to know about my own origins...

"Then the night after Manny Byrd pushed me off the

subway platform, I had the nightmare at home in Chicago and saw more details than I'd ever seen before. It was the first and only time that I actually saw the coil of brown rope in my dreams and thought it was a snake that was going to crawl toward me. I must have passed out when it really happened to me as a little girl, because I don't remember anything else...

"But I *always* saw the island and the white house in my nightmare...the dream always started with that. That's why I don't understand why I didn't recognize the island we just saw. It's so close to these ruins, which are clearly the ones where I was taken. But it just doesn't ring a bell at all."

By this time, Leah and Lawrence had missed Mac, and they walked around to the back of the house to see what was happening. Avalon explained the situation, and Lawrence walked over to her and put his arm around her shoulder solicitously.

"Poor girl," he said. "But I wonder why you didn't recognize this place when we first walked up to it, Avalon. With such terrible, vivid images in your memory, it seems it should have set off an alarm immediately. I wonder why it didn't..."

Mac said, "Well, twenty years *is* a long time ago, and I think it's a wonder she remembers anything at all, considering how young she was."

Leah agreed but went on to suggest that perhaps Avalon might have seen the ruined house from a different vantage point, which would explain it.

"If that horrid man deserted you here at the back of the house, then maybe he brought you in from the back.

Is that possible?"

They all looked out across the back yard toward the woods beyond. It was impossible to see any farther than the first line of tall trees where the lawn had ended originally and the forest began. Lawrence suggested that they do a little exploration to see if there might be another way of getting onto the property.

Avalon said she would prefer to wait in the car, and Lawrence thought Leah should stay with her. So the two men headed into the wild growth that surrounded the ruins, while the two women walked slowly back to Avalon's car.

It was nearly half an hour later when they saw Lawrence wearily trudging toward the car, alone. Avalon sat up and stared, her heart beating faster. Where was Mac? As soon as Lawrence was within earshot, she called out to him:

"Where's Mac?"

Lawrence came on to the car before answering her. Then he shook his head and said:

"I left him behind to keep an eye on the island."

"*What?*" Avalon and Leah said it simultaneously.

"There *is* another way to get onto that property, from the back. Mac stayed there to keep an eye on things, and he wants us to drive around by the road to meet him there."

Lawrence looked at Avalon thoughtfully, then said slowly:

"There's something else you should know before we drive around there, Avalon. Not only could we see the island from the spot behind the ruins, but it looks entirely different from there...

"And there's something on it that we couldn't see from where we were looking earlier. It's hard to tell what it is, but I'll bet you anything it's a house like the one in David's painting. It almost has to be, since you've found your ruins so close by."

Leah breathed, "No!"

Avalon was glad she was sitting down.

"The only question left now is how to get onto the island to check it out. We didn't see any means of doing that, at first glance."

Avalon roused herself from her reverie to say in protest:

"You can't just go barging onto somebody's private property – especially on an island! You might have a hard time getting off of it without getting into trouble. Southerners are the friendliest people in the world, but they take a dim view of trespassers unless they know for sure you're tourists. And even then, they don't much like people coming right up to their houses without an invitation, and I can't say that I blame them."

Avalon really believed what she was saying, but she knew there was more to her protest than concern for others' privacy.

"Well, I think we should drive around there right now and pick up Mac, no matter what we decide to do about the island. He'll swelter in this heat and be eaten up by mosquitoes, waiting for us that close to the water. Come on, Avalon, get your keys out, and let's go."

Avalon smiled at Leah, loving her for her concern for Mac. She got behind the wheel of the Maserati and started the engine. She hadn't driven it much until today; Mac had claimed that prerogative more often than she had.

Lawrence got into the front seat, and Leah stayed in the back. It was quite a long way to the spot where Lawrence had left Mac, and Avalon thought it was almost like a maze; she wondered how the two men had ever found it. She had to make several turns and go down more than one little road to reach it.

But finally, they drove out into a clearing and saw Mac sitting on a stump beside the water. Leah jumped out of the car as soon as it stopped and ran to him. He got up and hugged her, then said to the others:

"I've kept a close watch on that island ever since you left, Lawrence, and I haven't seen a single movement that would indicate that anybody lives over there. I haven't even seen any animals, much less human beings."

Avalon turned to Lawrence and said, surprised:

"But I thought you said there was a house over there."

He shook his head, laughing a little.

"No, I said there probably is, since the ruins that you recognize are so close to it. I said we could see something that might be a house…"

He put his hand on Avalon's shoulder and turned her toward the island, pointing.

"See over there, through the trees? I think I see something white…hard to tell what it is, from here. But doesn't it stand to reason that this must be the island in David's painting, since it's so close to these ruins, where you were left?"

She nodded and agreed that this was a reasonable conjecture, but she honestly didn't see whatever it was Lawrence saw in the distance and said so.

Mac and Leah were eager to get back into the car, since Mac's ankles were itching like crazy, he said. Leah was swatting insects, too.

Avalon said to Lawrence:

"How would that man have carried me to the ruins from here? I don't see a path, or a road leading to the house..."

He turned her toward the woods and pointed to a clearing about fifty yards away. She started walking toward it, and he followed, talking.

"Mac and I walked all the way up to the old house from here, through these woods. I suspect that the man rowed you over from the island there, and took you in through the back way. That's why you didn't recognize it at first."

They reached the edge of the lawn of the ruined house, and Avalon gasped.

"You're right, Lawrence! This is exactly what I remember from my nightmare! If we had approached the ruins from this direction, I'd have known the place instantly. It's slightly more decayed now, but it's not that different...

"Now my only questions are: why did he do it, and why was I not left there? And why was I so traumatized by the sight of the island and mansion in David's painting? I don't remember anything about that!"

He put his arm around her shoulders as they started

back to the car.

"I don't know, Avalon. But I want to help you find the answers to those questions, if I can."

He pulled her a little closer.

"I think we should start by finding somebody in White Castle or maybe even Donaldsonville who's likely to know more about these old places than the average resident around here does...

"I suspect this little town is like most places – the people who live here don't pay much attention to the tourist attractions. They're used to them. Not that the island would be one, but somebody who knows the old houses in the area just might be able to tell us something..."

She nodded, and when they got back to the others, she told them what she'd seen, and what Lawrence had suggested. Mac and Leah agreed.

"How about going through Nottoway? If we do a tour there, we're bound to meet somebody who knows about the other old places around here. At least, that's the way it is in Natchez," Leah said as she looked at her watch. "It's too late to do one this afternoon, though. It's past six, and most of these places close at five or a little after. I imagine Nottoway does, too. In fact, they may not be open at all on Sundays."

Mac started the car, and they headed back toward town. When they were almost to the turn-off for the motel on the highway, Leah said:

"On second thought, why don't we go on to Nottoway just in case there might be somebody still there who could tell us something?

"Those tour guides sometimes hang around for a few minutes after they stop taking people through. It wouldn't hurt to check."

Mac followed her directions, and when they turned onto the grounds of the huge house, they saw several cars still there.

"Oh, goody," Leah said, hopping out of the car as soon as it stopped. "I'll go ask. Anybody want to come in with me?"

Lawrence said he would, and they walked together up to the door of the small office and disappeared inside. Avalon and Mac were tired and didn't talk much while the others were gone. Leah and Lawrence were back at the car in less than ten minutes, excited.

"You're not going to believe this," Leah said, beaming. "One of the people here not only knows about the island – she lives on it!"

Avalon was stunned.

"You've got to be kidding," she said incredulously.

Leah grinned and shook her head.

"I'm not. Her name is Monica Linton, and she's about our age. She lives there with her father and a housekeeper, and she wants us to have dinner with them tomorrow night. How's *that* for progress?"

CHAPTER
TWENTY-TWO

Avalon wasn't sure whether the next day was too long or too short. She both desired and dreaded their evening engagement.

When the time came, they approached the island by a route completely different from the one they'd used yesterday, following the directions Monica Linton had given them at Nottoway.

It was still broad daylight at 7:20 in the evening, and Avalon was straining with all of her might to see the island, but she recognized it no more today than she had yesterday. She didn't know whether to be disappointed or delighted.

At the end of the road, Mac turned onto a paved parking pad next to the water's edge and pulled in beside three other vehicles already parked there. One was a new black BMW convertible; the other two were ordinary sedans.

Monica Linton met them promptly at 7:30 – in a motor boat. None of them had quite realized until that moment that there was no bridge or causeway to the island at any point, and it was with a feeling of both anticipation and apprehension that Avalon let Lawrence help her into the boat.

It was the first time she and Mac had seen Monica, and it was abundantly clear, even at first glance, that this young woman had been cut from a very different bolt of cloth than had Avalon.

Petite, but with an excellent figure, her short, dark hair framed a piquant, pixie face that seemed to hold a perpetually provocative expression. She exuded a spirit of sly, elfin mischief.

Avalon, who liked almost everyone she met, wasn't sure how she felt about Monica Linton, but she was certainly willing to give her the benefit of the doubt. And Mac, who usually reserved judgment until he knew someone well, seemed to decide against her instantly.

Only Lawrence and Leah appeared to be completely comfortable with their hostess for the evening, and the three chatted companionably as Monica steered the small craft slowly but expertly toward the island.

"Most days I take the rowboat back and forth for the exercise," she turned to say loudly, over the sound of the motor. "It keeps me in shape for more important sports." She said this with an impish grin, her white teeth flashing.

Avalon noticed that Lawrence blushed and thought it might be because Monica had been giving him little sidelong glances ever since they had left the shore behind. Lawrence was exceptionally good-looking, she reminded herself, and it was only natural that women would want to look at him.

She doubted that Monica had any idea of any kind of special relationship between Lawrence and herself – and in fact, there really was no official commitment. So why shouldn't she feel free to look?

Mac, on the other hand, was certainly not unattractive, but there was no comparison between his and Lawrence's appeal. And perhaps Monica had already sensed Mac's antagonism to her blatant personality.

Besides, it was patently obvious that Mac and Leah were engaged – Leah's diamond ring proclaimed it to all observers, and Avalon thought she might have informed Monica of this already. For whatever reason, Monica ignored Mac altogether – and came close to ignoring Avalon as well, except for the slightly troubling innuendo deliberately made audible to everyone in the boat.

They were about halfway across the expanse of smooth water when Avalon noticed Monica turning the motorboat to the left, to go around the island and approach it at a point invisible from the road. Apparently, whoever had built the original house before the Civil War had wanted it to face away from all signs of civilization.

No wonder she and the others couldn't see the house from where they'd stood yesterday afternoon! But how could Lawrence have seen "something white" on the island, if the house were on the far side?

As they rounded the island, the tall, unmowed grass and kudzu ground cover gradually gave way to a very different scene indeed. Wide lawns and shrubbery were manicured to perfection, as smooth as green satin.

And the house! As it loomed into sight, white and grand, set well back from the water, Avalon thought it shimmered in the setting sun like an imaginary palace rising out of a dream sea.

But she knew it wasn't imaginary, nor was it a dream. For, in spite of dramatic differences, it was the place in her nightmares. The dream always started with a glimpse of this house, as a tiny girl twisted herself around in the arms of a man rowing a little boat away from the island.

This was the place in David Daniels' painting that had hung in Megan Marshall's upstairs hallway – the painting that had caused her to pass out, apparently from memories so painful she could never consciously recall them.

This was the place the old man named Joe had described to David nine years ago – the place Joe had run away from, to avoid retribution for rescuing Avalon and failing to follow through on her murder.

The heavy jungle-like atmosphere that had almost choked her in her dream had disappeared, and the Greek revival mansion that was nearly hidden in David's painting was perfectly visible now, beautifully lighted by soft spotlights efficiently concealed in the shrubbery all around the house.

But it was the place, all right – the place she'd been almost holding her breath to see, and now that she was seeing it, nearly took her breath away.

Should she somehow let the others know? Lawrence had been watching her closely until just a minute ago. Had he seen her eyes widen, or heard her sharp intake of breath? She couldn't be sure. She made a swift decision to say nothing to anyone until they were off the island.

There was a multi-craft dock at the bottom of the sloping lawn in front of the mansion, and as Monica guided the boat toward one of the slips, a huge alligator slithered into the water close to them, making waves.

They all jumped, and Mac exclaimed: "Whoa! That was one big brute!"

"Oh, that's just Bruno," Monica said. "He's ancient and almost a family pet. But there are plenty of others around here who aren't!" She laughed.

When she docked the boat, Lawrence got out to help Avalon step up onto the pier, smiling warmly into her eyes as he did so. She thought he seemed to be trying to tell her something silently – to apologize or sympathize: she wasn't sure which.

Mac assisted Leah, and Monica reached up for Lawrence's hand before he could walk away. He leaned down to help her, and when she sprang onto the pier, she fell heavily against him, laughing lightly at her own clumsiness. Avalon saw Lawrence frown slightly as he helped her to regain her balance.

Monica led them briskly up a long, brick-paved walkway toward the house, chattering cheerfully as they went along, stopping once to flirt with a good-looking young gardener who was evidently enamored of his employer's daughter.

And when they finally reached the verandah, she stopped again, this time to pick up a large, beautiful white Persian cat that was sunning itself on a cushioned rocking chair.

"This is my very special kitty, Lady Godiva," she said in a voice softened by affection. "I call her Lady for short. I think I would just die if anything ever happened to her! She's my baby. She's a real little cuddle cat, and I love her dearly."

Monica caressed the cat close to her face and crooned to it. Avalon was amazed at the sweetness in her voice and face as she did this. She seemed so soft and vulnerable...almost a different creature.

Monica finally opened the front door of the house, and the middle-aged housekeeper met them just inside. The woman, whose name was Glenna Henry, was built like a tree trunk, sandy-haired and ruddy-complexioned.

It was immediately apparent that, although she seemed somewhat shy and silent, she occupied a responsible position in the household. Monica gave her taciturn employee some final instructions for dinner and then took her new acquaintances on a brief tour of the first floor of the mansion. It took them nearly half an hour to tour all of the rooms.

By the time they were settled in the dining room, Avalon was convinced that, while this was definitely the *place* in her nightmares, these were just as definitely not the *people*. Something had happened since this had been a hidden house on a jungle island.

Well, why should she be surprised? After all, it had been twenty years. She began to relax and enjoy the elegance of the gorgeous, high-ceilinged room they were occupying, as well as the unusual food.

"Since you all seemed so interested in the history of this area, I decided to ask our cook to fix a Cajun meal for you tonight. Like it?" Monica asked between her own big bites of soft-shell crab with slivered almonds.

Avalon had almost ruined her appetite by consuming so many appetizers, but it had been impossible to resist the grilled shrimp and scallops wrapped in bacon, and her mouth was full at the moment Monica was asking her question.

Leah responded for all of them by saying:

"It's marvelous! But surely you don't eat this way every day?"

Monica laughed, a delightfully unaffected and spontaneous sound that made Avalon lift her head to look at this paradoxical person. She was actually beginning to like the girl.

"I could if I dared," Monica said. "But I don't. I'd be as big as a barn if I did! But it's tempting sometimes. The only things I don't like are jambalaya and boudin. And our cook loves to make both of them, so Bruno eats well."

"You actually feed the alligators?" Mac said incredulously. "Doesn't that attract more of them? I thought you said there were already a lot of them around the island." Avalon could tell by Mac's tone of voice that he hadn't altered his opinion of their new acquaintance yet.

They discussed the flora and fauna of the region at length, until Lawrence cut into the conversation to say:

"I understood you to say yesterday when we met, that you lived here with your father and a housekeeper. I believe we met your housekeeper – Mrs. Henry, wasn't it? I hope we'll have the chance to make your father's acquaintance before we have to go back tonight."

It was a statement and a question at the same time,

and it could hardly be ignored as such.

Monica said formally, almost coldly:

"I'm afraid not. My father's in Europe right now, on a business trip. He won't be back until later this week – Friday, I think he said."

She changed the subject abruptly, and Avalon realized that Lawrence had been rebuffed. She wondered why.

"Are all of you through school?" Monica asked, patting her lips lightly with a linen napkin before she took another sip of her white wine. Evidently, she always had wine with her meals.

It hadn't seemed to phase her when all of her guests declined the wine, one by one. It occurred to Avalon that Monica might be accustomed to drinking alone...and perhaps eating alone, as well. She almost pitied her.

Again it was Leah who responded to Monica's question:

"I think we are...out of school, I mean. Avalon just graduated from Elmhurst College this past May with a degree in Music Education, and Mac graduated from Northwestern University two years ago and is an architect in downtown Chicago...

"And, let me see, I got my graduate degree in Art from LSU in Baton Rouge nearly two years ago, just before I moved to Chicago – and Lawrence –"

Leah turned to him and said, "I'm not sure I've ever known where you went to college, Lawrence."

She seemed surprised by her own ignorance and waited for him to respond. Avalon saw him blush.

"You've never known, because I didn't go to college. Except for a two-year stint in the army, I've been working ever since I graduated from high school. That was ten years ago. I'm twenty-eight."

There was a regretful silence around the table, as they all realized what Leah had done. There was certainly no shame in not going to college – especially these days – and Avalon knew that Leah would never have deliberately hurt Lawrence.

Avalon reached over and laid her hand on his, something she'd never done before. Lawrence responded by turning to her with a sheepish smile and saying softly, in a voice audible only to her:

"I told you I wasn't good enough for you. See how embarrassing it is?"

"How can you say that? As if I estimated people's worth by their education!" She looked at him almost resentfully, but relented when she saw the sad bitterness on his handsome face.

Leah, painfully aware of her mistake and always quick to alleviate others' discomfort, was eager to get the conversation back on a pleasant track.

"Let's see now...Lawrence is twenty-eight, and I'm twenty-four. Mac is twenty-four, and Avalon is – how old are you, Avalon? I'm not sure I've ever known."

"Twenty-two, as far as I know." Avalon paused for a moment, deciding whether or not to go on. "I – as you know, I was abandoned as a baby, and I've never known exactly how old I really am. The doctors told my adoptive parents they thought I was probably about two-and- a-half when somebody left me on the back pew of a church they were pastoring at the time.

"We always celebrated my birthday on February 14th, so it would fall on Valentine's Day. I guess they chose that date because it's a time when everybody's talking about love. And they certainly did love me....I miss them so much." She stopped, her voice breaking.

"Your parents are dead?" Monica asked in the same softened voice she had used with her cat, Lady Godiva.

Avalon nodded. "They died in a plane crash earlier this summer...just a matter of weeks ago. I still can hardly believe they're really gone for good."

"I know the feeling," Monica said. "My mother died when I was born, but I've always been watching for her, hoping that what I was told wasn't true, and that one day she would just re-appear out of the blue...

"My father wasn't here when I was born – I was two months premature, and when he heard that my mother had died in childbirth, he became ill and wasn't able to travel, so he didn't get to see me for a long time after I was born."

"And when *is* your birthday, Monica?" Lawrence asked quietly.

She looked at him coldly. "August 8th. I turned twenty-three this month."

Then she rose from the table and disappeared momentarily into the room next to the dining room. When she returned, she had a framed photograph in her hand, and she walked past Lawrence to show it to Avalon. Avalon smiled up at her, touched by Monica's desire to share it with her.

She first noticed the feminine, sweeping signature at

the bottom: "To My Beloved Ralph – With All My Love, Victoria". Avalon looked for similarities between the mother in the picture and the daughter standing in front of her. There was the same short, dark, spiky hair, and a sort of wide-eyed pertness which she supposed could have been passed on to Monica.

But Avalon had a hard time focusing on the face in the photograph as soon as she looked at the hands. They were resting across the forearms, as women often pose in formal portraits.

That was when she saw the ring on the woman's finger – a large marquise diamond set in white gold, surrounded by almost equally large emeralds.

It was identical to the ring Lawrence had given her – the ring that was lying at the bottom of her overnight case at this very moment, back at the motel.

CHAPTER
TWENTY-THREE

That night when they got back to their motel, Avalon lay awake in the darkness thinking about that ring long after Leah was asleep. She'd been quiet after dinner all the way back from the island to the motel, and Lawrence had asked her what was wrong. But she hadn't told him, and he hadn't seen the photograph.

What did it mean? He'd told her the ring had been his mother's. Surely the woman in that picture wasn't Lawrence's mother! That would make him Monica's brother, and that was utterly impossible – there wasn't the slightest similarity between them.

Lawrence was blonde and fair with blue eyes, while Monica was dark – black hair, olive skin, deep brown eyes. If one were looking for a resemblance, there was far more between Lawrence and Avalon herself.

She closed her eyes and tried to remember details about the photo Monica had shown her, which she'd held in her hands for such a short time, but which could ultimately have a long-term impact on her life.

Under a sudden impression, she got quietly out of bed and slipped to her knees in front of her suitcase, to dig around and finally pull out Lindsay's photograph. Then she tiptoed into the bathroom and went through her overnight case until she found the little velvet case containing Lawrence's ring.

She sat down on the side of her bed with both of them in her hands and gazed long and deeply into the smiling face in the photograph – the beautiful, fresh face of her mother at eighteen, young and carefree.

And she prayed. The Lord knew how important this was. And only He knew the truth about the past, and how much she and Johnna and Valerie did or didn't need to know. And only He knew what had happened to Lindsay...

She surrendered it all to Him, asking only that He would have His way in her own life and future, and theirs. And then she put the photo and the ring away and lay down again on the bed, where she fell almost immediately into a deep and peaceful sleep.

Five hours later, she was awakened as fully and instantly as if someone had spoken distinctly into her ear, and she sat up, wondering what she'd heard. But there had been no sound – only thought. And it came clearly: "Victoria"...

The woman in the photograph hadn't been smiling, so there were no dimples, and no perfect white teeth gleamed. The hair was all wrong – it was the extreme opposite of long, smooth and blonde. The name was all wrong – and all right at the same time: "Victoria".

Her mother had been hiding from her family throughout her married life, for fear they would find her and her much-loved "Lancelot" and force her to give him up. Naturally she would not have used the name "Lindsay". She'd needed another name – and what more appropriate pseudonym than the beloved English Queen's name, Victoria?

She looked much older in Monica's photograph, but wasn't that natural? Lindsay's own mother, Valerie Herrington, had aged ten years almost overnight when she realized that in spite of their recently raised hopes, they still might never know what had happened to her beloved elder daughter.

Even with her disguise and pseudonym, Lindsay must have lived under great stress. After all, Andrew Herrington was one of the richest and most powerful men in the state of Louisiana and had searched relentlessly for his young daughter and the husband he felt had stolen her from them.

Lindsay was so young and smiling in the photograph Megan Marshall had given to Avalon. In the photograph Monica had shown her last night, Lindsay looked at least ten years older, and very mature. Avalon now considered another possible explanation for this, besides a stressful life...

Monica had been told that her mother died giving her premature birth, twenty-three years ago this month. But twenty-three years ago, Avalon hadn't even been born yet, according to the doctors who'd seen her right after she was abandoned. And there could be no doubt that Lindsay was her mother.

So if the woman in Monica's photo were Lindsay Harrington, then she was not the woman who had died giving Monica birth – and she might still be alive! That picture could have been taken much later, when she was actually as old as she appeared to be.

Avalon went to her suitcase and pulled Lindsay's picture out again. Then she found a sheet of notepaper and a ballpoint pen in the drawer of her bedside table and started sketching short, pixie-style dark hair around her mother's face, which showed through the cheap, thin paper.

It made a dramatic difference in her appearance, and Avalon would almost have wagered her very life that the woman in Monica's photo was Lindsay Herrington. That meant she wasn't Monica's mother, though it was remotely possible...and strangely enough, Avalon realized with a shock that she would rather Monica were her sister than Lawrence her brother, and it had nothing to do with romance.

But why would Monica's father tell her that the woman in the picture was her mother and that she had died giving her birth? Avalon didn't understand this at all. And how on earth did Lawrence come into it?

She still didn't understand how he had come into possession of the diamond-and-emerald ring. There was so much she still didn't understand.

She replaced the photo and ring where they'd been before and crawled under the covers. She had turned on only one little light, and now she turned it off and waited in the dark silence for daylight.

She drifted off to sleep and woke up only when Leah shook her by the shoulder. Leah was bright-eyed and already dressed.

"Hey, sleepyhead, you'd better rise and shine! The guys are taking us to breakfast at Nottoway this morning, and believe me, you don't want to miss that.

Pain perdu – that's French bread battered, buttered, fried and sugared, and smothered in homemade maple syrup; then fresh homegrown watermelon, sweet-potato muffins, good strong Louisiana coffee that'll float an egg, and – "

"Stop, already!" Avalon laughed and held up both of her hands. "You're making me too hungry to wait for clothes! But I'm not going."

She was almost as surprised by this decision as Leah was, but she meant it. "There's something I need to do today that I need to do alone. Tell Mac and Lawrence I'll see them at lunch."

She swung her legs out of bed and rubbed her eyes as she yawned hugely. She must have been awake longer last night than she'd realized.

"Avalon, you've been acting strangely ever since we came back from the island last night," Leah said. "Did you see something you recognized, after all? You never said anything, so Mac and I just assumed you didn't. Did you?"

"Now, Leah...you'll know when I have something to tell you and Mac. I'm fine. I just have something I need to do – that's all. Don't worry about me, please."

Leah sighed and shook her head.

"Well, Mac's not going to be happy when you don't show up with me. He loves you like a little sister and feels responsible for you, Avalon. He'll probably be mad at me for not making you come with me. Can't you wait until after breakfast to do whatever it is you need to do?"

Avalon laughed and stood up to hug Leah.

"Stop worrying! Tell that big lug of a cousin of mine

that if I've survived Chicago for the past twelve years, I'm quite sure I can survive Cajun country for one morning...

"You all just have a wonderful time doing whatever it is you have planned, and I'll catch you later – at lunch, as I said. I'll be back here at the motel by noon, so you can pick me up then."

She glanced at her watch.

"It's already 8:30, so that's less than four hours for Mac to worry."

Leah seemed resigned, and when she finally left, Avalon got dressed quickly. Then she sat down on the side of the bed and dialed a phone number she'd found in the local directory.

Fifteen minutes later, she was in the back seat of a taxicab on her way to the first point from which she and Mac and the others had seen the island. It was quite a few miles from the motel and would be expensive, but she felt sure it would be worth it.

She'd chosen this point for several reasons: the island was closer from there than from either of the other places; no one would see her approaching the island from that point; and she had seen a small rowboat pulled up into some bushes there. She just hoped there were oars, too.

Avalon wasn't sure just what she was looking for on the island, but she knew she had to get there alone. She didn't trust Lawrence completely, and Mac was too protective. She had to know if her mother had ever been there, and where she was now.

How she was going to determine this, she didn't have

the foggiest idea, but she had to try. She knew Monica would be at Nottoway all day, and the man she still thought of as Monica's father was still in Europe. The only people who might be on the island were the young gardener and the housekeeper, and maybe the cook, all of whom she considered irrelevant to her purpose.

The cab-driver was a middle-aged black man, the talkative type, and he told her about the area as he drove.

"You need to be careful if you're rowin' over to Imitation Island," he warned her. "The water around that place is infested with the biggest alligators in this part of the state. Miss Monica makes pets out of 'em, and they get fat and sassy. Like spoiled kids, but a whole lot more dangerous."

"Why do people call it Imitation Island?" Avalon asked, leaning up from the back seat. "Doesn't it have a real name?"

The cabbie chuckled. "Some folks think it oughta' be called 'alligator alley'! But no, ma'am, it's been called Imitation Island ever since I've been in these parts, and that's a good long while now.

"I guess they started callin' it that back in the 1890's. That's when the folks came over from England and built that big white house that's there now...

"They built it on the ruins of a real old mansion that was deserted and pretty much fell down a few years after the War Between the States. So to us locals, it's just a imitation – see?"

"You say the people came from England!" Avalon exclaimed, startled.

"That's right. They didn't stay long, though...only about twenty years. After they left, the house was empty again for many a long year. It musta' took a powerful lot o' fixin' when Mr. Ralph Linton moved in there...

"He hadta' get his materials from Baton Rouge, though, 'cause we never saw 'im in White Castle or even down in Donaldsonville. I guess it was about five years before any of us ever laid eyes on Mr. Ralph or his daughter."

"How long ago was this? When did the Lintons move to the island?"

"Oh, let me see, now...it'd be somethin' like twenty-five years ago, maybe. I don't recall exactly. It was while the war was goin' on over in Europe, though. World War II, I mean...

"I recollect that much 'cause I saw Mr. Ralph at the airport in Baton Rouge, takin' off for England when the Germans were bombin' London – said his fam'ly had lots o' property around there, and he needed to go back and check on it."

Avalon's mind was racing with all of this new knowledge. Twenty-five years ago was exactly when Lindsay had left home to elope. Her husband had been from England, a member of one of its wealthiest families, according to the letter by Andrew Herrington, Sr., in which he explained why he had encouraged Lindsay to elope and not to bother taking any money or jewelry with her.

Was Ralph Linton the man Lindsay had married? If so, he was Avalon's father. And Monica thought he was *hers*.

Avalon was glad when they got to the end of the road where she would get out. She paid the driver and reminded him to pick her up at this same spot in two hours. They synchronized their watches. It was 9:15 a.m.

When the cab was gone, Avalon went immediately to the bushes where she'd seen the rowboat. It was still there. And thank the Lord, there were oars! She'd decided that if there weren't any, she would go into the woods and find a big stick and pole her way across.

She was determined to get to the island today. This was Tuesday, and Monica had said her father would be back from Europe on Friday. Avalon wanted to find out as much as possible before she met Ralph Linton. That meant she had just three days in which to do it.

Despite the August heat, she'd worn a long-sleeved shirt with her jeans and loafers to keep from being carried away by insects. As she climbed into the boat, she refreshed her memory on the efficient use of both oars. She needed to go straight to the island as quickly as possible without any wandering about, considering the hindrances she might encounter on the way.

She hoped Monica had fed Bruno a Nottoway breakfast this morning that would keep him lying somewhere on the other side of the island in a satisfied stupor.

She started rowing slowly and picked up speed as she went, looking behind her frequently. She dodged logs covered with turtles that were lined up in a row like so many black-clad chorus girls. Avalon thought she saw an otter once, and she spotted several deer in the woods she'd left behind. Blue herons stood at the edge of the water, graceful as gray ghosts in the morning mist.

She was wiping perspiration and swatting clouds of insects by the time she started into the homestretch. She was almost ready to row in among the tall reeds surrounding the island when she noticed something rough and brown that looked like logs protruding from the shallow water ahead.

Not wanting to endanger her boat, which was her only means of escape from the island, she looked for a route around them. Then the "logs" began to move, and Avalon realized she had company.

"Oh, Lord, help me," she prayed under her breath, her heart beginning to pound. She tried to remain calm, knowing the alligators could sense and even smell fear, which wouldn't help matters.

She began to gently row forward, as if returning to the shore she'd already left. Perhaps the huge reptiles were protective of the island and wouldn't pursue her if she rowed away from it.

Oh, why hadn't she thought to bring food to throw to them, since they were accustomed to being fed? They were probably expecting her to feed them – and that's why they were coming toward her. She could see that they were huge – some of them ten or eleven feet long, at least.

Avalon had been attacked by a black drunk in a Chicago ghetto and a white drunk in Uptown, and threatened by militant Maoists at the University of Chicago; and twice she'd been nearly murdered by a hired killer in the past few weeks. But she'd never felt as vulnerable than she did at this moment.

And when the 'gators began to churn the water around her with their heavy tails, several swimming close enough to bump her boat with their big, brutish bodies, Avalon forgot that she was trying to get on the island secretly and started shouting, "Help! Help!" as loudly as she could.

But her screams seemed to shrink away into the swamp surrounding the island, and the last thing she saw was one of the alligators with his huge jaws opened wide, as he heaved his big body out of the water and lunged at her.

CHAPTER
TWENTY-FOUR

Frozen with fear, Avalon cringed and closed her eyes tightly, bracing her body for the brutal blow – but it never came. Someone was shouting, but it took her a few seconds to open her eyes and see who it was.

When she finally dared to look, the young gardener was standing on the shore throwing big chunks of food to the alligators around her boat. They swam toward him instantly, moving their tails so fast that the rowboat rocked.

She held onto the sides until the rocking subsided and expelled the breath she'd been holding, her heart racing. When she recovered a little, she rowed slowly on into the reeds around the island, careful to avoid the alligators in their feeding frenzy.

Avalon was so relieved to be rescued from danger that she didn't even try to dissemble about her purpose for being there. The gardener stopped feeding the 'gators long enough to help her out of her boat, and she wasted no time in putting some distance between them and herself, after her rescuer helped her pull the boat farther out of the water.

When the young man had finally gotten the alligators to move away, he turned to Avalon, a question in his eyes. The only time he'd ever seen her was last night when she'd been Monica Linton's guest for dinner. He didn't seem to know quite how to handle the situation, so Avalon took the initiative.

"Oh, thank the Lord you showed up when you did, Mr. – Wilson, isn't it? I honestly don't know what I'd have done if you hadn't."

She reached out to shake his hand, but he held it up in protest, showing her the residue of the raw meat he'd just been handling.

She laughed shakily. "Better that meat than me. I felt like alligator bait there for a minute or two. Would they really have attacked me?"

He wiped his hands on a towel hanging at his belt and moved in her direction. They fell into step together and started walking across the island.

"I think that's what they were doin' when I heard you yellin', wasn't it?"

At first, she couldn't tell whether he was being serious or sarcastic and finally decided on the former. She concluded it would be safe to enlist his help.

"I'm sure you must be wondering what I'm doing here, Mr. Wilson."

"Chad. Call me Chad."

"Oh, OK, Chad…anyway, I wanted to tell you why I rowed over here today. I'm – interested in the history of the island and wanted to take a look at the family cemetery, if there's one here. Do you think that would be all right?"

She held her breath, waiting for him to say, "Well, Miss Monica would have to say it's OK" – but he did no such thing. He just shrugged and said:

"I don't see why not. It's not very big. Not too many people have lived on this island. Just the ones back before the War Between the States – " he hesitated and corrected himself. "I mean the Civil War – you know."

Avalon smiled at him and said:

"I don't mind hearing it called the War Between the States, Chad. That's what it was. I'm just afraid that someday we're *all* going to pay the price for *both* reasons for the War: slavery, and the federal government's desire for power."

She thought he might respond, but he just stared at her dumbly, and Avalon decided to be more discreet about what she said to him in the future.

Finally, he continued:

"Anyway, I was fixin' to say, when the house fell down after the War, nobody tried to re-build it for another twenty years. It was really just a pile of ruins. So when the Lintons came in the early 1890's and built this place, they hadta' build a whole new house from the bottom up.

"They only stayed about twenty years and went back to England for some reason. Then the place was empty for nearly thirty more years before Mr. Ralph came and made it like new again."

"But I thought – " Avalon started to say she was under the impression the Lintons had first come to the island in the 1940's, but she decided against it. She would just listen and learn all she could.

"I only know what Miss Monica has told me, you understand," Chad Wilson said. "I don't come from

around here, and I never knew any of the Lintons 'til I
met Mr. Ralph a few years back, when I needed work."

By this time, they had reached the mansion, and
Chad stopped and pointed to a small fenced enclosure at
a little distance from them, behind and beyond the
house.

"That's the cemetery over there. As I told you, there
aren't a lot of graves in it. But as far as I know, you're
welcome to look. I've gotta' get back to work now, Miss
– uh," he had apparently forgotten her name, and
Avalon didn't remind him of it.

"Thank you, Chad...I guess you might have saved
my life today. I'll always appreciate that, believe me!"

She smiled at him and moved away toward the
cemetery, glancing back at the house once. It looked
peaceful and empty. She wondered where the
housekeeper was at this hour of the morning. Perhaps
shopping in Donaldsonville?

It was hard for Avalon to picture Glenna Henry
rowing or even steering a motorboat to the mainland
parking pad and driving a car into town. But surely she
had to do it once in a while, if she ran a house as grand
as this one almost single-handedly.

Then Avalon looked again. There seemed to be
someone standing at a window on what appeared to be a
third floor of the house, a floor she hadn't seen from the
front. Someone was holding the curtain slightly aside
and looking out on the lawn.

She thought at first glance that it must be Glenna,
since that was the only other person who would be on
the island right now, except perhaps the cook. And Ava-

lon thought she'd heard that their cook was a man.

But a closer look at the distant figure made her catch her breath and ask: *was* it Glenna? This woman seemed to be younger and slimmer, and her hair was definitely lighter in color than the red-haired housekeeper's.

Avalon's heart almost stopped as she considered another possibility: her mother! Last night when she had thought of the alternative explanation for Lindsay's appearing to be so much older in Monica's photo, she'd thought perhaps the picture had been taken later, and her mother might still be alive.

Could Lindsay Herrington still be somewhere in that huge house? Avalon didn't know how she would manage to get inside, but she was determined to do so – today, if it were humanly possible. The very thought of it made her weak in the knees. But first, she would need to follow through on what she'd told Chad Wilson was her purpose for being on the island today.

When Avalon reached the cemetery, she opened the little wrought-iron gate at the entrance and stepped inside. This small plot was so extremely different from the huge Herrington family cemetery that she couldn't help but make the comparison.

There were several paved streets in the Herrington cemetery, and even a formal mausoleum. She would never forget when she'd first seen that cemetery on her visit to the Hall, never dreaming that she was a member of the family and might be buried there someday.

Here, there was only one slightly overgrown path between the tombs in the family plot, all of which were above-ground. She had seen this kind of cemetery in

New Orleans. That one was almost a small city in itself, with some tombs holding entire families.

Here in this cemetery, the dead were laid in individual crypts, and Avalon walked along slowly as she read the names and epitaphs engraved on them.

Most of them dated back to the mid-nineteenth century – the 1830's to the 1860's. There were no Lintons in these graves.

Then there was a gap in time of about forty years, and there were one or two dated during the early 1900's. These were Lintons. There was no grave at all dated past 1910.

She recalled hearing that no one had lived in the house between 1910 or so and the early 1940's, when Ralph Linton had moved to the island and restored the house, so naturally there would be no graves for that period. But what about after that? Apparently no one in the family had died during these past twenty-five years – between 1941 and 1966.

But wait! Monica had said that her mother died in childbirth twenty-three years ago, in 1943. Monica's birthday, she remembered, was August 8th. Even if the woman in Monica's photograph were Lindsay Herrington and not Monica's mother at all, Monica surely had had a mother, so where was she buried?

Or was she still alive? Monica had told Avalon that she was always looking for her mother, hoping she wasn't dead, after all.

The old man named Joe, who had described this island and house to David Daniels, said he could have been a rich man if he'd been willing to go through with a "spot of murder", and that there was still a great deal of money involved in the situation here.

If the Linton family could afford to buy this entire island in the 1890's and re-build the mansion from the ground up after it had fallen into ruin following the Civil War, and if Ralph Linton could afford to come here and refurbish it so luxuriously in the 1940's and remain a man of leisure, which apparently he was, there must indeed be a fortune in the Linton family.

Johnna's grandfather, Andrew Herrington, Sr., had said in his letter that the man Lindsay married was part of one of England's wealthiest families. If that were really the case, who could tell what might have gone on here during the past twenty-five years?

She was just about to turn away and walk back along the pathway to the entrance of the cemetery when she happened to glance over and see Monica's white cat, Lady, perched placidly on top of a nearby tomb.

And while Avalon was looking in that general direction, she spotted a sort of outbuilding situated some distance beyond the cemetery itself. It was built of dark gray stones and appeared to be very old.

What on earth was it? She stared hard but couldn't identify it from this distance, so she decided to investigate. But first, she walked over to pet the beautiful long-haired Persian.

Lady Godiva was not the typical independent cat of Avalon's experience. She meowed loudly and licked Avalon's hand, even placing her paw on Avalon's arm, seemingly in an appeal to be picked up.

So Avalon lifted the big cat into her arms and carried

her along, talking to Lady softly as she made her way toward the old building. On approaching it, she realized it was an ancient mausoleum.

This has to pre-date the cemetery, she thought, searching for a plaque or marker of some kind. Thick, green ivy covered the building in many places, and no marker was visible.

Several steps led downward to an ornamental cast-iron door into the mausoleum, but there was a heavy, old padlock on the door itself. Avalon walked down the steps and tried it, almost dropping Lady when the lock came apart easily in her hands.

Amazed, Avalon pushed on the door, thinking it, too, might be easy to open. But the door was heavy and cumbersome and more resistant to pressure than the dilapidated lock had been, and it took her some time and physical effort to get it to move, even without a lock on it.

She had to put Lady down while she was trying to open the door, but the affectionate feline simply rubbed her fur against Avalon's legs and purred, staying close.

It was dark and slightly dank inside, and she hesitated momentarily on the threshold. Why was she even doing this? If the mausoleum pre-dated the cemetery, whom did she expect to find in here? Certainly not a Linton! And would she even be able to read the names on the vaults?

Avalon vacillated for another moment, and Lady Godiva took that opportunity to dash into the mausoleum, apparently seeing something worth chasing in the partial darkness. The cat howled, and there was a scuffle.

Avalon shuddered and started to back out of the place. But she couldn't just close the heavy door and leave the cat trapped here!

She called to Lady, but the cat refused to come to her. Avalon looked around for something to prop the door open, so Lady could leave whenever she chose. She found a limb on the ground that served the purpose.

Then, since she had good light with the door partially open, and her hands were free, she decided to step inside briefly and look at the names of those interred here.

The dead here had been laid to rest in separate crypts containing their caskets, big containers that would normally have been placed underground in most parts of the country. But here in south Louisiana, and especially on this low-lying island, that was not advisable. She wasn't sure just why these few happened to be placed together in the old mausoleum instead of in separate tombs like those in the cemetery, unless they were older.

On the name plate attached to the first one, she saw a family name and date similar to those in the pre-Civil War section of the cemetery she had just left. Lady came back to her now, wanting to be picked up and held, and Avalon was ready to leave the mausoleum when she both saw and heard something strange.

What she heard was a crackle in the nearby woods, as if someone had stepped on a limb and broken it. And then silence. What she *saw* held her rooted to the spot with an emotion she would never be able to describe.

There, engraved on one of the vaults, surrounded by

the dead of an earlier century, was the name of the one she had hoped against hope she would not find under these circumstances.

She knew her own heart then, as she had never known it before. For here, where she had least expected to find her, lay her mother...the one who had actually given birth to her and named her Avalon.

The metal plate read: Lindsay Anne Herrington Linton, May 11, 1923 – August 8, 1943. There was also a quote: "She died for those she loved – Lancelot and Avalon."

Avalon leaned her head against the cold stone and cried. She had never met this woman and had never wanted to know who she was – hadn't wanted to admit to herself that she even existed! And yet – she wished now with all of her aching heart that she had found her alive somewhere – not here.

She knew now that the woman she'd seen at the top-floor window of the house couldn't have been her mother. Her mother had been right here for the past twenty-three years.

She stood there, lost in grief and regret, until Lady Godiva begged to be picked up, putting her paws up on Avalon and crying pitifully. Avalon had just picked up the cat when she saw a shadow flit across the door to the mausoleum.

She rushed to the door instantly and called out: "Who's there?" When no one answered, she ran up the few steps and looked around. But the shadow had disappeared.

CHAPTER
TWENTY-FIVE

Or had it? She could have sworn she saw a shadowy figure moving in the woods, away from the mausoleum. Whoever it was hadn't wanted Avalon to see him – or her. Who on earth could it be?

Avalon decided to follow. As she moved quickly through the woods, she strained her eyes to keep the elusive shadow in sight, and when it seemed to run, so did she.

The woods were dark and dense, with huge old trees whose exposed roots ran along on top of the ground, and it was hard to keep from stumbling over them. She was soon breathless from running.

She looked back once and realized that she had covered quite a distance already, since she was deep in the woods. The trees towered over her, so thick that even the strong summer sunlight barely showed through the tangled vegetation overhead. And when she finally looked forward again to find the fleeing figure, whatever she had seen was gone.

What she saw in its place, however, was so intriguing that she almost forgot she'd been following anyone. For there, barely visible from where she stood, was what appeared to be the end of the island – and as she came closer, she saw a rope bridge hanging between a huge oak tree on the island and another enormous tree on the other side of the water. The bridge led to a tiny, tumbledown cottage surrounded on three sides by dark, marshy, virtually impenetrable woods.

Whoever or whatever she'd thought she saw in the woods had simply disappeared, and it was so perfectly quiet all around her that she wondered if it could have been her imagination. She stood listening for a few moments, but there was nothing to be heard or seen.

The bridge looked sturdy and safe, and she hesitated only a moment or two before deciding to cross over and examine the cottage. The ropes swayed with her weight, and she held on to the sides tightly, moving slowly, carefully toward the other side.

About half-way across, she began to wish she'd thought about it a little longer. There below, less than three feet under her own feet, were her "friends" from the other side of the island – at least, they were alligators, whether they were the same ones or not.

Lady Godiva saw them and squirmed in Avalon's arms, meowing fearfully. Avalon held onto Lady more firmly and wished fervently that she had left the cat behind.

The thirty feet of water that separated the mainland from the island was chock-full of the reptiles, and she wondered why, since there was no one living nearby to feed and spoil them. The cottage itself was obviously deserted. The dark green shutters hung crazily on rusted hinges; the pointed roof looked as if it might cave in at any moment.

Avalon breathed a sigh of relief when she reached the other side and stepped off the swaying bridge onto solid ground. The cottage was just a few yards from the edge of the water, so she immediately tried the front door, which opened easily. She felt safer once she and Lady were inside, out of sight of the aggressive reptiles that surrounded the place.

The feeling of safety didn't last long. When she'd satisfied her feminine curiosity about the interior of the tiny cottage, which was essentially empty except for a rusty, sagging bed and a table and chair in the tiny kitchen, she glanced out the front window, and her eyes bulged with shock.

The rope bridge was gone! How could that be? She looked around desperately and saw that it had been untied from the tree on the island and was now dragging in the water, where several alligators were nosing it curiously.

Her heart nearly pounding out of her chest, Avalon tried to think rationally. Who on earth could have done that? Surely not Chad Wilson! He'd saved her life when he could easily have stood by and watched her being drowned – or worse – by half a dozen hungry, angry alligators. She didn't know much about him, but he'd seemed friendly enough, and she couldn't imagine any reason why he might wish to do her harm.

Glenna Henry? Somehow Avalon couldn't picture that tree-trunk of a figure being agile enough to run like a wraith through the woods, or fast enough to dismantle a heavy rope bridge that quickly. And why would she do it, anyway?

Whoever had detached that bridge had clearly meant to trap Avalon here – but *why?*

She looked at her watch and realized she was supposed to meet the cab driver at their appointed rendezvous a half hour from now.

What would he do when she didn't show up? Just leave and say nothing? He had no reason or obligation to do otherwise.

But if he did that, how would anyone ever know where she was? She hadn't given Leah the slightest hint about her plans.

How long could she last here with no food and no drinking water? She had checked the kitchen cabinets and pantry out of curiosity, and they were as good as empty. A couple of cans of broth sat in a dusty corner on one shelf, but there was no can-opener in sight.

And she certainly wasn't going to try swimming to the island through thirty feet of alligator-infested water! Not only that, the cottage was surrounded by dense, swampy woods that were totally unfamiliar to her.

Avalon knew from her years of living in Louisiana that it would be even more dangerous to wander around out there and risk falling into a bog than it was to sit tight and hope someone would show up sooner or later. The only problem was: how much later would it be?

She dreaded the thought of nightfall almost as much as she dreaded the thought of hunger and thirst. She had often noticed how intensely dark the woods in Louisiana were at night, and there was no electricity in the cottage, nor had she seen any candles.

She shrank from the thought of trying to sleep on the

rusty bed with its stained, sagging mattress.

And how would she feed poor Lady Godiva? The beautiful white cat clung to her affectionately, and Avalon knew that putting her out into the woods to find her own food would be a death sentence for the pampered pet.

Not only were there wild animals in the woods capable of killing the cat, but now there were alligators sunning themselves all over the ground outside the cottage. If only she hadn't picked up Lady in the first place!

Avalon opened the back door of the cottage to look around, hoping against hope that she might spot a boat of some kind that she could use to get back to the island. But would she really risk running a gamut of alligators again? And how would she row, holding onto a nervous cat? She was almost glad there was no boat, so that she wouldn't have to make that life-and-death decision.

She could scream and yell, but who would hear her? She was a long way from the mansion now. She had never heard anyone even mention this place. It was utterly uninhabitable, with its roof about to cave in and great gaping holes in the walls.

Did Monica or Ralph Linton even know about the cottage? It appeared to be the kind of property that gets left behind and forgotten for years. Perhaps forever.

Finally she sank down onto the filthy floor of the front room and leaned her head back against a section of the wall that didn't have any holes in it. Lady Godiva jumped into her lap and went to sleep there almost immediately.

Even under their desperate circumstances, Avalon cherished the feeling of the cat's warm, furry body against hers. Lady was purring like a motorboat.

Motorboat. Her rowboat! Surely someone would see it and wonder about her. Chad Wilson knew she was on the island! Surely if he saw her boat still there long after she should have finished looking at the cemetery, he would come looking for her.

But Chad Wilson didn't come to check on her. No one came at all, and as the day wore on, with all of the typical heat and humidity of an August day in south Louisiana, Avalon was thirstier than she'd ever been in her life.

She'd been so eager to investigate the island that she hadn't eaten or drunk a drop of anything this morning before starting, and rowing to the island in the hot sun and then running through the woods had taken their toll.

By nightfall, she was even tempted to try avoiding the alligators that lay around the cottage, in order to dip her hand into the water that surrounded the place. It was only a few yards from the front door. But the water itself was brown and covered with algae, and she just couldn't bring herself to do it.

And once it was finally dark, she didn't dare walk outside the cottage. At least the walls, dirty and disgusting as they were with their horrible holes, provided shelter from the alligators and snakes.

If only there were moonlight! But darkness descended on her like a sooty blanket, heavy and black, smothering Avalon's last hope of getting out of the place tonight.

She could hear scuttling and scurrying noises from inside the walls of the cottage, and she shivered at the thought of what might be living there. She just hoped and prayed that nothing would crawl on her during the night. She thought she could stand anything but that!

She could almost hear Johnna's sweet voice that day at Herrington Hall, after Avalon told her how she wanted to turn her own nightmare into Johnna's dream, using her knowledge of the island in David's painting as an inducement to get the Herringtons to let Johnna marry him.

Johnna had said: "Your nightmare into my dream... I hope it doesn't turn into a *real* nightmare for you, Avalon...I'd feel so guilty."

Avalon remembered replying:

"No, don't even think that, Johnna. The Lord knows everything that's happening to both of us right now. It's going to be all right, whatever happens...I'm sure of it."

Now she wondered: had she really meant "*whatever* happens"?

It was a long night, and Avalon sat against the wall with her eyes closed, fighting her hunger and thirst in the darkness. She kept saying to herself, "The Lord is my light and my salvation, whom shall I fear?" She knew the Lord was with her; but for the first time since finding the island, she began to sense the presence of an elusive human enemy.

Amazingly, Avalon drifted off to sleep in spite of her intense discomfort. Even more amazing were her dreams. Familiar voices wove in and out of them, saying things that made no sense.

She heard Lawrence say:

"If you don't...I'll be back...cops...the hour. My fiancée...on this island....I don't intend....without her."

Avalon smiled in her half-sleep, thinking Lawrence was indulging in wishful thinking, saying she was his fiancée!

Then she heard other murmurs. Mac's voice –

"She has to be...saw her rowboat still....left it...this island somewhere."

And was that Leah?

"...all over the house...cemetery, and the guys have...island itself...not a sign...has to be somewhere!"

Finally, she could hear Monica shouting shrilly:

"Lady! Lady Godiva! Come here, little kitty girl! Here, kitty, kitty, kitty! Here, kitty, kitty!"

Monica's calls to the cat in Avalon's lap were perfectly audible, and she finally woke up completely and realized that the voices she'd been hearing were not part of her dreams, but just across the water from the cottage!

She sat up and shook her head to wake herself up completely. Just before she could start shouting to let them know she was there, she heard Monica say in a voice like frosted steel:

"If my cat is over there and one of those alligators gets to her before we get this stupid bridge fixed, somebody else is gonna' be dead around here, and it won't be me! It took you long enough to find this place for us. Now, *move!*"

Someone else responded:

"I just don't see how anybody could be over there, Miss Monica, with no bridge to go across on – there's no other way in or out of the place! Nobody would swim across with all those alligators in the water."

Avalon finally recognized Glenna Henry's voice sounding shaky and nervous and far more frail than Glenna herself had appeared to be. Then there was silence.

Lady Godiva had heard her mistress's calls and perked up. It took Avalon a minute or two to stand up, she was still so stiff from her long night on the hard floor. At first she staggered and almost fell, but then she made her way slowly to the front door to let them know she was inside.

Almost before she could get the door open, Mac and Lawrence were across the restored bridge, and they rushed toward her. Blinded by the bright sunlight that had come while she slept, she couldn't see anyone but Mac.

Then Lawrence and Leah claimed their hugs, and Monica rushed to take Lady out of her arms. Avalon relinquished the cat somewhat reluctantly, since Lady had been her comfort and companion for – how long had it been? She looked at her watch and was surprised to see that it was not only morning, but nearly noon!

They made their way back across the bridge carefully, one at a time, and when they got to the other side, Lawrence glared at Glenna Henry.

"How on earth could this happen?" he said sharply to the older woman.

Glenna was standing a little apart from the others and had said nothing at all to Avalon yet. Now Glenna came closer to her and asked:

"How did you get over there, Miss? Wasn't the bridge detached?" She appeared to be genuinely puzzled.

Avalon said:

"No, it was up when I first saw it. I – I was looking in the old mausoleum behind the house, and I thought somebody came to the door, but when I went outside, they'd disappeared. Then I thought I saw someone moving through the woods, and I followed him – or her, I don't know which. Honestly, I'm not even sure it was a person…

"Then I crossed the bridge to see the cottage, and when I looked out the window just a minute or two later, the bridge had been taken down, and it was trailing in the water."

Glenna stood there shaking her head in bewilderment, and Monica stared back across the water at the abandoned cottage with avid curiosity. It was obvious she'd never laid eyes on the place before.

Avalon turned away from the others toward Mac and said very softly:

"I found my mother in the old mausoleum yesterday…she's been dead for twenty-three years. She must have died when I was born. You can't imagine how much I dread telling Johnna and Andrew…but especially Valerie. She's going to be devastated."

Avalon's face was sad as Mac placed his husky arm around her slim shoulders, and they moved away from the others a little distance, talking quietly. Avalon didn't see the intense scowl on Monica's face, nor the worried look on Glenna's.

Lawrence and Leah were discussing the rope bridge and how it could have been taken down. Could someone have done it without realizing Avalon and Lady were across the water at the cottage? Leah said she thought it was the only explanation.

Lawrence was more deeply disturbed by the incident than anyone, even Mac. No one could doubt that he was sincerely shaken by the whole situation and more horrified than any of them by the bare possibility that Avalon might have been stranded indefinitely in that deserted spot.

By the time the four of them had returned to their motel in town, she had nearly forgotten her suspicion of him. But her melancholy thoughts about her mother reminded her of Monica's photograph of Lindsay.

And thinking about the photograph reminded her of the ring she'd seen on Lindsay's finger. She still needed to know about that ring, and she was determined to ask Lawrence about it just as soon as possible.

CHAPTER
TWENTY-SIX

"You haven't asked me yet why we came looking for you on the island today...don't you want to know why you didn't end up thirsting to death over there in that God-forsaken spot?

"Your cab driver came to pick you up at your designated meeting place at 11:15 yesterday morning, and when you didn't show up, he waited for about half an hour, and then he came back to the motel to tell us you were missing. If he hadn't been kind enough to do that, we wouldn't have had the slightest idea where you'd gone!

"He said you seemed like 'such a sweet, helpless young lady' he didn't like to think about anything happening to you. *I* could have told him a few stories!

"Why do you *do* things like this, Avalon? The very idea of not letting any of us know where you were going! You could have ended up rotting in that place!

"What if somebody had removed your rowboat so everybody would assume you'd already left the island and were out of the area? Huh? We didn't know that cottage even existed!

"If Monica hadn't been so frantic about her precious cat and hadn't been convinced that Lady was with you, we'd never in a hundred years have found it...

"Glenna Henry didn't seem to want to show it to us at all. I thought Monica was going to kill her before we finally got there!"

This was one of Mac's typical tirades in response to Avalon's occasional escapades; but this time, she felt it was completely justified. He was right: they almost certainly would have found her eventually, but it might easily have been too late. She felt humbled and deeply grateful that it hadn't been.

"I know, Mac. You're absolutely right. I'll be more careful in the future...I promise. But no place is really 'God-forsaken', you know." She tried softening him with a smile, but he was implacable.

They were having a late lunch in the restaurant on the grounds of Nottoway. Monica had gone back to work after taking several hours off to help them search the island for Avalon.

Mac and Leah and Lawrence had concluded reluctantly that if Lady Godiva hadn't been with Avalon, she might have been stranded in the abandoned cottage for a very long time. Taking the cat with her had probably saved her life.

When the cab driver had told them about dropping her off across from the island, Lawrence insisted that Monica come with them, since she knew the island so well. But she hadn't done much to help them yesterday.

It was only today, when Monica finally realized Lady was really missing and must be with Avalon, that she'd been willing to search every inch of the island. She'd been strangely silent after all the commotion, submerged in a morose mood.

Nothing more had been said about how Avalon came to be stranded at the old cottage in the first place. There seemed to be a tacit agreement that someone – Chad Wilson, apparently, since there was no one else on the island who could have done it – had taken the bridge down in ignorance of the fact that he was marooning Avalon and Lady over there.

It was very hard for Avalon to accept that idea, since Chad had called off the alligators earlier that day and knew she was looking through the cemetery. But she supposed it was possible.

Obviously, she hadn't said anything to him about exploring the mausoleum, or about going deep into the woods and crossing the bridge to check out the cottage, since she hadn't known of its existence. So perhaps it wouldn't occur to Chad that she might be there.

Despite the stuffed crabs, oysters, crawfish bisque, shrimp, seafood gumbo, garlic bread and the ever-present sweet Southern tea set out on the table in front of them, nobody felt much like eating, except Avalon.

She found she was both dehydrated and famished after her experience, and she had to exercise extreme self-discipline in drinking and eating slowly and lightly while the others picked absent-mindedly at the food on their plates.

"Leah and I want to run up to Monroe and see David and Johnna this afternoon, Avalon. But I'm not going anywhere until you promise me you won't step foot on that island while we're gone. Will you promise me that?"

Mac was in his fatherly role, and Avalon thought all he needed was a pair of glasses to peer over as he lectured her. He'd been trying to boss and protect her since she was ten and he was twelve, and although she usually ignored him, she loved him for it.

"I promise I'll be very careful while you're gone, Mac. That's the best I can do under the circumstances. I definitely want to meet Ralph Linton, since there's not much doubt now, that he's my father...

"But he won't be back until Friday, according to Monica. That's day after tomorrow, and I can't think of a reason in the world why I would need to go back to the island before then. And surely you'll be back by then, won't you?"

"We should be back by Friday morning at the latest, so wait for us!" Mac instructed her forcefully.

"I'll do my best to stay out of trouble, I can promise you that easily enough, after what I've just been through! So please just go on to Monroe and don't worry about me – and be sure to give Johnna and David my love."

After they dropped Mac and Leah at a car rental in a suburb of Baton Rouge, Lawrence suggested that he and Avalon take a leisurely drive back to see the Chapel of the Madonna a few miles north of Nottoway.

"It's supposed to be the smallest church in the world, so it might be interesting. What do you think?"

"I'd love to see it," Avalon answered promptly. She'd been afraid Lawrence would insist on her resting all afternoon to recuperate from her trauma.

But Lawrence wasn't Mac, and she was glad. Maybe

the Chapel of the Madonna would be an appropriate place for them to discuss Lawrence's mother's ring. Looking over the chapel would give her time to decide how to broach the subject.

They put the top down on her convertible, and Avalon drove about thirty miles an hour. It was a lovely day, and it felt good not to be in a hurry. The world seemed all new to her after her near-disaster.

She wanted to soak up everything around her – the dazzling sunlight and turquoise sky, the drifting clouds and the luxuriant green woods on one side of the road, the mighty Mississippi on the other. She wanted to savor it all in slow motion.

When they arrived at the Chapel, Avalon pulled off the road and parked in front of the microscopic building, shaking her head in amazement at its size.

They got out of the car, and Lawrence opened the gate of the fence that surrounded the tiny chapel. There was a wooden box mounted on the wall to the right of the door, and he reached inside to see if there were a key.

There was, and when he had unlocked the door, they stepped inside, one at a time. The chapel was about the size of Leah's kitchenette back in Chicago.

Avalon chuckled and said:

"I feel like Gulliver in his travels to Lilliput! This is incredible, isn't it? I'm surprised they can get this many chairs in here."

There were several candles on the altar and three straight wooden chairs on each side of it. Avalon sat down in one of them with a sigh.

"Tired?" Lawrence said solicitously, sitting down in the chair next to her.

"No, not tired...just – oh, I don't know, Lawrence. Just troubled, I guess."

"Troubled? About what? Not that you shouldn't be, after what happened to you yesterday. Terrible!"

Avalon shook her head.

"No, that's not what's bothering me right now. It's something that happened when we had dinner with Monica on the island."

"Dinner?" he said, sounding surprised. "Oh, you mean Monica? The way she threw herself at me?" He shook his head as if in disgust at the memory. "I certainly hope you didn't let that bother you, Avalon. You know I never look at anyone but you."

He took her hand and smiled into her eyes affectionately.

She pulled her hand away.

"No, Lawrence, it wasn't Monica. It was something Monica showed me after dinner. That photo of her mother. Did you see it? I don't think she showed it to you – did she?"

She looked at him to see his reaction before he answered. His handsome face was blank.

"No, why? Should I have looked at it?"

"I sort of wish you had."

"Why?" He sounded sincerely curious.

"Because there was something in it that maybe you should have seen."

"Avalon, what are you talking about?" He was looking at her with a puzzled frown. She found herself thinking that either he was honestly ignorant of the matter, or he was an excellent actor.

"The woman in that picture was wearing a ring – a ring that looked exactly like the one you wanted to give me as an engagement ring. It had a large diamond in the middle and a dozen emeralds – at least, it looked like a dozen to me – surrounding the diamond."

At first, Lawrence's face registered surprise, and then a certain wariness, or so it seemed to Avalon, who was watching him closely.

"Is that all? Avalon, there must be a hundred rings like that in the world! My mother's ring certainly wasn't custom-made."

"But all of the stones are much larger than usual – and usually the diamonds in a ring are the smaller stones in the ring and surround the larger central jewel, like an emerald or sapphire or ruby...it's usually the other way around – not like that ring. I know I'm not describing it very well, but I could have sworn it was the same ring you gave me."

"But how could it be? The ring I gave you was my mother's ring. I don't even know Monica's mother! I don't really understand what it is that's bothering you so much."

"I guess it's because I think the woman in Monica's photo may not be her mother at all, but mine. The woman in that picture, wearing that ring, may be Lindsay Herrington. My mother. So how could you have gotten her ring, unless she's your mother, too?"

The words sounded foolish when spoken aloud.

"Lindsay Herrington my mother! *Your* mother *my*

mother? Oh, Avalon!"

At first, Lawrence seemed stunned, then relieved, and he laughed uproariously, apparently amused by the ridiculous nature of Avalon's concern.

He kept laughing, shaking his head, as he reached into his back pants pocket.

"I'm sorry, Avalon. I know I shouldn't laugh, if this has had you worried for even a minute. But the whole idea is so ludicrous I just can't help it – I'm sorry."

He had retrieved his wallet with one hand and put his other hand over hers with an apology in his eyes and voice as he said: "Forgive me for laughing?"

He was still grinning, but Avalon was so reassured by his reaction that she relented.

"Of course I forgive you if it's really that funny. But you have to admit the ring is a strange coincidence. What were you going to show me just now?"

Lawrence opened his leather wallet and found a wallet-size photo, which he pulled out and handed to Avalon almost reverently. Avalon looked at his face and was amazed at the softness and tenderness she saw, even though she had seen those expressions there for herself more than once.

His voice was gentle as he said:

"*This* is *my* mother, Avalon."

She looked, and there could be no doubt at all that the woman in the picture was, indeed, Lawrence's mother. She looked about twenty years older than he, but enough like him in facial features to be his twin sister.

Lawrence looked as much like his mother as Avalon

looked like hers. The only difference was their coloring: Lawrence's hair was blonde, while his mother's was dark brown.

There was not a vestige of doubt in her mind that this woman was Lawrence's biological mother, and she certainly wasn't Lindsay Herrington. Avalon looked up from the picture into Lawrence's smiling face and wondered why she didn't feel more relieved.

"You seem to be amused by all of this," she said, somewhat aggrieved.

He stopped smiling and carefully replaced his mother's photo in his wallet, then put the wallet back into his hip pocket.

"I'm sorry, Avalon. It's just that I have – or had – a perfectly good mother, a beautiful, wonderful mother – and I certainly don't need to share one with you or anyone else in the world...

"I guess I'm just amazed and appalled that you could think such a thing! Did you honestly think I would want to marry you if you were my sister? That would really make me angry, if it weren't so comical."

"Lawrence, I realize now that I was wrong. I believe that woman is your mother, and she's beautiful. I wish I could have met her before she died. But you must admit that you and I do look a lot alike – enough for those people back at the motel in Memphis to think we were brother and sister."

"Oh, that!" Lawrence scoffed. "Nosy old busy-bodies."

"And do you remember what you told me at J.J. Biggs in Chicago that night when you wanted to give me the ring? You said your mother had been born to money and was disinherited by her family when she married your father. Well, that's exactly what happened to my mother – Lindsay Herrington. So is it any wonder I thought what I did?...

"Besides, you've never shared anything with me about your background – where you were born and grew up, or where your mother died. I've known you for months now, and I hardly know anything about you!"

"Well, I was born in Detroit and lived there most of my childhood. When my parents finally divorced, I stayed with my mother, and we moved to Chicago. I spent some summers with my Dad in New York, and I was with him when he died, but only for a few days. And then my mother passed away last year, and I was truly alone in the world. Until I met you..."

He looked at her so lovingly that Avalon felt almost ashamed of her suspicions.

"I'm sorry, Lawrence. I know your life has been so different from mine."

"Yes, it has. Maybe that's the reason – or at least one of the reasons – I want so much for my life to change. I want to share it with you. I want you to be a part of it. You're so beautiful that life with you would inevitably be beautiful, too."

Avalon simply smiled in response and said nothing. They sat in silence for another minute or two, with Lawrence's arm around her shoulders. And then they rose and got back into the Maserati and drove back to the motel.

They parted outside her room, and when she stepped

inside, Avalon locked the door and sat down on the side of her bed.

She couldn't deny that her fears had been greatly assuaged by what she'd learned inside the miniscule Chapel of the Madonna. The picture of Lawrence's mother had dispelled the last shadow of a doubt about his being Lindsay's son.

And the more she thought about it, the more she had to agree with the others that it was at least *possible* that she and Lady had been stranded at the cottage across from the island by accident. It was certainly a more palatable theory than a few others she had considered.

Just before she finally lay down to rest, Avalon unzipped a side-pocket in her purse and pulled out a small slip of paper. She'd hardly given it a thought since Sunday, but now she laid it next to the telephone on her bedside table and stared at it. Cameron Evans's name and phone number stared back at her, an assurance of active concern, a promise of protection and strength.

She had no plan for the conversation and no idea of what reason she would give for calling, other than to tell him what had happened to her on the island. But as she slipped into sleep, her last conscious thought was that the name and phone number written on that little slip of paper were really amazingly comforting, almost like a message from home...

She would call him as soon as she woke up.

CHAPTER
TWENTY-SEVEN

Avalon made the call as soon as she got up a couple of hours later, but she didn't get to talk to Cameron. There was no answer at his home, so she called the church where he was an associate pastor, but he wasn't in his office, either.

She left a message with the church secretary, asking her to tell Cameron she'd called and was all right, but that she did want to talk to him about something strange that had happened to her recently. She left the name and number of her motel with the secretary and hung up, disappointed.

Then she called Lawrence in his room to tell him that she was still tired and didn't really want to go out to eat tonight. But if he'd like to take the car and pick up something for both of them, she could certainly eat some supper.

He said he'd be glad to do that, and they ate cheeseburgers all the way with fries and Cokes in the motel's small hospitality area.

"I was getting a little tired of Cajun food and thought you might be, too," he said with a smile as he handed her the take-out from a nearby drive-in.

"I was. I've had enough of it in the past few days to

sink a barge. This looks good. Good old all-American food! Thanks, Lawrence."

When they'd eaten the burgers and were finishing up the fries and Cokes, Lawrence said quietly:

"You know, you need to be thinking about what you're going to say to Ralph Linton when you meet him on Friday. Apparently he's your father and not Monica's – unless she's your sister, and I'll never believe that...

"So why does she live there, thinking he's her father, and being told all of her life that the woman in that picture – Lindsay Herrington – is her mother, who died when she was born? There's something very strange going on here, wouldn't you say?"

"Of course there is, Lawrence – that's obvious. But I'm not going to just barge in there on Friday and confront Ralph Linton or Monica with what I've found out. That might even be dangerous until we know a little more, don't you think?"

Surprisingly, he shook his head.

"I think that the minute Ralph Linton sees you, he's going to know you're his daughter, because you look exactly like your mother. And you brought that photograph of her with you, didn't you? The two of you look like identical twins. How could he deny it?"

"He probably wouldn't, but what happens then? Monica believes she's Ralph Linton's daughter and that the woman in the picture who called herself Victoria is her mother. That means that either someone has lied to her, which means there's an adult with a reason for doing so; or she herself is in on the deception...

"I've never met Ralph Linton and have no idea what he's like. But I *have* met Monica, and I wouldn't turn my back on her any more than I would a hostile Doberman! To be honest, I kind of feel sorry for the girl, but I don't trust her an inch.

"Besides, the old man who told David about the island said there was still a huge fortune involved in the situation here. He'd been asked to do away with someone – me, apparently! – but he didn't follow through with it, and he was afraid for his own life – that was the only reason he wouldn't tell David where the island was...

"So don't you think it might be wise to try to find out a little more before we just march in and blow the lid off what could be a keg of dynamite? I'm still just a little jittery after my recent experience – I'm not exactly eager to have another one like it anytime soon, thank you." Avalon shivered.

Lawrence put his hand over hers and smiled at her tenderly.

"I'm sorry. I shouldn't even be talking about it tonight. I'd forgotten about the money part of it. You're probably right. I won't mention it again. I certainly don't want to give you nightmares! You've had enough of those to last a lifetime, haven't you?"

They talked a while longer, and then Lawrence walked her to the door of her room and kissed her "good-night" gently. She tried to call Cameron Evans – again without success – and finally went to bed for the night.

She did have her nightmare again several hours later,

but this time, it didn't begin with a view of the island and the mansion from a rowboat, as it always had before. It started at the old ruins where she'd been deserted on a dark night, left all alone next to the jagged, broken column.

At first, she was terrified, hearing movements and cries of animals in the surrounding woods and watching the brown coil of rope she still thought was a snake. But then, a handsome, dark-haired man strode up the steps, reached down and picked her up, comforting her kindly.

He looked a little rough, but he was gentle. And again at the end of the dream, she heard Lindsay's voice say, "I love you, little Avalon. Never forget that."

She had forgotten that part of her nightmare and was almost glad she'd had it. She lay drowsing, a sense of melancholy stealing over her now that she knew for sure she would never hear that voice in real life. She almost hoped she'd keep having the nightmare so she could hear her mother's voice again.

The next morning she and Lawrence had breakfast at Nottoway; and while they were eating, Monica came into the restaurant and walked over to their table with a sunny smile on her face.

She seemed almost a different person from the quiet, moody one they'd last seen yesterday after Avalon's rescue from the abandoned cottage.

"I have good news for you," she said cheerily. "My father made it back from Europe a day earlier than he expected! I remember you said the other night at dinner that you wanted to meet him, Lawrence...

"So it looks like you'll get to, if you can come to the

island tonight for dinner. I suggested inviting you tonight, because I wasn't sure exactly how long you planned to stay in the area..." She looked at them uncertainly.

"Oh, that's too bad, Monica," Avalon said with sincere regret. "Mac and Leah drove up to Monroe to see her brother, and I don't think they'll get back in time for dinner tonight. They'll be back tomorrow, though – couldn't we do it tomorrow night instead?"

Monica's face fell.

"Oh, I've already told Daddy about you all, and he's really looking forward to meeting you! He has to leave again for New Orleans tomorrow morning, and he said he wouldn't be back again until late next week.

"Please come tonight! I've already talked to our cook, and he's planned a really special meal. We'll all be so disappointed if you can't come. Couldn't the two of you come tonight, and then maybe everyone can come again before you all leave town for good?"

She looked so forlorn and appealing that Avalon hesitated, finding it hard to say 'No'. Lawrence took advantage of Avalon's hesitation, jumping at the chance to meet Ralph Linton.

"I accept for both of us," he said immediately, and then ignored the look of surprise on Avalon's face. "What time do you want us to be there?"

"How about sevenish? I don't get off work today until after six-thirty, and I can meet you at the landing around seven. I always leave one of the boats there. Daddy has his own, of course."

"We'll be there," Lawrence said.

When Monica left, Avalon turned to him, her lips tight.

"Why did you do that, Lawrence? You didn't even give me a chance to say No!"

"Yes, I did. You know you hesitated, and I knew that meant you really wanted to go. So we're going...

"Avalon," he went on, suddenly serious, "you need to meet your father. I know it's going to be hard for you, under the circumstances. But everything will be all right – you'll see. Your father will be ecstatic to see you after all these years. And I *will* take care of you. Nobody on that island is going to touch you – I'll see to that." His voice had steel in it.

She looked at him without speaking for a long moment and then nodded.

"All right, you win. I'll go. But I insist that no matter what happens when we meet Ralph Linton, you'll let me handle it, OK? He's *my* father."

He assured her that he wouldn't do or say anything to interfere, and she felt somewhat relieved. Mac had told her not to step foot on the island until he got back, but she simply had to meet Ralph Linton before he left again.

How she was going to manage things, she had no idea. If Lawrence was right, she might not have to say a thing: her father would know who she was the instant he saw her. The only question was: how would he react?

She was still a little nervous about the whole thing as she dressed for their dinner on the island. She and Lawrence had spent most of the day driving around looking at antebellum houses along the Mississippi, and late this afternoon, while she was in her room at the motel resting, she'd tried again to call Cam Evans.

Where on earth *was* the man, she wondered as she hung up after her third try. He'd seemed so genuinely concerned! He'd given her his number, but what good was it if she could never reach him? She had left two messages now, the second more urgent than the first.

As Lawrence drove the Maserati toward the point where they would take the motorboat to the island, Avalon tugged at her dress and straightened her jewelry for the third time since leaving the motel.

When she reached up to smooth her hair once again, Lawrence laughed and said:

"Relax! Why are you so nervous?"

"You'll never understand, and I can't explain it. I'm about to meet my biological father, and I don't even know yet if he'll be glad to know I'm alive!"

Her voice broke slightly as she voiced the thought that had haunted her ever since she'd known they were to meet Ralph Linton tonight...

For a moment, she was transported back to a time when she knew beyond a shadow of a doubt that she was dearly loved by a father – Eric Evans. But he was gone now, and so was her mother. Both mothers...

Lawrence reached over and put his hand on hers comfortingly.

"He'll not only be glad you're alive, he'll love you at first sight – almost as much as I did." His voice was gentle, and he sounded sure. She hoped he was right.

When they reached the end of the road and pulled onto the parking pad next to the water, they saw that

Monica had gotten there ahead of them, and she was already in the motorboat, ready to go. Avalon thought she looked even more impish than usual as they stepped into the boat with her.

She certainly seemed to have shaken the melancholy mood that had made her so morbidly silent yesterday. She was as sprightly and spirited tonight as when they'd first met her – was it possible it had been only three days ago?

Avalon hoped the lightheartedness was a good sign. She only wondered how long it would last. Apparently Monica was enlivened by Ralph Linton's presence, so she must care for him. Avalon prayed that she would know how to handle things tonight in a way that would be the least hurtful to Monica.

As the motorboat moved smoothly and swiftly through the water, she saw that the house was lit up like a country church, and Avalon smiled at the thought. She wouldn't have traded one year in the little country church near Columbia with Eric and Lora Evans for a hundred years in that mansion, even with Lindsay and Ralph Linton!

So what was she doing here, anyway? She already knew her mother was dead, and Lindsay had been the real object of her search. But she wanted to meet her mother's "Lancelot" – the one for whom she had given up her home, parents, little sister, friends and inheritance. It was important for her to know him: Johnna and Valerie would want to know what he was like. And, after all, he *was* her father...

They docked, and Lawrence helped them both out of

the boat. Avalon was glad to see that there was no seductive stumbling tonight. They talked about the weather as they made their way up the long brick walk to the house.

There were severe storm warnings for later that night, and Monica voiced her concern that they might have a rough time getting back to the mainland if it hit while they were at dinner.

As she climbed the steps up to the wide verandah, Avalon was touched by the sight of Lady Godiva curled up in her favorite rocking chair, just as she'd been that first night. She walked over and petted the cat's soft, warm fur, and Lady looked up at her trustfully with big blue eyes.

Avalon shuddered slightly at the memory of what the two of them had shared so recently, but she smiled at Monica and said:

"I'm thankful to see Lady again, safe and healthy. She was a great comfort to me when we were stranded in that awful place. I'll never forget her."

Monica smiled, but Avalon thought the smile didn't seem to reach her eyes. As soon as they walked through the front door, Monica called out to Glenna Henry that their guests had arrived and they would all be ready for dinner in a few minutes.

Avalon's eyes were everywhere at once, anticipating Ralph Linton's appearance. Her heart was beating fast with agitation. What would he say when he first saw her? Would he think she was her mother come back to life? They certainly looked enough alike for that.

But no one came into the hallway, and when Monica led them into the dining room, Avalon saw that the table was set for only three. Her heart sank, but she said as lightly as possible:

"I thought your father was here, Monica. Isn't he eating with us?"

Monica shrugged. "I'm sorry to disappoint you, but he couldn't make it to dinner tonight, after all. I didn't find out until it was too late to let you know; and besides, I had such a special meal planned for you that I didn't want to waste it. And I didn't think you'd want to cancel our engagement, either. So – I'm sorry, but all of this is just for us."

She gestured toward the long table, elegantly set with elaborate silver candelabra and fresh flowers, tall crystal goblets and antique china.

Avalon did her best to hide her disappointment from their hostess. But when she looked up at Lawrence, she was alarmed at the expression on his face.

And after they were seated, and the dishes were being passed around, she was even more alarmed when she felt a folded piece of paper under the bottom of a dish he passed to her.

She slipped the paper onto her lap, and a minute or two later, she unfolded it furtively and read the words he'd scrawled there:

"Don't eat/drink – find restroom/lock it".

CHAPTER
TWENTY-EIGHT

Avalon hoped her face didn't reflect the shock she felt when she read Lawrence's message. She put her hand to her face and felt the warm flush there.

She'd already drunk nearly all of the water in her goblet, which was the only drink at her place setting, so there was nothing she could do about that.

And what danger could there be from a slender girl her own age and an overweight, older housekeeper? It didn't make any sense to her, but the grim, watchful look on Lawrence's face was a first: she'd never seen it there before, so he must know something she didn't. But what?

Avalon toyed with her food for a moment or two longer without eating anything and then said quietly, with sincere self-consciousness:

"Monica, I'm afraid I need to find your powder room – I apologize for interrupting our meal, but I'm not feeling very well. Is there one on this floor?"

She pushed her chair back and stood up unsteadily. At first, she thought Monica was going to refuse to tell her where it was, but finally she said:

"Yes...I'll show you."

"No, no," Avalon said quickly, holding up her hand

to forestall their hostess, who was about to get out of her chair.

"There's no need for that. I'm sure I can find it on my own. Please – don't leave Lawrence here to eat alone – I wouldn't want that. Just tell me how to find it."

Monica hesitated for a moment and then looked at Lawrence, seemingly reluctant to leave him alone in the room. She gave Avalon directions, and Avalon left the room without a backward glance.

She made her way swiftly down the long hallway to the last door on the same side of the house as the dining room and slipped inside quickly, locking the door behind her.

Once inside, she was calm enough to think. And her first thought was: how was she any safer here than in the dining room? Surely Glenna Henry or Monica would have the key – and besides, there was a window in this room.

Avalon went to it and looked out, and she saw that it wasn't far from the ground outside. The window was locked, but what would keep anyone from breaking the window and climbing through it to reach her, if they really wanted to?

There was no doubt in her mind that Lawrence was right in sensing danger, but this room certainly wasn't going to be sufficient to protect her from it.

She took a deep breath and then prayed, asking the Lord to help her know exactly what her next move should be. For a few more moments, she stood quietly, thinking.

Then she took the low, cushioned stool at the mirrored dressing table and placed it in front of the window. Quietly turning the lock, she lifted the sash all the way to the top and climbed onto the stool gingerly. Then she hoisted herself onto the wide windowsill and looked out.

This room was on the side of the house opposite where the boats were kept, and she would have to pass outside the dining room to get to them, but she was determined to do it, and without delay.

She thought she'd be less likely to run into Glenna or Chad or the cook if she took this route, rather than going around the back of the house where the informal living areas were.

The predicted storm was in the air, and Avalon saw black clouds hanging over the island. The sooner she could get into one of the motorboats and make her way back to the mainland, the better.

She'd seen Monica leave the key in the ignition of the boat both times she'd ferried them across to the island, so that would be no problem.

And she had her car keys in her small evening bag, which she had naturally taken to the powder room with her. She would drive back to the motel and wait for Lawrence there.

What he would tell their hostess, and how he himself would get back, she couldn't begin to imagine, but that didn't concern her now. Apparently she was the one in danger.

Carefully Avalon let herself down from the window to the ground outside and pulled the bathroom window

all the way down behind her. She crouched low against
the house and began to make her way stealthily past all
the rooms, until she reached the dining room and
recognized it by the color of the drapes.

This was where she would have to be especially
cautious, she knew. The tall windows had been open a
few inches at the bottom when they'd sat down for
dinner.

She almost held her breath as she started past, and
then she was arrested by the sound of Lawrence's voice
from inside the room.

Avalon had never heard him speak so coldly, his
words as sharp and brutal as a knife attack.

"Back off, Monica. You know you're making a fool
of yourself. You could come on to me from now 'til
doomsday, and it wouldn't get you anywhere."

Monica sounded incredulous, but also irritated.

"Oh? Why not? You don't give two hoots about that
sanctimonious little prig, and you know it! I'm much
more your type, and I knew it the first time I laid eyes
on you.

"You know it, too, or you wouldn't be so intent on
resisting me. Look at me and tell me you're not attracted
to me – I don't think you can!"

She was taunting him now, and Avalon had stopped
in her tracks to hear their conversation. She crouched on
the ground directly under the window, where she could
hear every word. She had never eavesdropped before in
her life, but somehow she knew she had to do it this
time.

"Oh, yes, I *can* tell you I'm not attracted to you, and

I *am* telling you," he said ruthlessly. "I'm also telling you that whatever you and your mother have planned for me and Avalon tonight, you're a couple of idiots if you go through with it."

"My *mother!* What are you talking about?" Monica's voice had changed from that of a playful kitten to that of an angry cat. "My mother is dead!"

"I'm talking about Glenna Henry, and you know it. I doubt you knew she was your mother until Avalon showed up, and Glenna had to enlist your help in getting rid of her – and fast, before Ralph Linton gets back tomorrow.

"She must have recognized Avalon instantly, because she looks exactly like Lindsay. I was afraid of that. I knew Glenna wouldn't know me, though, since I took after my mother instead of Joe.

"Besides, Glenna hasn't seen Joe Martin for twenty years – ever since he rescued Avalon from her and wisely disappeared. And of course I've been using a different name – Masters instead of Martin."

There was total silence on both sides of the wall after Lawrence's words. Avalon's own heart had nearly stopped beating when she heard them.

Lawrence was old Joe's son! The old man who had described this island and house to David Daniels nine years ago in Nachitoches – Lawrence was his son! She was stupefied with shock.

Monica seemed to be wordless with astonishment, too. Finally, Avalon heard her say breathlessly:

"I don't know what you're talking about. You just wait until my father gets back, and I tell him…"

Lawrence laughed.

"*Your* father! Your father is never coming back, Monica, because Joe Martin has been dead for the past six months. I should know, since he was my father, too, and I was with him when he died.

"How do you think I knew about this place? I spent my summers with him and decided years ago that when he died, I'd come here and blackmail Glenna with what she'd done…

"Poor old Ralph Linton! He must have felt like a dove that finds a cuckoo in its nest all these years. It's no wonder you're such a flirt – he's probably never been able to bring himself to love you like a daughter, so you're still looking for every man's approval and admiration. He must have wondered how on earth he and Lindsay Herrington could possibly have produced a piranha like you.

"Well, they didn't, of course. That old red-haired biddie who calls herself a housekeeper threw herself at my father, though I'll never understand why he gave in – and you're the result. Not a very pleasant one, I must say. I wouldn't be attracted to you even if you weren't my half-sister.

"Joe would've done better to stay with my mother, even if he didn't deserve her. At least he was married to her – a dubious honor he never gave *your* mother." His voice was bitter when he mentioned his mother.

Monica burst out:

"Glenna Henry my mother! Me your half-sister! You're lying! You don't know what you're talking about. You don't know anything!"

Lawrence continued implacably:

"I know everything. I know that your mother was here when Lindsay – otherwise known as Victoria – gave birth to Avalon prematurely and died.

"Glenna was already pregnant with you then, but nobody knew it. When she realized that Ralph Linton wasn't coming back to the island for a long time after Lindsay died, because the news of her death had made him too ill to travel, she got the bright idea of getting rid of Avalon and putting you in her place. Who could tell one baby girl from another?

"She would have done it much sooner if our father hadn't stopped her several times. He rescued Avalon at least twice, but when your mother knew that Ralph was finally on his way back to the island, she got desperate and hired that thug from New Orleans to get rid of her.

"He left Avalon at the old ruins to die of exposure and starvation, but Joe slipped away and rescued her again. He risked his life by taking her to St. Francisville and leaving her at that church – if Glenna could have traced him, he'd have been dead. He never went back to the island after that, because he knew what a monster your mother was.

"Avalon was small for her age because Glenna deprived her of proper care for the first three years of her life, so the people who found her thought she was only two. And you seemed about the right size for someone who'd been born prematurely, since you were actually six months younger.

"So when Ralph finally came back to the island, Avalon was gone, and you were presented to him as his daughter. What a disappointment you must have been to him all these years!"

Monica was choking with fury as she sputtered:

"So why are you telling me all of this? And why are you trying to protect that – that –"

"Because you and your stupid mother are about to kill the goose that laid the golden egg, that's why."

He snorted derisively.

"You'd never get away with it even if you killed both of us tonight and made us disappear somehow and told everyone we'd never been here. Mac Evans and David Daniels would never let it rest until they found out the truth, I can assure you. You'd lose it all – money, freedom, everything.

"But if Glenna lets us go, I plan to marry Avalon, and once I'm in her will, and she's out of the way, I'll have access not only to the Linton fortune, but one that's about ten times that size!

"For your information, Avalon has just inherited two hundred million dollars from her mother's side of the family – the Herringtons. What can Ralph Linton give you or leave you in his will that begins to compare to that?"

Avalon felt faint. The black clouds overhead had burst, and the rain was falling fast now. She was getting soaked, but she leaned against the wall like a limpet, listening.

"So why are you offering to share with us at all? Why not just walk away with your precious Avalon and forget all about us?" Monica sounded bitter, but it was clear that she believed him now.

"Two reasons, really. One – I know Glenna's not planning to let us leave the island alive. That's why we're here tonight, as you well know.

"And my father warned me about her so often over the years, I know she's perfectly capable of murder – look what she tried to do to Avalon the day before yesterday...

"In fact, if Lady Godiva hadn't been trapped over there with her, *you* probably would have been glad to let Avalon rot in that horrible hovel!

"And secondly, why not spend two fortunes instead of one? My original plan – I confess – was to get rid of Avalon first and then come here to blackmail Glenna with what I knew. I didn't want Avalon showing up some time down the road and tearing up my playhouse.

"I knew there were good pickings to be had, from what my dad had told me about how wealthy the Lintons were – and I was sure of it after Glenna sent me that diamond-and-emerald ring as a first bid to keep me quiet.

"But I made the mistake of hiring that same stupid thug from New Orleans that Glenna used twenty years ago – I guess I should have known he'd blow it in Chicago, too, and he did.

"He tried twice to kill her and bungled it both times, and he got arrested the second time. He'd done a few jobs there already, and the police kept the $3,000 I'd paid him up front, and for all I knew, they'd be able to keep him, too.

"So I decided to get close to her myself, and take care of things if I had to. But Manny had a good lawyer with mob connections, and they wanted him on the street. So I paid him again, and he started all over.

"Then, the very next day, I found out that Avalon had inherited two hundred million dollars – and I had a hit man on the street looking for her! I almost had a heart attack then and there.

"I knew I had to stop Manny Byrd quickly, and I did. Fortunately for me, he was willing to meet me in the middle of the night on a bridge over the Chicago River, and I was able to get my money back and take care of things. I didn't know at the time that the mob had gotten him out only because they wanted to get rid of him, or I'd have let them save me the trouble."

"So now you're not only a blackmailer, but a murderer," Monica said scornfully.

"And *you're* a rank imposter – even if you *were* ignorant of that fact until three days ago! Are you willing to give it all up to become an honest but poor woman? I'm telling you that you can have it all, if you can stop Glenna tonight from doing whatever it is she has planned for us.

"I knew the minute you told us Ralph wasn't here after all, that it had been a trick to get us here. What was it going to be? The alligators? I'd face a thousand alligators for two hundred million dollars!"

Avalon could almost hear the sneer in Monica's voice as she said:

"No. That method would be highly suspect at this point. Glenna's much too smart for that. And she'll be here in about two minutes, if my watch is correct…

"And I assure you that even if she *is* my mother, and

you were to threaten to snap my neck, she'd still find a way to get rid of you. She doesn't love me *that* much."

In spite of the pathetic irony in the girl's voice, Avalon's pity for her had long since dissipated. She was shivering uncontrollably now, both from the drenching rain and the horrifying revelations she'd just overheard.

And she realized with a start that whatever had been placed in her water tonight was beginning to take effect. She was feeling drowsier by the moment. If she didn't start moving now, she probably wouldn't live to tell anyone what she knew.

But when she tried to get up, her feet and legs were so numb, she almost fell. It was a second or two before she had the strength to walk, and even then, she moved almost on all-fours in order not to be seen.

She had just cleared the house and was stumbling toward the water and the boats when she heard Monica scream shrilly from inside the house:

"Oh, my God, she must have heard us!"

"Yes, and 'my God' is going to help me get away from you," Avalon muttered as she ran, her high heels sinking into the wet earth with every step. Finally, she kicked them off and kept running, barefoot.

She looked back long enough to see both of her enemies poised at a window of the dining room, Monica pointing toward her with a look of horror on her face.

Avalon turned back toward the water just as Lawrence catapulted himself over the window sill and out onto the lawn, where he began chasing her in a race for the boats. She reached the pier first and flung herself into the closest boat, frantically grabbing the ignition key to start the motor.

But before she could get it started, Lawrence seized the steering wheel to stop her, exclaiming plaintively:

"Avalon, wait! I don't know what you heard, but I can explain...please!"

CHAPTER
TWENTY-NINE

He didn't hang on long. The ring Avalon was wearing was large, the diamond and emeralds sharp and protruding, and he pulled his hand back instinctively when she gouged him with it, just long enough for her to get the motor going and put the boat in reverse.

She pulled away from the dock and headed out across the water with the throttle pushed all the way forward, glad she'd decided to wear her mother's ring tonight – on her right hand, of course. She knew Lindsay would have been proud of her for thinking to use it just now, even if the jewels *were* slightly bloody.

How conceited could a man be? She was sickened by the memory of Lawrence's protest and plea. Did he really think she'd ever believe anything he said again, after this? Incredible!

But he didn't know for sure what she'd heard. He'd only seen her after Monica screamed, so he couldn't know for sure if she'd heard anything they'd said, or how much. But he knew now that she had run from him, not with him.

Would his inconceivable conceit keep him from believing she'd heard enough? If he was right behind her, would he try to explain – or try to get rid of her?

One thing was certain: as soon as she reached safety, she would expose him as a blackmailer and a murderer. She was aghast at the realization that it had been Lawrence who'd tried to have her killed in Chicago!

No wonder she hadn't wanted to get serious about him! It was appalling to think she'd ever felt the slightest attraction to him. But he was a plausible devil, no one could deny that.

He'd told her once that his father was a "good-looking loser", but old Joe had been a far better man than his son, since he had risked his own safety to rescue Avalon more than once, and Lawrence had been willing to kill her!

She looked back toward the island only once and saw Lawrence in another motorboat, coming toward her fast. She barely pulled the throttle back before she got to shore, running the boat up onto the land and jumping out almost before it stopped.

She'd pulled her car keys out on the way, and now she ran pell-mell for the Maserati. She was inside starting it while Lawrence was still in his boat.

He jumped out and raced toward the car just as she was backing out of the parking space, her tires squealing. She locked her doors instantly and put her foot on the accelerator. Lawrence threw himself in front of the car and stood there, framed in her headlights like an apparition from Hades.

"Oh, dear Jesus, please make him get out of my way!" Avalon prayed. "I don't want to have to hit him, but I don't dare stop! Please, please!"

She pressed the accelerator hard, and the car lurched

forward. At the last possible moment, Lawrence hurled himself out of her path, rolling over and over as he fell.

She knew he hadn't gotten the keys to Monica's car, or he'd be in it by now. That meant he'd be without wheels long enough for her to reach the motel ahead of him. Lawrence would have to take the boat back to the island and get Monica's car keys. She wondered if he'd get them at all.

Still, she didn't relax completely until she pulled into the parking lot at the motel where they were staying. And then, she was so thrilled by what she saw, she almost cried.

Not only were Mac and Leah back from Monroe and standing just outside her room, David and Johnna were there, too. And amazingly, Cameron Evans was with them, all of them talking animatedly.

She blew her horn briefly and waved to them all, smiling. Their eyes widened with disbelief and relief, and as Avalon got out of her car, they rushed to her. Mac didn't even start to scold her until he'd hugged her, and then the others shut him up as they embraced her ecstatically.

Avalon and Johnna were both crying with joy at seeing each other, and Cam just stood there beaming. His relief was so conspicuous that Avalon hugged him, too.

"Lawrence killed Manny Byrd," were the first words out of her mouth when she could finally speak. "I need to tell you that right now, because he might be right behind me, and he's going to do his dead-level best to talk you out of believing what I say. But I know. I heard him tell Monica – "

Mac stopped her.

"You don't need to convince us of anything, Avalon. We know, too. When we showed David and Johnna the snapshots we've taken on this trip, David recognized him instantly as the boy he saw that summer with old Joe.

"He was younger then, of course, and dark-haired; but David has an artist's eye for detail, and he knew him immediately. We drove like bats out of you-know-where to get here. And when we did, Cameron was already here waiting for us."

Cameron said:

"I'm so sorry I didn't get to actually talk to you when you called, Avalon, but I had an out-of-town emergency and was gone for a couple of days. But when I got back and saw you'd called twice, I knew something had to be very wrong, so I made arrangements to take another few days off and came down here as fast as I could to check on you and help you if you needed it...

"And when Mac told me about Lawrence being that old man's son, it just confirmed something I'd suspected. But I had no hard evidence for it, and that's why I was so reluctant to warn you against him without knowing anything for sure."

"What are you talking about?" Avalon asked, puzzled.

"That night when the four of you had dinner at Antiques & Ambrosia – remember? I stared at you all so rudely, you couldn't help but notice. It was Lawrence who puzzled me.

"His face seemed familiar to me, but it was all wrong, too. I mean, his hair was blonde, and he didn't have a mustache, and the person he reminded me of had had dark brown hair and a mustache. He looked like the same person without looking like him, if you understand what I mean."

"But where did you recognize him *from*?"

"He came to our church one day last winter – six months or so ago, I guess it was. It was on a weekday, but we're all in the church offices from eight to five on a pretty regular basis, so I was there when he came by.

"He seemed deeply distraught and was in a great hurry, and he told us his father was dying. He said he was trying to find a friend of his father's, who had taken in a little girl who'd been left there at our church, about twenty years ago.

"He said he couldn't recall the man's name, but the little girl had been blonde and about two or three years old. He wanted to get in touch with this friend of his father's, to let him know that his father was very ill and wanted to see him again before he died.

"Well, of course your story was well-known by everyone around St. Francisville, and certainly to many people in our congregation. And there didn't seem to be any reason not to tell him, so the church secretary looked up your parents' current address in Evanston and gave it to him.

"He seemed like a nice, normal young man who was just trying to follow through on his father's wishes, and none of us gave it another thought...

"That is, not until that night when I saw the four of

you at Antiques & Ambrosia and thought I recognized him – and yet, he was so different, I thought it must be my imagination.

"And, of course, I didn't know who you were that night; and even after we met and had lunch together after church on Sunday, I still didn't know there had been recent attempts on your life. So I really had no reason to suspect him of anything.

"It did cross my mind that his blonde hair and lack of a mustache might be a disguise, and I wondered why he would be using one. But people do change the color of their hair and their appearance all the time – even men. And from the way you talked about him, he didn't sound dangerous or even suspicious-acting.

"I gave you as much of a warning as I felt was justified by my own suspicions. I – didn't want you to think I was trying to turn you against him for my own purposes...but I did want to protect you."

Avalon blushed a little and said softly,

"I guess that's why he didn't want to come to church with us in St. Francisville this past Sunday morning – he was afraid someone might remember his coming there and getting directions to our house in Evanston...

"And they would have wondered, just as you did, why he was blonde and without a mustache now – especially if I had told anyone about the recent attempts on my life.

"You know, there was always something that held me back from trusting him completely. I know the Lord protects His own, and I guess this was one of those times. I wouldn't have gone to the island with him alone tonight, except for the fact that I really did want to meet my father...

"We were fools to fall for Monica's bait, after what happened to me on the island. Lawrence probably did suspect even before we went, but he wanted to make a deal with Monica and her mother so he could have access to both family fortunes. No wonder he was so outraged when Glenna stranded me in that awful cottage...I was his ticket to easy street!"

"Now *we* don't know what *you're* talking about, Avalon," Leah said, smiling. "But don't you think we'd better go inside instead of standing out here where we might have to deal with Lawrence in public? Besides, you're all wet – and where on earth are your shoes?"

Avalon tried to tell her as they all trooped into Mac's room. Leah got a towel and a thick pair of socks for Avalon, and they sat around the table in front of the picture window.

Every now and then, Mac pulled the drapes back just enough to see if Lawrence had pulled into the parking lot yet. Avalon repeated as much as she could remember of Lawrence's and Monica's conversation, and they were all as appalled as she'd been.

Leah said:

"No wonder he was so stunned at Gino's that Sunday, when Mac told him you'd just inherited all that money! We all thought it must be because he felt inferior and unworthy of you – and that's what he told you, wasn't it, Avalon?

"And all the time, he was being quiet because he was frantically trying to figure out how to find Manny Byrd and stop him from killing you – which was what he had paid him to do!"

"And I wondered why he sounded so cynical when we were talking about the South and small towns," Avalon said. "Of course, we had no idea he'd ever lived in one. But apparently he spent every summer with Joe, and they must have moved from one little town to another, always on the wrong side of the tracks, always dirt poor...

"Remember, David said he felt sorry for old Joe, living as he did in that little shack in Natchitoches nine years ago. That business about receiving an inheritance from his mother was just a blind. Lawrence must have decided money was worth killing for, after all."

"I guess that's why he didn't want to go to Herrington Hall on our way down here – he was afraid of seeing David," Leah said. "Or rather, he was afraid of David's seeing him...

"And when he saw Lindsay's picture at Megan Marshall's house, he was shocked by your resemblance to your mother because he knew Glenna Henry would recognize you immediately!

"Lawrence had apparently planned to win your love and confidence and then present you to Ralph Linton as his daughter. He must have thought his reward would be Ralph's gratitude and acceptance, and eventually your hand in marriage – but he knew he had to get you safely past Glenna Henry, and that scared him."

Mac called the White Castle police, who sent two officers to the motel. They were both stationed outside, watching for Lawrence. Avalon had told them everything she knew about Lawrence's activities in Chicago, and the authorities there had already been contacted.

She also described Monica's BMW convertible, and more officers were watching for it on the road to the island. By now the storm was raging so wildly that they didn't dare try to reach the island itself in a boat.

Everyone was hungry, since no one had eaten anything all evening, including Avalon, who by now was truly drowsy and fighting sleep with all her might. They sent Cam for take-out, and when he got back, they sat around the large round table in Mac's room, eating – and waiting.

Avalon finally went next door to her own room and succumbed to sleep. Johnna and Leah followed an hour later and lay down to rest on the other bed in her room.

And Mac, David and Cam all sat around the table long after the young women had left, discussing the situation. The two police officers watched and waited.

But Lawrence never came.

CHAPTER
THIRTY

It was a long night, and when Avalon woke up the next morning, she was alone with Leah. Mac and Cam had gone out to the island with the police at about four o'clock this morning, when the storm had abated enough for them to take a boat safely.

David and Johnna had followed them a few hours later, leaving Avalon to rest a little longer, with Leah to keep her company.

Avalon could hardly wait to get out to the island with everyone else and find out what had happened after she left. Had Lawrence simply walked away instead of going back to the house for car keys? He and Monica certainly weren't on the best of terms, and there was no guarantee she'd help him in any way.

It had been a long walk if he had walked away – more than seven miles to White Castle, and farther than that to any other point of civilization. Avalon certainly wouldn't have wanted to do it herself, on such a treacherous night.

She hoped and prayed he hadn't done that, because if he were still out there somewhere, she'd be watching for him the rest of her days, or at least until he was apprehended. If he'd taken a car, at least they would be able to trace that.

And would Monica and Glenna try to brazen it out at the house, going right on as if nothing had happened? They'd gotten away with it for a long time. They might think they could bluff their way out of what had happened last night.

If Lawrence had run away, all they'd have to do would be to call Avalon a liar – and perhaps a thief, as well, since she was in possession of Lindsay's diamond-and-emerald ring.

But no, they'd know they couldn't do that, with Ralph Linton coming home today. The minute he laid eyes on Avalon, he'd know Monica was a phony, if he hadn't already figured it out.

Avalon wondered what time his plane would arrive. She wanted so much to be there to meet it. She said as much to Leah as she dressed for the day.

"I'm going to call the Baton Rouge airport and find out if there's a flight coming in there today that originated in London. That cab driver said Ralph Linton owned a lot of property around London and flew back to check on it from time to time. That's probably where he's been this time, too."

She made the call and learned that there was a flight coming in at two o'clock that afternoon from Atlanta, via New York, originating in London. They gave her the gate number, and although it wasn't the same as Eric's and Lora's had been, it gave her a sense of *déjà vu*. She would be driving to an airport to pick up a parent...

A parent. It seemed so strange. Especially since this parent wasn't expecting her – wasn't even aware of her existence! Would he be glad? She realized suddenly that she was nervous, thinking about meeting her father.

She hadn't given him much thought when she'd made the commitment to Valerie and Johnna to try to find the island in David's painting and learn what she could about her mother. She'd been looking for Lindsay and had found Ralph.

She had found Lindsay, too, but not alive. Mac was the only one she had told about finding her mother's tomb...until last night, when she had finally told Johnna.

It had been so hard! Johnna had wept as if for someone she had seen every day of her life and had loved dearly. They were both deeply dreading the moment when Valerie would have to be told.

Mac and Cameron had taken the rental car to the island, and David and Johnna had their own; so Avalon and Leah still had the convertible. The storm had passed completely during the night, and the air smelled so sweet and fresh that she decided to put the top down.

They found a drive-through donut shop in White Castle and got cinnamon rolls and coffee on their way out of town. Once they were on the road again, Avalon said to Leah, smiling:

"I know this isn't a very healthy breakfast, but I feel like celebrating just being alive, after last night."

The warmth of the hot coffee in her hands was a poignant reminder of last night's cold, drenching rain. The whole thing seemed almost like a fantasy this morning. Today's weather was so mild, the sky so clear, it was hard to realize that a thunderstorm had raged so fiercely last night.

And it was even harder to believe she had raced along this road just hours ago with a murderer behind her! Everything looked perfectly peaceful today, and Avalon thought again how quickly things can change and how deceptive outward appearances can be.

They were soon at the parking pad across from Imitation Island, and Avalon saw that the only vehicles parked there were the police car the two officers had come in, the rental car that Mac and Cameron had driven, and David and Johnna's car.

Where was Monica's BMW? And Glenna's sedan? And the third car which they had assumed belonged to Chad Wilson or possibly the cook? They were all gone this morning. She supposed she wasn't surprised, but she was curious.

Avalon pulled into a parking space beside the others, and she and Leah got out and looked around for a boat to take to the island, but there wasn't one.

"Maybe we should have gone around by the other road and taken your little row boat!" Leah laughed. "How are we going to get across?"

They didn't have to wonder long. A motorboat was coming their way, with Mac at the wheel. He looked grim and gloomy, and Avalon's heart sank.

What had they found?

On reaching shore, he throttled back and called out to them over the noise of the motor:

"Get in! I'll take you across."

They climbed into the boat, and as soon as Mac turned it around and headed back toward the island, he said:

"I'm glad you're both here. Avalon, you need to brace yourself for a shock. We came over this morning to see if we could find Lawrence and the two women, and we found – more than we'd bargained for."

He stopped speaking abruptly and didn't say another word until they docked in front of the house. He helped them both out of the boat, giving Leah an affectionate smile when she gave him her hand. He dropped his eyes when Avalon gave him hers.

She searched his averted face as she got out of the boat, wondering what on earth they'd found, to make him so reluctant to tell her.

The three of them walked silently together up the long walk toward the house, just as they'd done when they came to dinner as Monica's guests the first time. The difference was that Monica and Lawrence had been with them that night. Avalon was beginning to dread whatever it was Mac had to tell her.

As they climbed the steps to the verandah, she glanced over at the rocking chair where she'd always found Lady and saw that it was empty. Mac opened the front door and held it for the two young women, then closed it behind them.

He walked ahead of them down the long hallway toward the last room on the left, which Avalon knew was the Library. She couldn't keep from glancing inside the dining room as they passed it.

"Mac!" she exclaimed when she realized what she was seeing.

The beautiful, high-ceilinged room had been stripped

bare – of china, silver, candelabra, paintings, marble busts, the small bronze figurines Avalon had admired just last night – everything portable and of value had been removed. No wonder all three cars were gone!

"I can't believe it! They must have worked all night without stopping, to take that many things."

She had stopped in her tracks, and Mac paused long enough to say:

"You haven't seen anything yet, Avalon. That's just one room. They took everything that wasn't nailed down and could be sold. The amazing part is that they were able to transport it in the boats without having them sink under the weight of all that stuff. They must have used all the boats and still made a hundred trips."

"No wonder you didn't want to tell me. Poor Ralph! When he gets back this afternoon, he's going to be so shocked and disappointed. Not only about the robbery – but imagine finding out that the girl he thought was his daughter was an imposter! And that the housekeeper he must have trusted had been deceiving him all those years – not to mention trying to kill his real daughter.

"I know he'll recognize me because I look just like my mother, and I hope he'll learn to love me as a daughter. But surely he must have come to care for Monica, after twenty-three years. I just feel so sorry for him."

"I know. So do I. But come along...there's something else you need to see."

He stood aside at the huge door of the Library, and she and Leah walked in ahead of him. Everybody else was there, standing around looking sober ... Johnna and

David, the two police officers, Cameron, and someone else who looked official – someone she'd never seen before and didn't know from Adam.

And then they all moved aside, and she realized that the official-looking person must be the coroner. For there on the large library table, which had been cleared off for the body, lay Lawrence. Avalon caught her breath and put her hand to her mouth.

Then she walked over to him, staring down into his face – almost unable to believe that he was really dead. It was a face with the profile and features of a Greek god, a face that had once expressed love for her so convincingly. His bronzed skin was pasty and white now, his clothing wrinkled and still damp.

"What *happened?*" she asked in a soft, horrified voice. "How long – how long has he been dead?"

She turned automatically to Cameron for an answer, even though Cam had been the last one to become involved in the situation. He walked over to her and placed a gentle hand on her shoulder.

"We don't know what happened, but the coroner told us he's probably been dead since about one o'clock this morning. Mac and I got here around four, and we found him still in the water, floating face down."

Avalon felt nauseous, picturing it.

"Where?" she asked weakly.

"Down by the boats. At first we thought he might have been shot, but there are no marks on the body at all. There are no signs of any kind of foul play – he seems to have just stepped off into the water and drowned. It's peculiar, to say the least. The alligators weren't even interested in the body – thank the Lord," he added under his breath.

"Lawrence didn't just step into the water and drown himself," Avalon said with spirit. "He wasn't the suicidal type. Monica and Glenna did something to cause it – I can almost guarantee that. It was probably Glenna. She's always specialized in the indirect murder attempt.

"With me, she hired someone to leave me at the old ruins when I was just a baby, and again the other day, she stranded me at that old abandoned cottage – but she never took direct action.

"She probably did something indirect this time, too. But unless we find her and Monica, we'll probably never know just what."

Avalon was suffused with sadness as she looked at Lawrence's handsome features, now so ghostly and gray. His life had been a tragedy – so different from hers, as he himself had agreed that day in the tiny Chapel when he'd shown her the picture of his mother.

And yet – Avalon's hadn't always been a bed of roses, either. The difference had been the Lord.

Cam said softly, seeming to understand her feelings:

"It's tragic...I feel it, too. But at least, this way you won't always be wondering if he's coming after you because you heard him confess to murder. You need to remember that, when you start feeling heavyhearted about it all."

She nodded. "I know. I *am* relieved, in a way. I guess that's only natural. But I regret so *much* not being more alert to his real spiritual condition! He just seemed so normal and sane!

"If I had recognized the reality, maybe I could have helped him find a relationship with the Lord that would have freed him – set him free from his violent – I can only call it *lust* – for money! The Lord could have given him something so much more *satisfying* – something that would have made him so much happier! I can't help but think of the Scripture that says 'the love of money is a root of all kinds of evil'..."

"People often misquote that, you know," Cam said, "saying money itself is the root of all evil. But that's not what the Bible says at all. Money can be used for great good, and often is...

"It's the *love* of money – a kind of obsessive craving for the luxuries money can buy and for the power and prestige it gives, making it the goal of life, being willing to compromise our principles and sell our soul to get it – *that's* what destroys people, the poor just as surely as the rich."

Avalon nodded. "You know, I think – I *hope* – this will teach me a lesson. I have a tendency to assume that the people around me are doing all right spiritually and share the same general values and principles – especially the people sitting next to me in church...

"But you never know what deadly soul struggles someone may be going through! Or how close they might be to simply stepping off into an abyss of one sin or another! Everyone is spiritually vulnerable until the day they die..."

They stood silently beside Lawrence's body for a few more minutes. When they finally turned away, Mac was walking toward Avalon to hand her something.

"I thought you might like to have this. We found it when we were searching the house. It was on the floor in the hallway near one of the upstairs bedrooms. I took it out of the frame because somebody had stepped on the glass and smashed it to bits. If you needed any more proof that she once lived in this house, you have it."

Avalon looked down into the face of Lindsay Herrington – blonde and beautiful, dimpled and smiling. The photograph was signed, "To My Beloved Lancelot, With All My Love, Lindsay."

CHAPTER
THIRTY-ONE

The coroner finally removed Lawrence's body from the table in the Library, and Cameron offered to take Avalon back to her car on the mainland in one of the boats. She was going to drive to the Baton Rouge airport to meet Ralph Linton – alone.

Johnna had said, "I think we need to give him a little time to adjust to having a daughter who looks enough like Lindsay to be her ghost, before he actually has to meet one of the Herringtons, don't you?

"David and I will wait at the motel until about six this evening, which should give you time to pick up Ralph and tell him everything that's happened. Then we'll come back here to the island and meet him. I can hardly wait, but I think it's best I stay in the background at first."

Cameron didn't say much until they were nearly to shore, and then he throttled back so that it was quieter.

"Avalon, I don't quite know how to say this, but I don't want to lose track of you now. You didn't really need me to rush down here, I guess, but I wanted so much to help.

"I feel responsible for your ending up in such a precarious position last night – if I'd gone ahead and told you what I suspected about Lawrence, probably none of it would have happened. You could have been killed! Can you forgive me for not saying more?"

She smiled. "I forgive you for being hesitant to judge someone quickly and for not having a suspicious nature – I don't have one, either. But I have to admit that I did have my suspicions about Lawrence, long ago. So I have no one to blame but myself. I think the Lord just protected me emotionally – and I know He protected me physically...

"There may come a time when you and I are far less trusting of our fellow human beings, but I hope it won't be too soon. I've heard psychologists say that people tend to 'project' their own personality traits onto other people and assume that other people are just like themselves; so I guess that means that those who are trustworthy tend to be more trusting. That's the way I like to think of it, anyway."

He helped her out of the boat, and they walked to her car. The top was still down, so he helped her to put it up. The sun was high in the sky now and beginning to bear down, hot and humid. The air conditioning would be welcome on the way to Baton Rouge.

"You'll bring him back here to the island, won't you?"

"I will if he still wants to come back after hearing what I have to tell him about Monica and Glenna. But I'm sure he will – after all, it's his home."

As she started to get into the car, he took both of her hands in his and said soberly:

"You will keep in touch with me, won't you?"

"Of course I will. You're almost family, you know."

Cam smiled. "I'm glad to hear you say 'almost'."

Avalon thought about that nearly all the way to Baton Rouge. She knew what he meant. She liked him, too. But it was too soon to be getting attached to anyone yet.

She still felt a little sick inside about Lawrence. She hadn't been in love with him; but remembering what he had done and had tried to do to her was still painful right now. And seeing him lying dead on the table in the Library had hurt even more.

Besides, Avalon wanted to concentrate on her father. He was all she had left now, in terms of parents. He would need her, once he found out about Glenna and Monica.

On reaching the airport, she parked the car in the covered area and locked it, swinging her purse over her arm for the short walk to the terminal.

It was cool and dim inside after the glare of the August afternoon heat; and in just a few minutes, Avalon was seated in the waiting room watching for her father's flight.

She still had nearly half an hour to wait, and she pulled out her mirror and checked her make-up one last time. She was aware of being more nervous than usual, so she concentrated on sitting as still as possible to compensate for it.

The minutes ticked by uneventfully, and finally the flight arrival was announced over the loudspeaker. She got up immediately and watched as the plane taxied to the gate. The steps were let down, and passengers began descending onto the tarmac.

Avalon could feel her breath coming quickly, and her fingertips tingled. There had been no way to let Ralph know she would be there to meet him – or even that she was alive.

She hoped he wouldn't be too shocked at the sight of her. She really didn't even know for a fact that he would be on this flight, but she believed he would.

Then, just as the passengers started coming through the door into the waiting area, she realized something that simply hadn't occurred to her before. She had no idea what Ralph Linton looked like!

It was a blow to her system when the thought hit her. How could she have completely ignored something so crucial?

But there had been no one to ask, anyway. Glenna and Monica certainly wouldn't have told her, and Lawrence would never have admitted knowing anything about Ralph Linton, even if Joe Martin had described him.

Apparently, the people in White Castle didn't see him often enough to tell her much about him – at least, that had been her impression. And she'd never seen a picture of him at the house on the island. She didn't know which rooms were his and certainly wouldn't have felt free to invade them if she had known.

She stood directly in front of the doorway into the terminal so that no one coming in from outside could avoid seeing her. It was a full flight, and dozens of passengers were dispersing in every direction.

People all around her were embracing their families

and friends and walking away together. She scrutinized every middle-aged man carefully, making certain every one of them looked her full in the face before he walked on.

Avalon needn't have worried. She knew Ralph Linton the instant she saw him, because he stopped dead in his tracks when he saw her, staring as if at a ghost, and clutching his chest as if about to have a heart attack.

CHAPTER
THIRTY-TWO

Ralph staggered and closed his eyes and would have fallen, but Avalon ran to him immediately, taking his arm and helping him to a nearby chair in the waiting area.

He was a slender man of medium height, in his fifties, with thinning gray hair and a complexion that was probably always pallid but which was a ghastly gray now. Impeccably dressed and with perfect posture, he still had a look of vulnerability about him.

She felt such a rush of affection at the sight of him and his reaction to seeing her that her eyes filled with burning tears, and she had to brush them away in order to see where she was going.

She put her arm around her father and pulled him toward her gently, amazed at the feelings that flooded her.

"I'm so sorry I was such a shock to you...Father. But I had no way of letting you know I would be here...are you going to be all right?"

Ralph drew a deep breath and opened his eyes slowly, like a man waking from a dream and still unsure of reality. He turned to look into Avalon's face as if at a vision from heaven. She realized that he still thought she was Lindsay.

"Did you call me 'Father'?" he asked weakly, sounding confused.

She nodded, smiling.

"I'm the baby girl Lindsay couldn't wait to name Avalon. I'm Avalon! Your daughter…"

He continued staring at her as if he couldn't get enough of her face.

"I don't understand," he said, shaking his head slightly.

It was another hour and an entire trip back to the island before he did; and even then, he still seemed to be in a sort of daze. Avalon didn't say a word about what Monica and Glenna had done to the house – stripping it bare of every portable treasure.

Ralph Linton was her biological father, and she already loved him, feeling more for him than she'd ever imagined possible; but she had to remind herself that he was not Eric Evans – a man who had viewed everything on this earth only in the light of its effect on human souls and their eternal destiny.

Ralph Linton was a wealthy, worldly man to whom the news of such a loss would be a blow. The extreme luxury and elegance of the house on Imitation Island told her that much. She guessed the robbery would be too much to add to his burden of surprise at this point.

Ralph told her that he had always believed Monica to be their – his and Lindsay's – daughter, but he'd always wondered where she'd gotten her looks, character and personality. She certainly hadn't resembled anyone in the Linton family, but he hadn't known any of the Herringtons except from Lindsay's descriptions.

He had truly tried to love Monica like a daughter and had failed; but he had done his best to treat her right. Avalon knew that Monica had suffered; but so had Ralph. And it was all Glenna's fault.

Glenna had been with the Lintons for years, Ralph told her, and so of course she knew Lindsay before she dyed her hair black and changed her name to Victoria. She also knew that the Herringtons were looking for Lindsay.

Glenna had told Ralph that before Lindsay died, she changed her mind about wanting their little baby girl to be called "Avalon". She'd been afraid, Glenna said, that the name might lead her parents to her, since they knew, and her best friend Megan Marshall knew, that she'd always planned to use that unusual name for her child.

Glenna told Ralph that Lindsay had chosen the name Monica instead, and Ralph believed her.

"At that time, I would have believed almost anything, I was so confused and devastated by Lindsay's death. I had planned my trip to England in such a way that I could be back in plenty of time for your birth. But you came two months early...so I wasn't there."

"I'm so sorry. I wish I hadn't. I may have been the reason she died." Avalon felt like crying.

"No, no...you mustn't think that...babies come early all the time, and most mothers don't die from it. Lindsay was always so fearful that her family would find her and force us to give up our life together. I think the stress of that insecurity might have weakened her health.

"When Glenna told me that Lindsay had died in childbirth, I became so seriously ill that I was bedridden for nearly a year. And after that, the thought of going back to the island without Lindsay was just impossible. It was a full three years before I could bring myself to face that house without Lindsay in it...

"I know I should have thought of you, but I wasn't myself, Avalon. I hope you can forgive me. If I had been there when I should have been, as your father, none of those terrible things would have happened to you. I'm so sorry for that, and so very, very thankful God took care of you when I didn't."

His voice broke with the last words. He reached for her hand, and she grasped his warmly, feeling a connection with him that was more than physical. If she felt this with her father, what would she have felt with Lindsay?

"We had something so special, your mother and I. But it nearly broke my heart to take her away from her family – especially her grandfather. They were so close!

"But he encouraged her to elope, since her parents refused to give her permission to marry me. I don't know why he actually urged her to just go away with me, without regard to her parents, or why he didn't tell them about my family – unless he was afraid they might make our mutual fortunes an issue that would cause us grief through the years...I don't know."

Almost before she knew it, they were at the end of the road, with Imitation Island in sight. She saw that someone had made sure a motorboat was there for them, and she took Ralph's few pieces of luggage out of the trunk of her car and put them in the boat. He had told her that he came here so seldom and stayed such a short time, he didn't need much.

As they sped across the short expanse of water, Avalon almost had a sense of surrealism. And yet, with her father beside her, it seemed that the torn tapestry of her life was at last being pieced together in a comprehensible pattern.

She knew that her adoptive parents would have been so happy for her if they could have known! But Lora would have been deeply grieved that Avalon had found her mother in a vault in the old mausoleum, instead of alive.

When she and Ralph walked together through the front door of the house, she didn't have to tell him about the robbery. He saw the results immediately, and it was nearly the *coup de grace* to a day of staggering discoveries.

He seemed almost as stupefied by the loss of so many of his family's priceless treasures as he'd been by his first sight of Avalon, especially the Faberge egg that had been given to a Linton by a member of English royalty in the distant past, and the set of old Paris Sevres China, Rose Pompadour design, that had been handed down in the family for generations. He'd treasured a few of the priceless Italian bronzes that were missing, too.

She encouraged him to go into the den and lie down before going upstairs. He preferred his big chair in the Library, he said; but Avalon couldn't bear to go into that room, where she'd last seen Lawrence's body laid out.

She hadn't told Ralph about Lawrence and his death yet; and when she did, he shook his head at still another unhappy revelation and agreed that they shouldn't go there.

That was how they ended up in the Music Room, which is where Ralph was still resting on the sofa, and Avalon was playing her mother's piano, when David and Johnna arrived.

It gave Avalon intense pleasure to introduce her father to her mother's baby sister; and in just a few more minutes, Ralph was sitting up, his elbows on his knees, his hands clasped in front of him, talking to Johnna about Lindsay.

"Lindsay missed you terribly after she left home," he was saying to Johnna. "I think that's one reason she was so eager for us to have a baby right away – and she wanted a little girl, she said. Not only to use the name Avalon, but to try to compensate for losing you. I think she missed her baby sister 'til the day she died."

Johnna had tears in her eyes as she listened.

Avalon had begun playing the piano very softly in the background. She'd found a portfolio containing some of Lindsay's favorite pieces, according to Ralph; and the sweet, mild nature of most of the music – Beethoven's Sonatina and *Fur Elise*, Hugo Wolf's Lullaby, Clementi's Prelude in D Minor, Rimsky-Korsakov's *Scheherazade*, Mozart's Sonata I, Schubert's Unfinished Symphony theme, J.C.F. Bach's *Anglaise,* Schumann's Melody & First Loss, J.S. Bach's Prelude in C Major, Godard's *Berceuse*, Morovsky's Adagio in A Major, C. P. E. Bach's Pastorale and *Lento Affettuoso* – all told Avalon more about her mother in that hour than she could have learned in a lifetime!

Ralph told her that Lindsay had always felt she should have at least an hour's worth of gentle classical pieces in her repertoire; and it had been, in fact, her favorite music. It was music she had played as a girl, and it always brought back memories of her old home and family without seeming to make her sad.

"Sometimes I can almost hear her playing, and I've felt her presence in this house so forcefully that I couldn't bear it, and I'd go back to England sooner than I had planned," Ralph said. "You might think that feeling her near would be a comfort, but it isn't – it's just pure agony, when I know she's not really here, and never will be again. You can't begin to imagine how lonely my life has been without her...

"That's one reason I came so seldom and stayed such a short time. Part of it has been because of Monica and Glenna, of course...I could never feel comfortable with either one of them. But part of it has been the feeling that Lindsay was here, and yet not here...it's hard to explain.

"When I first came back from England three years after Lindsay died, the initial feeling was so strong that I made Glenna open up the mausoleum so I could look inside the vault that had Lindsay's name on it, to be sure her body was there and she was really dead. I think Glenna thought I'd really lost my mind then!

"Of course, Lindsay's body *was* there...and she had been buried in her wedding dress, as she'd always said she wanted to be. At least Glenna had remembered that much. Lindsay was the most sentimental person I ever knew. That was just one of the things I loved about her.

There were so many."

His voice trailed off, and Johnna reached across and patted his hand briefly in sympathy.

Johnna glanced over at Avalon and smiled. So that's where Avalon had gotten her soft heart. Johnna had suspected it before, but she had been only three years old when Lindsay had eloped, so she'd never really known her sister except from their mother's description and the photograph of Lindsay at eighteen, which she'd seen only recently.

The strains of the beautiful music filled the room, and the atmosphere seemed to be one of peacefulness instead of pain, so Avalon played on. She could hear her father saying to Johnna:

"It will be hard to leave this house, with Lindsay's tomb here on the island. But I don't think I can bear to come back here again, to be completely alone...

"And somehow I can't see Avalon living out here in the middle of nowhere, even with me. Besides, as beautiful as she is, I'm sure it won't be long until she's married...

"No...I think it's time to move on. This house has too many memories. And this island has been an imitation too long...not only the house, which the locals always looked at as a phony, since it wasn't really antebellum, but the life we lived here, after Lindsay died...

"Monica was an imitation daughter, and Glenna was an imitation friend – and I guess I was an imitation, too. I had no real life here, without Lindsay. The only real reason I came back was to 'do the right thing' by

Monica, because Glenna told me she was Lindsay's and my daughter.

"It's still hard to believe Monica fooled me all these years. But of course, she was fooled, too, poor girl. I guess my eyes and heart were so dull with indifference by that time, I didn't care enough to notice the things that would have told me the truth."

Avalon was starting to feel forlorn at the thought that Imitation Island might be deserted almost as soon as she had found it, when she became aware that someone else had come into the room. She stopped playing the piano long enough to turn around and see who it was.

She felt a twinge of fear that it might be Glenna or Monica, come back for no good purpose. But it was just a woman she'd never seen before, with medium-length white hair and wearing a simple kind of dress and sandals.

She was middle-aged – probably in her fifties, Avalon guessed at a glance – but still slender. She seemed unsure of herself as she stood in the doorway, or at least unsure of her welcome.

Could she be Lawrence's mother? Lawrence had told Avalon his mother was dead, but he'd told her a lot of things that weren't true. Could the poor woman have come to take her revenge for his death?

Avalon had stopped playing the piano abruptly in the middle of the piece, and the others were looking toward her to see why she had stopped. And then their eyes followed hers to the doorway.

Avalon looked around at all of them: did any of them

know the woman? They didn't seem to. They just sat there staring at the stranger stupidly, apparently waiting for her to tell them who she was and what she wanted.

Avalon wondered how she'd gotten there: had they left one of the boats at the parking pad? She couldn't remember…

Time seemed to hang suspended in the music room for a long moment of uncomprehending silence. And then – just when Avalon opened her mouth to speak to the woman, since no one else seemed inclined to do so, she heard Johnna say incredulously, in a voice choked with emotion:

"*Lindsay!*"

CHAPTER
THIRTY-THREE

There was shrieking on every side then, and running feet and loud exclamations, as they rushed upon the lone figure, who stood uncertainly in the doorway of the music room where she had played the piano so often before being shut off for so long from the rest of the household by a whole floor and heavy doors, and even seclusion at a location off the island itself.

Ralph Linton was already weak from the shocks of the day, and he fell back, nearly fainting at the sight of the wife he'd thought dead and buried for the past twenty-three years.

But somehow, he managed to hold out his arms to her, and he gave her such a look of inexpressible joy that she flew to him and fell into his arms with sobs of relief.

Lindsay Herrington was no longer the blonde beauty she had been when she'd eloped with Ralph Linton twenty-five years ago. Her hair was pure white now, and she looked much older than her forty-three years.

But she was still slim, with pretty features; and Avalon realized with a jolt that this was the light-haired woman she'd seen standing at an upper window at the back of the mansion the day she had rowed to the island alone and searched the cemetery and mausoleum.

So it had been her mother, after all! But how was that possible? Her mother had surely seen her wandering around down there. Why hadn't she motioned to her or tried to make contact with her?

Lindsay extricated herself from Ralph's iron grip long enough to rush to Avalon and embrace her so tightly that Avalon could scarcely breathe. She seemed to have read her daughter's mind.

"I wanted to warn you, my precious Avalon...that day when I saw you down there exploring the cemetery behind the house. I was afraid that wicked woman might try to get rid of you somehow!

"But I was so terrified that if you knew it was me, or even suspected as much, you might actually come into the house, and Glenna would never have let you leave alive once she got you here alone, especially if you hinted that you'd seen someone at a window on the top floor of the house!

"Oh, Avalon, my little baby girl...I just can't believe it! She told me you died when you were born, just as she told Ralph *I* had died. Oh, how can God be so good to me?"

She was weeping with joy now, and Avalon wept with her, their arms around one another, seated side by side on the piano bench.

"It was your playing my favorite songs that lured me here," Lindsay said happily, wiping her eyes. "I had to be cautious, because I didn't know who might still be in the house. I didn't dare show my face to Glenna...

"It must have been Chad Wilson who unlocked my door...I don't think Monica ever knew I was here. Chad knew, but he was crazy about Monica, so Glenna was able to keep him quiet and use him.

"I didn't know it was unlocked at first – I must have been sleeping when he did it. At first, I thought Glenna had unlocked it and was trying to lure me to my death...

"She's wanted me dead for so long, but she didn't have the nerve to do anything herself. But she might have arranged an 'accident' for me – she's done it more than once over the years."

Ralph Linton still seemed to be somewhat bewildered, but he spoke now, haltingly:

"I always felt your presence, Lindsay. I could hardly bear it at times, and that's why I didn't come here more often or stay very long when I did come.

"But how could you actually have been here in the house all those years without my knowing it? It just seems too wonderful to be true..."

Lindsay went back to him and sat close beside him on the sofa, laying her head lovingly against his shoulder.

"I was never here in the house when you came home, Ralph. I was always moved out before you arrived – there's a way to get off the island without using the boats. You and I never knew about it, but the cook discovered it years ago, and he's Glenna's boyfriend.

"The two of them hid me in an old wreck of a cottage over on the mainland whenever you were coming back to the island. Glenna always removed the rope bridge, but she needn't have worried. I gave up trying to escape, years ago....

"I doubt Monica ever knew I was here in the house...

I never laid eyes on her. It was just a coincidence that I'd gotten out of my room and was standing at the window that day and happened to see Avalon when she came to look around the cemetery."

Avalon thought: "A coincidence is a miracle in which God chooses to remain anonymous." She knew it hadn't been just a coincidence, especially when Lindsay went on to say:

"You can't begin to imagine how much good that did me! Just knowing my child was alive, after all – and actually on the island! I've tried to escape so many times, I'd given up long ago...

"But that day was a turning point for me...I started to pray that Avalon would find me somehow, without getting herself killed in the process! And God was merciful and answered my prayers."

She turned and looked at Avalon with so much love in her eyes that Avalon knew she would never again have trouble calling Lindsay "Mother".

"I remember one day just a few years after Glenna shut me away, I was so lonely and desperate that I cried out to you, Ralph – and to Avalon...

"I shouted just as loudly as I could, 'I love you, Ralph!' And 'I love you, little Avalon. Never forget that!' I knew nobody could hear me, but it helped...."

Ralph said, "But how on earth did she ever get you up there in the first place?"

"It's a good thing Glenna doesn't have whatever it takes to get rid of someone directly, or I'd have been dead long ago, and Avalon, too. But she's an expert at taking advantage of people at their weakest moments...

"And she took advantage of my weakness after Avalon was born, to move me all the way up to those third floor rooms at the back of the house. I thought I'd go crazy! I actually looked forward to being moved when you were coming to the island, just to get outside for a breath of fresh air...

"You know the Lintons shut off that part of the house sixty years ago, and nobody ever went there. She told *you* that I had died in childbirth. And she told *me* that Avalon had died at birth. We were so isolated here, she got away with it...

"I was a prisoner in my own home, and you never knew! I was fed, but if I ever tried anything – on the island, or off of it – I was punished severely for it. She starved me for days afterward.

"Do you remember when you asked Glenna to open the mausoleum for you, to prove that I was really dead, and you looked inside that vault that has my name on it?

"A woman's bones were in there – dressed in my wedding clothes. Glenna came upstairs afterward and told me about it and gloated. How did that terrible woman get a body for that? It horrifies me to think of it..."

She began to cry weakly, her head still against Ralph's shoulder, and Avalon went to her and touched her on the shoulder gently. It was obvious to her that this poor woman who was her mother was utterly exhausted by the stress of her captivity, and even by her unspeakable relief and joy at seeing her husband, child and sister.

"Lindsay ... Mother ... you're weary, I know. Why

don't you lie down here and rest for a while, and let me play for you?"

Lindsay nodded, reaching up and touching Avalon's face lightly with her thin hand. And Avalon played.

But it wasn't any of Lindsay's favorite classical compositions that she played, although Avalon herself loved them, too.

It was "Amazing Grace", the song she felt best described what was happening in all of their lives right now.

She decided to sing the words as she played, her sweet, pure voice floating out across the room to comfort the souls that had suffered so severely from the sins of others.

'Amazing grace, how sweet the sound that saved a wretch like me. I once was lost, but now am found – was blind, but now I see!

'Twas grace that taught my heart to fear, and grace my fears relieved. How precious did that grace appear the hour I first believed.

'Through many dangers, toils, and snares I have already come. 'Tis grace hath brought me safe thus far, and grace will lead me home!

'When we've been there ten thousand years, bright shining as the sun, we've no less days to sing God's praise than when we first begun.

'The Lord has promised good to me, His Word my hope secures; He will my shield and portion be as long as life endures."

The song was so reassuring that she repeated the stanza that meant the most to her at this moment:

'Through many dangers, toils, and snares I have already come. 'Tis grace hath brought me safe thus far, and grace will lead me home!'

Dangers and snares...the Lord had brought her through so many! Both in Chicago and here on the island, things could have gone so differently for her – at the old ruins when she was a child, her sabotaged car and the wreck on Lakeshore Drive, Manny Byrd's near-fatal success in the subway, the attack by a group of spoiled and hungry alligators, being trapped at the abandoned cottage, and the night she'd heard Lawrence's confession to murder...

The Lord had been so good to her! Protecting her as a little girl and giving her Lora and Eric Evans all of those years, who had so much love to give her and who introduced her so beautifully to Him; then protecting her as an adult and returning her to Lindsay and Ralph – these parents who had needed her so much!

She hadn't wanted to know them. She'd been so fearful of her past, so afraid of devastating discoveries about herself and her birth parents. She had avoided and resisted that knowledge with all of her might and had resented their very existence.

She hadn't felt she needed them or their love. If it had been entirely up to her, she'd have gone on her selfish way forever. She had wanted to forget that part of her life – to pretend it had never existed.

But the Lord had intervened in many ways. He'd known how much they needed her...how much they needed each other. Ralph and Lindsay had been suffering all of those years when she'd been so happy!

If she had refused to look for the island in David's painting, they might have gone the rest of their lives in the same situation – her mother trapped upstairs, her father dying of loneliness inside, Monica inheriting the Linton fortune, and Glenna exploiting it in dreadful ways.

Now, instead, Avalon had a chance to love them back to a normal life and help them to forget the past. She could hardly wait to let Andrew know about Lindsay, so he could break the wonderful news to Valerie...

She could almost hear Lora Evans's voice saying softly: "Life is so short, Avalon...and we all need each other's love so much. It's utterly impossible to please God if we don't deeply and truly love the people He puts in our lives here on earth.

"But sometimes it seems that the people we should love the most – those closest to us, those who look to us for acceptance and affection, those who most need our love in spite of their faults – are the very ones we sometimes belittle or hold at arm's length.

"I don't know why that is...maybe we expect too much from each other. But I do know that the very special, unconditional love you and your Daddy and I have shared is a gift from God, and I can only pray that it will somehow overflow to others who need it, too. There are so many people who feel unloved and alone in this world...

"You know, it was nothing short of a miracle that you came into our lives, and I believe God let it happen for a reason that goes far beyond us and our little lifetime – I do hope and pray so, because we've had so much more than our share!"

When Avalon finally stopped singing, her memories running parallel to the music, she turned around on the piano bench, and Johnna caught her eye and smiled. The two of them knew that "amazing grace" and its Giver personally and would do their utmost to share it – and Him – with these precious loved ones who'd been so wonderfully restored to them.

"Sing that verse again, Avalon – the one about the Lord promising good to us," Johnna said from the arm of the sofa where she was perched, smiling down at Lindsay as she softly stroked her sister's white hair. So Avalon turned back to the piano and sang again:

"The Lord has promised good to me, His Word my hope secures; He will my shield and portion be as long as life endures." As long as life endures…what a promise!

Avalon turned around when she finished singing the verse and was surprised to see Cameron Evans standing serenely in the doorway where Lindsay had stood so uncertainly just a few minutes before.

As he walked into the room and smiled at her, she felt that perhaps he was walking into her life for good, just as Lindsay and Ralph had…and Johnna and David…and Valerie and Andrew.

The tapestry of her life was complete now, with no more missing pieces. And with the Lord's continued grace and mercy, there would be nothing "imitation" about the life they would all have together.

EPILOGUE

Avalon and Cameron Evans were married nearly a year later, in late June. Valerie Herrington survived her cancer long enough to see Avalon's wedding day and died several weeks later in Lindsay's arms, content in the knowledge that she was loved and completely forgiven for all of the "lost years", not only by Lindsay and Ralph, but by the Lord.

Valerie and Lindsay were inseparable after Lindsay's rescue, and Andrew Herrington and his once-detested son-in-law Ralph Linton became nearly as close during that trying period in Andrew's life.

Lindsay and Ralph and Andrew all surrendered their lives to Christ completely at Valerie's deathbed, in response to her dramatically changed life; and Lindsay expanded her repertoire to eventually become the pianist at the little white country church near Herrington Hall, when she and Ralph moved there for Andrew's sake. Sarah Edwards and Megan Marshall were always her dearest friends.

Glenna Henry's and Monica Martin's whereabouts remained a mystery, as did the cause of Lawrence Martin's (alias Masters) death; but Ralph and Lindsay were able to recover many of the priceless Linton family heirlooms that the two women had stolen, since they had been sold to antique dealers in New Orleans, Baton Rouge and Natchez.

When Valerie died, Herrington Hall was temporarily left in Sarah Edwards's capable care, and the Linton mansion on Imitation Island was closed indefinitely, while Lindsay and Ralph accompanied Andrew on a long, quiet trip around the world, to help them all deal with their loss.

They visited the Girls' Christian Shelter in India that Avalon had supported, as well as Christian hospitals in Kenya, Africa and Okinawa, Japan and Christian schools in Haiti and Kingston, Jamaica; and they gave millions more to help in innumerable ways.

The three younger couples were all "just one big, happy family", as Avalon had hoped they would be, despite the geographical distance between them. Johnna and David stayed in Louisiana, and Mac and Leah married and moved to Lake Barrington, a far north suburb of Chicago. Avalon and Cameron moved to the far south side of the city for Cameron to do graduate work at the University of Chicago, and they were attending a black church in nearby Woodlawn during the eventful year of 1968...

And the painting – David's painting of Imitation Island hangs once again in Megan Marshall's upstairs hallway, where it serves as a poignant reminder to all, that –

"God works in a mysterious way,
His wonders to perform."

NEW YORK & NEW JERSEY

GETTING STARTED GARDEN GUIDE

Grow the Best Flowers, Shrubs, Trees, Vines & Groundcovers

First published in 2015 by Cool Springs Press, an imprint of Quarto Publishing Group USA Inc., 400 First Avenue North, Suite 400, Minneapolis, MN 55401 USA

The information in this book is true and complete to the best of our knowledge. All recommendations are made without any guarantee on the part of the author or Publisher, who also disclaims any liability incurred in connection with the use of this data or specific details.

Cool Springs Press titles are also available at discounts in bulk quantity for industrial or sales-promotional use. For details write to Special Sales Manager at Quarto Publishing Group USA Inc., 400 First Avenue North, Suite 400, Minneapolis, MN 55401 USA.

ISBN: 978-1-59186-912-2

Library of Congress Cataloging-in-Publication Data

Simeone, Vincent A., author.
  New York & New Jersey getting started garden guide : grow the best flowers, shrubs, trees, vines & groundcovers / Vincent A. Simeone.
      pages cm
  Other title: New York and New Jersey getting started garden guide
  Includes bibliographical references and index.
  ISBN 978-1-59186-912-2 (sc)
  1. Gardening--New York (State) 2. Gardening--New Jersey. I. Title. II. Title: New York and New Jersey getting started garden guide.

  SB453.2.N7S56 2015
  635.909747'1--dc23

                    2015014599

Acquisitions Editor: Billie Brownell
Project Manager: Sherry Anisi
Senior Art Director: Brad Springer
Layout Designer: Danielle Smith-Boldt

Printed in China
10 9 8 7 6 5 4 3 2 1

Disclaimer:
The opinions and statements contained in this book are the author's and do not represent the opinions and interests of the New York State Office of Parks, Recreation and Historic Preservation.